The God

Gene

DNA Helix 2012

Wendy Pagdin

With the shift in human consciousness predicted by many disciplines to be happening in 2012 many people all around the world began working unconsciously, to prepare for this change. Having arrived at this point in time we now need to understand what is happening and why. This is the story of one of those segments of preparation and the energies and insights applied to the tasks. In reading this book an awakening process will begin leading you into greater awareness of the changing world in which you are an integral part.

ISBN: 978-1-291-59522-2

PublishNation, London
www.publishnation.co.uk

Biographical details of the author

Wendy Pagdin has been a healer and spiritual teacher for the last twenty years. Before that, her varied career included being a scientist, driving profiler, artist, technician at a school, wife, mother and last year a grandmother. Throughout all of these varied transformations Wendy has been a writer and a poet.

In 1987 her book 'A Piece of Thyme' was one of the first books to be published by the then new, desk top publishing technique. Since then although the manuscript pile has increased, no attempt at publication has been made.

Wendy Pagdin lives in small village in Hampshire, where, along with her husband, she runs a successful healing practice. In the grounds of the house they have built a large stone circle with blue stone, the same stone as at Stonehenge. Some of the exciting events that happen in this stone circle are related (albeit in story form) in the "Goddess Gene."

"The end is in the beginning and the beginning is in the end. Cycles of life happen Time and Time Again.   Sometimes we remember them."

If we stop and take the time to make the thought process manifest and coherent, we can change not only our lives, but the field in which we all exist and to which we are all connected.   As in a hologram, if you take one tiny part of a hologram picture and look at it, you have a miniature version of the whole picture – not just a part, but a small version of the whole. The micro reflects the macro and the bindings are magic.   Nature works on a perfect repeatable pattern. We are all part of Nature.

Preface

Extract from the Chronicles
(Part of the Arachne Archive given to David Appleby when the time was deemed right)

The Day the Plot Thickened: OXFORD 1990

"What do you mean Leonardo da Vince was a Buddhist?"

I was shouting. I knew I was shouting because the other people in the café were turning round to look at me. My enigmatic friend continued to stir her coffee

"You yourself told me it was more than likely that Jesus was a Buddhist and that he survived the cross and went to live in India."

"Well yes" I replied, "don't the Mormons believe he went to America ?"

"Probably. Anyway that is the premise for my next book"

"I take it we are back to Leonardo now, not the Mormons?" I wasn't shouting anymore and had decided to pour my tea "anyway you can't write that, it is too soon".

"Look you know we have to get this information into the mainstream or field or whatever you keep calling it. You know people are already writing about the Goddess stuff without of course calling it Goddess stuff"

"It isn't me calling it anything. You know very well it exists, this field of ...... other things...."

"God, I hope you are not calling it that? 'The field of other things', you will be having poor David change his name to Sam Grey or something!"

She leaned over to speak more quietly.

"You know we can't release any of this ourselves, it has to get 'out there' by devious means, via some kind of established person. Otherwise it will become another bloody religion and we will be at the start of another war which will lead to counter wars. You know by this time how it works."

"Oh yes I know how the holders of the idea or philosophy become the elite or high priests, then how those already in the power game raise objections, adopt a flag and symbol, then, a holier than thou attitude. Next, they have to protect their ideals and will fight in order to do that"

"Exactly! Anyway, all Leonardo's leanings are Buddhists principles, he just happened to live in a Christian society".

"He actually lived on top of the Pope ! Will you stop going on about Leonardo. Not that I don't agree with you, but we cannot start there. It is too radical and far too way out"

"That's what you said about some of those plays that we slipped Mr Shakespeare" she said smiling.

"Yes. Well not all those plays made it. Anyway we have to use the same principles with this guy we are going to meet. Don't for Gods sake start going on about Buddhism, just keep to art. Just re-remember sitting on that bench in Leonardo's studio whilst the master himself made rude comments about us and let him overhear that! David, I mean"

"Ok" she finished her coffee and I hurried to drink my tea.

"So are we ready for some serious swanning about whilst we look mysterious and enticing?"

"Too bloody right ! Then we will have to start on the serious hard work of getting his life to fall into order without it looking contrived"

"Work, work, work! We are always working. Although tonight isn't working, it is fun and you know it!"

She laughed getting up from the chair and slipping the elegant lilac jacket onto her shoulders "I must say I like your feathers" she said, "David Appelby won't know what has hit him, or who."

Chapter One

The Village Book Shop Brampton-on –the-Heath

David Appleby turned away from the computer as the bell and voices could be heard downstairs.

He walked onto the gallery landing and glanced down into the well where three women had entered Abra Chat and were looking along the book shelves ooh-ing and ahh-ing at the green geometric fabrics at the windows, on the tables and covering the chair seats. The white walls were a perfect backdrop for the green lines and reflected the light onto the wooden book cases spreading warmth from the early May sunshine which then caught fire in the copper kettles and tea pots exactly as Sara and Kelly had said it would.

"Ladies " he said skipping down the staircase and causing them all to look up and smile, as the sight of his dark, curly, unruly, hair and lithesome body often did. "How can I help you?"

Marian Bradley, one of his regular customers, moved forward to greet him. She was dressed, as always, as if she was about to open a garden fete. Resplendent in dark gold with orange swirls, jewelled wrists and the over the top wedding hat. David pushed his fingers quickly through the tangled hair and rolled his sleeves back a little more symmetrically.

"David!" she beamed, kissing the air just right of his left cheek "how nice!"

Did she mean he was nice? The shop was nice? Or she was nice?

"Marian" he responded without the kiss, "looking splendid as ever".

"Ugh" she waved her arm as if to dismiss compliments in general and his in particular.

"I have brought two very dear friends to browse a little and perhaps be allowed to visit the field?" The last sentence queried somewhat.

1

Marian's friends were always very dear. He wondered briefly if she had any cheaper ones.

"Of course" he said, bowing slightly to the two other ladies who were about Marian's late middle age and built in the same sturdy proportions. .

"Will you want some tea later?"

"But of course" she laughed. "The novelty of a bookshop, chat shop and teashop has to be experienced to be believed."

"Go through the house to the field" he said, checking the supply of Assam tea, "the French doors are open."

They went off with a series of thanks, whilst David thought some more about the field, both of the A-causal events and the one he had bought at the back of his garden.

The phone rang at the same moment as the kettle boiled. He managed to scald his hand, trip over yesterday's delivery of books, mutter "shit" three times and still miss the phone, because the door opened just as he was reaching behind - and hit him on the head!

"For Christ's sake!" he shouted at the startled, but still lovely features of Sally Weatherfield actually entering into his shop, just as he had pictured her doing many times before.

He stood stunned whilst she exclaimed "Oh my God! are you hurt?"

Was he hurt? Only by his stupidity and foul temper. Trying to work as a bookseller, host and writer all at the same time just wasn't what he could do. He was a man after all!

"No, no, I'm OK" he smiled a little shakily. The telephone stopped and the kettle turned itself off. Sally Weatherfeild brought the other lovely long leg round the door and shut it quickly.

"Have you got some ice or something?" she said.

"Ice?" his head was aching now. His hand went up to the temple. Did she want a quick G&T? Did he have any Gin?

"For your head" she smiled, sensing his confusion.

"Oh" he smiled back, using the most redeeming of all his assets; it lit his green eyes and removed the almost permanent frown that hovered on his brow.

"I'm fine" he said "please come in and look around – I'm making tea."

2

Christ! That sounds inane, as it he was a domestic nut or something.

"Sorry you missed the phone call" she said, tossing long blonde hair that was loosely caught in a ponytail, as she turned to look down the book shelves.

"If they want me they'll phone again" he said. It was probably a wrong number anyway, it usually was. Every agent and publisher he had ever contacted seemed to have lost his number.

"It's so pretty in here" she breathed. Her voice was very husky, he had noticed that whenever he had sat staring at her in the Rose & Crown. But she had never noticed him amongst the hundred other pairs of eyes that were eyeing her.

"Thank you – although I take no credit. Abra Chat is a franchise."

She looked puzzled "I thought you lived here?"

So – she knew he lived here! Joy.

He finished putting milk on the tray and took the tray to a table.

"I do" he said "would you like some tea?"

"No thank you" she said, "I just need a present for a friend – this will do fine."

She walked towards the counter and he had to hurry back. Damn! She would be gone and he hadn't even made an impression on her.

"Is it someone's birthday?" he asked as he put the book into the bag.

"David!" The stone circle is marvellous!" cried Marian coming back through the door.

"Oh hello" she beamed at Sally, "you live in Brampton Heath don't you?"

"Yes" said Sally, "I'm Sally Weatherfield". She held out her hand.

"How do you do" said Marian "Marian Bradley – doctor's wife – those are my friends, Fiona and Estelle."

Everyone nodded and smiled.

"Oh tea ......" said Fiona, or was it Estelle? David sighed and added another cup to the two he had placed on the tray. "Won't you stay Sally?" said Marian.

3

"No - thank you", she glanced at the clock, "I have to go". She moved towards the door.

"Thank you" she said turning towards David, "sorry about your head".

"So am I" thought David who could think of nothing to say, wishing his head worked better.

Chapter Two

"It's always the same" David complained next morning to Dez, the milkman whilst he took the bottles of milk and papers from him.

"I'm charm itself when I don't need to be, but just let it be important and "wham" ...... suddenly I can't think of one compliment or witticism."

Dez nodded sympathetically. He had no idea what Mr Appleby was talking about, people only told him half tales anyway as he was passing and delivering.

"You need looking after" he said wisely "go for a woman who can cook. Those long legged blondes are trouble – real trouble" and a far away look came into his eyes.

David was startled to think that perhaps Dez was more than he looked. Did he have a secret life over and above delivering milk every morning?

He turned to go inside and ponder upon the secret lives of those we know or think we know, but only see, when in the corner of his eye he caught sight of Louise Peabody coming round the corner of the milk van.

Damn! he thought, he hadn't got those books unpacked or washed up from yesterday yet and it must be Saturday already if Louise was here.

Dez was smiling and giving her some advice about something. Louise tossed her head and smiled, then headed towards him with her piercing, alert eyes taking in his unshaved, dishevelled state.

"Morning" she said.

"Morning, Louise ...... I ......er I haven't unpacked those books yet."

Her eyes disappeared into the back of her head and she tutted as only a fifteen year old with intellect and attitude can.

"The phone's ringing, David" she said.

"Shit" he said, he still could only just hear it. Young ears picked up high frequency better than older ones.

He missed it again and by the time he had disentangled the milk and papers and made the coffee, Louise had unpacked and stacked the new books.

"I put them in with "weird and wonderful"" she said, taking the coffee cup. "I've moved your stuff up to the end of the shelf."

"You mean behind the door where no one can see it?" he wailed in his best hurt voice.

"They all know you write stuff" she said soothingly "your fame is safe in Brampton."

He smiled and went to wash up before she reminded him it was his turn as she had done it last week. Louise lived a little way down the lane, with her father who was a violin maker, but was still next door. She also had some mysterious connection with the infamous Sara and Kelly, although quite what he had never figured out. His best bet was that they all belonged to the same witches' coven.

He smiled to himself thinking that.

"David Millhouse Appleby" said Louise from the shelves near the door "Millhouse?"

"It's from my Mother's line" he said "they are the mad ones who come from Ireland. The reason I had to run away and live in a caravan."

"Did you run away?" she said interested.

He looked up

"Why, you aren't thinking of running away are you?"

"No, of course not" she said "you did travel though didn't you?"

"Yes" he sighed. "After I had stayed at Oxford so long I just wanted to get away and see the world as they say."

"Is that where you met Kelly and Sara – in Oxford?"

"No, I met them at some writers' thing a long time after I had left Oxford, when I had done my wandering and was considering settling down."

"They had their first Abra Chat in Oxford you know, in an old Malthouse."

"So I heard. But not anymore?"

"No. They have moved on now – to other things."

The phone rang again. Louise answered it and David want back upstairs to the desk and the computer. He turned it on, thinking

6

about perception and how we tag the thoughts and stories to make them different from the events of our real life. We have to add time, linear time, because if we don't separate our memories into past, present, daydream, myth, history, film, book, then our thoughts have no framework in which to operate. Once inside our heads they are all the same. Just pieces of data, like inside the computer. It is only when we retrieve them that we need to re-label them and add the separating gaps like punctuation. Without punctuation, the understanding is lost.

"David"
Louise put the cup of coffee on the table next to him making him jump.
"Thank you Lou" he said, recovering himself "are you going now?"
She bent down slightly to look out of the window. Across the field the church spire could just be seen and the road was visible for a small stretch between the trees. No one was in sight.
"In a little while" she said straightening "Hanna is coming down."
"Oh, OK", he was a little crestfallen he had so much to do and
......
"I'll be here tomorrow" she said casually "Sara and Kelly are coming."
David nearly fell out of his chair. He looked guiltily at the screen, then at Louise. She was a girl old for her fifteen years, an obvious Taurus. Calm and placid with a frightening depth, unstoppable determination when she wanted something and an intelligence that made people remark knowingly that she had been here before – whatever that might mean.
She looked at him now her grey/green eyes framed by the warm apricot tinge of her dark hair.
"Kelly phoned earlier. She said she had tried several times since yesterday."
Damn! the ringing phone. David continued to look at Louise as if for some sort of explanation.
"They are bringing a film crew" she announced quietly, pausing for effect.

David jumped up "What ! What do you mean?" He sounded hysterical, what did they know he didn't know? Did he know anything? What were they going to film?

"Well" said Louise smiling sidewise, "not exactly a 'film crew' – you know how they love drama – just a man with a camera, I think."

"What for?" said David in a whisper.

"Oh they didn't say. Perhaps they are doing some advertising for Abra Chat. Anyway Sara is flying in from South Africa today and they plan to come tomorrow sometime. Is it alright if I go now" said Louise, her message delivered. "I can see Hanna walking down. We are going into town."

David glanced out of the window, thinking distractedly of what he should hide and how many discs it would take to off load the text. He could see the Louise look-alike walking down the hill. Was it the food? he thought. Was that what made these children grow so tall? He was 5'10" but these girls would be catching him up in no time.

"What did Kelly actually say?" he asked following Louise onto the gallery towards the circular staircase.

Louise moved herself round the stairs and repeated in a voice higher than her own with a touch of dialect.

"Tell DM we are both coming tomorrow with a film crew and to look his best."

But this was his best he thought, it doesn't get any better than this! My god, tomorrow!

Louise, with her normal tact, had been somewhat economical with the truth. What Kelly had actually said was

"Tell 'size 10' to get his act together. We are going to get a few shots in the can whilst the place still looks A OK. OK?"

But David didn't know that his nickname was 'size 10' a reference to the initials DM of the boots fame. And the quick-speak was only used between the two of them. .

She also knew the story of the meeting between 'the two' as she thought of them and the gypsy, David. She had been trying to extract information from him when she asked those inane questions. He obviously didn't realise that Sara and Kelly had known of Mr DM Appleby long before that first meeting. They had read his books on the origins of myths, fables and Goddesses, tales from long ago.

8

When Sara and Kelly had met each other they had soon realised that their secret writing passion was a shared one. When they decided to write together and wrote esoteric revolutionism – their words. Lou P – as they called her just labelled it 'weird'.

Their struggle to get other people to understand what they had written was 'ongoing'. However, needing to live meanwhile, they turned their creativity into design – the hope being that owning their own bookshop would mean selling their own books.

They wrote to David in those first years sending him the Plan of their proposed new work which covered myth, religion, history, geometry and cathedrals. But the Plan itself was thirty-nine pages long and if he ever saw it he had neither remembered nor mentioned it.

When he returned from his travelling quest of searching for connections and perceptions, they managed to get themselves, and him, invited to a publishing event. They had a small Desk Top Publishing business and were busy on plans for Abra Chat. He assumed the meeting was an accident of fate. They knew it was nothing of the sort. This collision, unlike their own, was preplanned.

"I wonder who planned ours" Kelly had once remarked.

"We, ourselves, are the only people clever enough to plan our meeting" had been Sara's reply.

Chapter Three

The village of Brampton-on-the-Heath was built around the Village Green. On one side was a row of neat shops with old fashioned bow windows. One was the Post Office -cum- local stores and one a butchers in the old style, with feathered birds hanging on hooks and sausages freshly made. There was also a Bakery where the bread was actually baked, whilst the last was a gardening tools and hardware shop. Very necessary, where the favourite pastime was gardening and then more gardening. On the opposite side of the green was the Rose & Crown. Not just a pub, but a well established restaurant with bed and breakfast facilities.

The green itself was cut diagonally by a small road on one side of which was a very ornate Victorian Bus Shelter. This enabled the local bus to pull into the stop without blocking the narrow roads on either side of the green. Cottages followed the high street in both directions up and down the hill, all gates and doors and window frames painted a dark green. Even the sturdy, once red old fashioned telephone box was green. The reason being, that all of these dwellings and shops were owned by the Estate. In fact most of the land belonged to the Estate. One cottage had winking, multicoloured lights in its small window. David had thought it was the local brothel – something else left over from the Victorian era – but it transpired on investigation to be nothing more exciting then a hair dressers. Since the thatched roofed village hall was only two doors away, it did very good business when 'events' were held. Apart from that, Friday and Saturday were the busy days when the Hampshire housewives got their hair "imprisoned" for the weekend jollies.

This weekend had seen the arrival of many visitors to the Estate House which was situated at the top of the hill, its long imposing driveway running down to the road opposite the church. The occasion was the 21st birthday celebrations of Richard Henry

10

Armstrong, the Heir apparent and darling of his much devoted mother.

The main cause of glee about these weekends was the business brought to Bramley Edge – David's converted Barn. It was situated on the road to the Estate House, neatly placed on a bend in the road which forced even the most unobservant driver to slow down and take a look. Having looked, it was only a matter of time before a pause in the House activities brought them back. Saturday afternoons seemed to be the favourite time.

Having calculated this business strategy to his own advantage, David locked the Barn and walked down to the Rose & Crown telling himself that even high powered executives had to stop for a lunchtime sandwich.

When David had finished and had exchanged pleasantries with the Landlord, he strolled back to the Barn thinking about the next chapter in his complicated plot. As he rounded the bend he heard a shout

"Pip! There you are, don't tell me you had forgotten."

David had been trying to work out who owned the Rover sitting in his drive. He had decided it must be an eager customer when the tall, blonde man wearing designer clothes unwound himself from the driver's seat.

"Ross!" he said, surprise giving way to panic. Christ! Saturday! "See you Saturday, will stay a few days …… Ross." Now he remembered the message. Was the spare room bed made up?

"Of course I hadn't forgotten – just lost track of the time – sorry. Great to see you."

Alexander Rossington and David Appleby had been at school together, then at Oxford. They met regularly and worked together when they could.

Ross smiled, the famous square jaw moving to reveal perfect teeth. The symmetry of face was a camera man's dream. He looked like a hero and to David's memory had lived as one for a long as he could remember. The strong physique was matched by the intelligent eyes. A smaller, lesser being, such as David could hate him, but you couldn't really hate old Ross, he was a true Alexander.

"I've been reading this manuscript of yours" he said following David into the Barn.

"Did I give it to you?" said David frowning.

"Well I didn't bloody well steal it!" said Ross "didn't you want me to read it?"

"I suppose I must have. What did you think?"

They went through the wooden door from the shop into the lounge beyond. David pointed to the whiskey bottle and Ross nodded, then sprawled himself onto the settee.

"It's very visual" he said, "no one has done the young Cleopatra you know. And that woman angle is intriguing – what made you think of it? It's very different from your dry, factual myths and fairy tales."

David smiled and poured soda into the two whiskeys, then brought them round the other settee and handed one to Ross.

"It just came to me" he said. He was worried a little by this turn of events – he had almost hoped to be able to keep his creation under wraps, but still ……

"Are you serious about it being visual?"

"Oh yes, I think I could do a screen play pretty quickly. It's just a matter of getting some TV company interested."

"Wow" was all David could think of to say.

Ross looked at him sidewise. David always looked shifty when he wasn't being quite honest.

"What is it you're not telling me?" he said smiling.

"How the hell should I know!" snapped David. "What are you talking about anyway", then smiled because Ross was already laughing.

"Look – I don't really care where or who you got the idea from, it's just fascinating."

"It's even more fascinating than you think" said David "but never mind that now, I thought you had come down to see my stone circle."

"Ah yes – another fascinating move by you – are you going to tell me about that?"

"Finish your drink, come and see the stones and then I'll tell you. Actually I am trying to write about all these series of weird events that have happened, before I forget about them entirely."

"What weird events?" said Ross following him through the French doors into the afternoon sunshine. He paused to look admiringly round the walled garden. It was full of trailing and hanging plants that followed the winding pathways as they disappeared and reappeared, making secret little arbours with seats and trelliswork. There was even a gazebo!

"Hey Pip, this is wonderful – who did it?" David paused and turned round to his friend.

"What makes you think I didn't?"

"Just a wild guess and a lot of background knowledge" smiled Ross.

"OK" sighed David continuing to lead the way to the back wall and the door to the field beyond. "You're right – it was already here and it seems to come with the original gardener who makes sure it stays like this."

"Its beautiful" murmured Ross "it's like the secret garden of childhood."

"That's what everyone says." David stood aside opening the door and allowing Ross into the three acre field.

The stone circle stood placidly in the sunlight neatly placed in the right hand lower corner of the field. There were sixteen stones in the circle proper and six stones in a line parallel to the large stone at the head of the circle.

"Wow" said Ross echoing David's earlier comment "your own Stonehenge."

"Not quite" said David dryly, "not quite the same size stones, not quite the same purpose and not quite as complicated. However," he paused beckoning Ross into the middle of the stones "I would like you to close your eyes and let your mind and body relax. Just 'feel' what it feels like inside here.

Ross followed and did as he was bidden. At first it just felt like closing your eyes. Lots of thoughts flashed through his mind like "where did he need to go on Monday?" "Where was his favourite shirt?" "Did he phone Jill?" "Was David mad?" "Would he meet a wonderful girl next week as he certainly hadn't this week?" "What was wrong with his leg?" "Was cancer catching ....?" But slowly the thoughts dried up and he relaxed. He could hear the birds shouting and arguing with one another. He could hear the distant sound of a lawn mower and somewhere cows lowing, an aeroplane's lazy drone was overhead and the scent of newly cut grass seemed to surround him. He could hear all these sounds, but he seemed to have the distinct impression of silence - a deep, deep silence. He sighed involuntarily.

David laughed "no matter how hard I try, I can never prevent that sigh from escaping."

Ross opened his eyes and looked at the stones. They were all different shapes and sizes yet they seemed to be part of a whole. They were no longer just stones in a circle, they were the Circle and they almost seemed to dance in the sunlight.

"It's a copy of a Neolithic circle in Wales" David said quietly "built on the same principles. A group of dowsers were looking into the power lines of this circle when it came to them that it was a healing circle. Each segment corresponds to a different frequency and those frequencies apply to certain parts of the body. So in fact, the circle acts like a giant tuning fork - each section vibrating at the correct note for a different organ. You are standing in the heart section so your heart is being tuned and is receiving energy from the earth vibrations."

"Does it work?" said Ross.

"Why should it not? Everyone who has come and stood in it for whatever reason seems to benefit from it in some way. It also acts by opening a channel for the mind. Because the body becomes tuned and sort of 'on line' and the frequencies stop any other interference from outside, it clears the mind, acting like a window to allow access to the universal. That's the background field to which we all belong, but which we need to refocus upon in order to see. A bit like those magic pictures that look like random dots of colour, but if you refocus your eyes, after a while you see a three dimensional picture. It was there all the time, you just couldn't see it."

Ross smiled slowly. "Will it bring me my heart's desire?"

14

"It's not a wishing well, you clot" David smiled "but it will help you to focus your energy on what you really want – as compared to what you think you want – that is half the battle in achieving anything."

"You still believe that we waste our efforts fighting against our own prejudices and fears then?"

"I don't believe it, I know it" said David. "Look, you stay here and make peace with yourself. I've got to go inside and see if customers have arrived. There's a chair over there." David pointed as he began walking back indoors. "Ask yourself questions and don't be surprised if you find you know the answers – and sit in that segment there" he pointed, "that should help that old rugby injury in your knee."

Ross smiled and went to get the chair. One thing you could definitely say about old Pip was that he was always learning something new and interesting. He put the chair down where David had indicated. Life was a funny thing, a series of bizarre events. Who would have guessed this time last year that he would be sitting in the middle of a stone circle in the middle of a field, trying to perceive the universal field of which he and his life were a series of events.

Chapter Four

"So come on, what gives with this new style of writing" said Ross taking another helping of the wonderful dish of pork and prunes served up at the Rose and Crown.

May evenings could be cold and they were glad of the log fire burning in the grate. The room was filled with the comforting hum of people eating and talking. As David suspected the afternoon had been very busy with visitors to the Hall liking the easy elegance of Abra Chat. They sat about drinking tea and eating Mrs Perkins scones, whilst buying books and crafts that David was sure they neither needed nor would ever read. Still, that was business, and this was supper.

"Like all good ideas, it happened by accident" David mumbled between mouthfuls. "or should I amend that and say by a-causal events."

Ross frowned.

"OK, let's call them coincidences. But these coincidences, once they begin, happen so quickly that you have to sit up and say – something is happening here. These coincidences are too coordinated – someone or something else is controlling these events."

Ross looked at him a moment, but he was entirely serious. "Who is it then?"

"I don't know. The Universe I suppose, the whole huge field of energy of which we are part."

Ross took a drink of wine and looked condescendingly at his friend.

"Go on then" he said putting the glass down.

David smiled "OK let's stick to easy things. I'll just tell it like it happened and leave the why's and wherefores for another time."

"Sounds good to me" said Ross continuing with his pork and potatoes. "I'm all ears."

David thought for a moment. Things had moved so fast that he really had to strive for the beginning.

"It must have been about two years ago. It was a cold January and I had returned to England for Christmas. I stayed with my family and I was really at a low ebb – you were in the States I think."

Ross nodded , remembering those heady days of wine and roses before his little Rose had turned into a thorn bush.

"I didn't know what to do – where to go. My life was a mess, aimless. I had wandered about as far as I wanted to wander. I sold the boat the year before and had been travelling in a camper van but I was sick of that. I wanted to settle down, but where and how I didn't know."

"Still hadn't found Miss Right then Pip?"

David smiled "I found lots of Miss Rights – unfortunately they all went wrong!"

They both laughed. Jane came and cleared away their plates and they settled down to finish the bottle of wine.

"Anyway, I got this invitation to a Publishing event in Oxford and not having anything else to do I thought it might be interesting – who knows who you might meet."

"Not to mention having your ego massaged by some publisher who may want to get you to write something for him."

"Yes. That too!" David laughed.

Jane came back and asked about sweets, but they had eaten more than their fill. "So off I went and while nibbling an hors d'oeuvre and trying to avoid a woman who kept telling me she had read everything I had written, I overheard a very amazing conversation."

"You 'overhead' " said Ross raising his eyebrows.

"Well, I stood unobserved and purposefully listened then". David poured the last of the wine into Ross's glass and topped up his own.

Bernie, the landlord, came over and stoked up the fire. They both complimented him on the excellent meal.

"Ah well, you were lucky" he smiled his round face glistening in the fire glow. "Mary overreached herself today, in case any of the Gentry came down and wanted something special."

"Their loss is our gain" said Ross as Bernie returned to the bar.

17

"So?" he said to David who was taking the pause in their conversation to quickly scan the other guests and what he could see of the front bar for any trace of the long legged Sally. She wasn't there.

"So" said David "these two women were having a very animated discussion about the Magdalene and the Madonna only they were talking about Leonardo Da Vinci as if he lived next door and they were remembering that he had said that they looked like the Magdalene and the Madonna.

"Did they?"

"Did they what?" said David distracted from his reminiscence of the scene.

"Look like the Magdalene and the Madonna?"

"Well – one was – is I mean – tall and dark, amazing green eyes – very attractive. The other one is small, rounded, blonde, attractive in a more gentle way not as threatening, but more ......"

"You liked her?"

"I could relate to her easier, but the dark haired one was stunning. Anyway it wasn't really how they looked – I mean they looked great individually, but together – they emanated this amazing energy. It made them bigger, brighter, more vibrant than anyone else in the room. They drew people's attention all the time, but they also were a little frightening. No one except me was anywhere near them."

"Are we talking about your own obsession here with things ancient. They sound like a couple of the Goddess's you are always talking about."

David smiled. "You are probably right, I have been looking for signs of the Goddess for so long." He hadn't thought about the experience from this angle until now. In fact he had never spoken of the 'event' at all and it was only now as he spoke of it and recreated the scene that he understood what he had seen – or what he had projected on to what he had seen.

"Yes! Of course" he said realising ; "they looked exactly like Artemis and Aphrodite or Diana and Venus – in modern dress, of course" he laughed.

18

Ross laughed and shook his head. His friend lived in cloud cuckoo land sometimes. "Go on" he said, "tell me what Artemis and Aphrodite were saying."

"Well they were actually arguing - in a friendly way. It was about Leonardo not liking them and being very arrogant and superior, but because he saw them sitting on a bench in his studio, he had sketched them – as far as I could gather it was the Leonardo cartoon. They were laughing about becoming cartoon characters. Then they switched to Michael Angelo and his Pieta. They said his reason for making his Madonna young. even when she held the adult body of her son – was that he realised about the immortality of woman.

Then they went on to Mark Antony and his broken nose that Michael Angelo also possessed.. They decided that that was why in Leonardo times she had been so attracted to Michael Angelo (even though it was to no avail) he must have been the reincarnated Mark Antony. Then they laughed and shouted because the initials were the same – MA and MA." David paused smiling at the remembered joy of their laughter.

"Then Aphrodite said she had also thought Mark Antony was a complete twerp and Artemis said how fortunate it was that they didn't like the same type of men." He stopped.

"Well" said Ross "what happened then?"

"Then they decided to stop arguing and do some serious swanning about while they could. They filled up their champagne glass, got a third glass and came over to me."

"They knew you were listening?"

"I don't know really. But if their conversation was contrived, it was very complicated and I don't think many people would have been able to make sense of it."

"Except you?" said Ross "did they know who you were?"

"Well I introduced myself and they gave me the champagne. They knew of my work – vaguely – they said. Then they started to tell me about Abra Chat and the franchise and if I was interested to get in touch with them."

"Then what?"

"Then I went home."

"Well that doesn't sound like a bizarre series of events" said Ross sighing.

Jane came over with coffee so they moved to the fire which would free their table for someone else. Ross sat down on an armchair and David perched on a stool next to him.

"Well you see at that point I had no house, no plans, no prospects and Abra Chat was just an idea. But – but the next day – I stayed in Oxford overnight and was looking around the town when I bumped into Charles Herding. He used to work in Oxford years ago, but had moved on and I hadn't seen him for a long, long time. We went and had a drink and he told me he was going to live in America – if he could only sell his house. It was a converted Barn. He was selling it cheap because he wanted to leave quickly. I went to see it that same day and loved it immediately. It was also perfect for Abra Chat. In fact, Kelly and Sara (Artemis and Aphrodite) had said the night before "a converted Barn with a gallery would be absolutely perfect – shades of Shakespeare and the 15th Century". Four weeks later I had moved in and they arrived just after to decorate Abra Chat."

"Very odd, but where did the writing style come in?"

"The more I saw of them together and the more they talked about various things and about their own meeting, the more my imagination was fired and my initial "listened in" conversation remained with me. That they were in fact two very different woman types, one the Virgin Queen – the warrior and lover, tall, dark, aloof. The other, soft and warm. The perfect lover/mother. Opposites, yet the same. I could see them as eternal. Place them in any setting, in any time and they could be there. Sara even looked like Cleopatra! Damn it, she even came from Africa – so the African Queen was an easy title. Kelly was full of mystery and magic. One was classical in approach, the other romantic which is why Abra Chat is so good. It is a tight, well run business, but it is also imaginative and flowing. They argue all the time, but constructively.   Watching them and remembering their two 'places in history' that I had overheard, one being Mark Antony and ancient Rome. The other Michael Angelo in the sixteenth century. I began to place them there". He paused and smiled at Ross, who was now fascinated himself.

"It was easy to do anyway – they helped me all the time."

"How?" said Ross.

"Well – they too write about myth and history and religion – although I have never actually seen any of their writing – but we took long lunch breaks and they gave me their theories about the history that isn't written – or should I say Herstory."

"You mean Goddess stuff?"

"Well – more the unwritten side from the female point of view. After all history is written by the Victors who, of course, change it to their own perspective. Besides it is always written from the male view point."

"Ah now I see! You are rewriting history from the view of the female."

"Well, a bit more than that. Sara and Kelly seem to think that history has been 'twisted' by the patriarchal society for its own material ends and to separate and 'keep down' women. They believe in the old 'wise woman' theory."

"What – that women know more about life than men do?"

"Something like that – and that men know this to be true and are afraid of them. They think that if you revisit history you will understand that the continuity of humans has always been in the hands of women."

"So this is the premise you are writing from?"

David sighed and moved his position on the stool. "Sort of – I am using these two 'types' as Goddess who appears again and again throughout history and who remember their times before and who are working to a 'larger' plan. They are here to progress the human consciousness by effecting history. But History has always been about the Victors in a battle. Power struggles the past being completely rewritten by who won which battle which means we are only ever seeing one perspective, that of the male. When in fact the women have always been there progressing life, always creating a pattern but we can not see it because we only have one version. Pieces are missing from our roots."

Ross looked at his friend and smiled. "You know Pip, if we do a television drama, none of that will come over. It will just be another adventure story."

"I realise that – but even so – it will be different. Not just the long hand of Rome subduing yet another civilisation. Don't you think ?"

"Oh yes, I think the sight of two woman plotting to change the course of history – whilst still being human and confused - will certainly come across. I'm impressed and intrigued."

David looked at his friend then reached behind to put down the coffee cup he had been nursing. It was late and they should be making tracks for home but he must tell him first.

"Ross" he began. Ross looked up from the fire where he had been visualising Cleopatra and her High Priestess – planning to reel in the big fish of Rome. David was looking at him with that 'I have a confession to make' gaze.

"What?" he said frowning.

"Kelly and Sara – my two models for all of this."

Ross nodded.

"They don't know."

"They don't know that you have been writing about them?"

David nodded his head.

"But you said they had helped. Told you of their theories."

"That's true, but they didn't know I was going to write about them". Did they? How could they?"

Ross thought for a moment. "Who else but me knows you have written any of this?"

"No one. In fact I had forgotten that in my enthusiasm I had given you a copy to read."

"OK. So if no one knows its you, and the style is different, you just change your name and I present it – I'll have to write the screen play anyway." He looked at him "Pip it's good – let's do it."

It sounded so easy – almost too easy.

"What shall I be called then?" David frowned.

"I don't know, but we can discuss that at home, tomorrow."

"Tomorrow! Oh my God" said David hitting his forehead with the palm of his hand. The voice of Louise once more in his head saying "I'll be here tomorrow, Kelly and Sara are coming."

"They're coming tomorrow!" He looked round hastily to see who was listening. To see if they had come already.

22

"Who are?" said Ross puzzled, also glancing round to see if they were under observation.

"Kelly and Sara" whispered David as if their names could be taken down and used in evidence against him "with a film crew" he said dramatically."

Ross looked alarmed "A film crew?!"

"Well – no – a person with a camera I suppose." He jumped up "Come on let's get back and off load all the text onto some discs. If we are going to do this we need to cover our tracks now."

Ross got up and took his wallet out of his pocket. David seemed to have forgotten about paying. In fact Ross laughed to himself at the thought of his friend who had been so inspired by two women that he had secretly written two books about them and was still terrified of them finding out. What difference did it make? Surely they would be flattered? Anyway it was not really them, it was just based on them – there was no reason to suggest that they would even recognise themselves.

But then Ross hadn't met Kelly and Sara, David had. He paid the bill and hurried after his friend who was already out of the door and his way home to hide the evidence.

Chapter Five

"Take the door as it opens. From here! Peter, he's coming!"

David stood behind the door for a moment and took a deep breath. The voice was unmistakable, besides it had a South African twang.

"Yees, that's right" could be heard as David took the plunge and opened the door.

"Why David" she beamed giving him the full blast of perfect teeth "looking elegant as ever I see".

"Mizz Abrams how nice" he returned the smile and was stunned as always by the Classic beauty in a pale lilac mini skirted suit, the legs made even longer courtesy of three inch high heeled shoes. Hope she hadn't worn those on the plant he thought distractedly. He moved aside to allow entrance whilst she flung her arms dramatically outward to take in everything that was Abra Chat.

"Circle it Peter – get the full effect of coming in."

"Where's Kelly?" David asked trying to avoid the lens. Were they on tape as well?

"Grovelling in the undergrowth" she said, plucking through the recent book additions on the shelf.

"I don't grovel" said a voice somewhere behind an armful of Moon daisies "I was picking these. Hello DM" she walked towards him and, crushing the daisies between them, gave him a kiss. He smiled at the warmth and scent of flowers that Kelly always brought, even when not holding a great bunch of them.

"Nice waistcoat" she breathed approvingly.

He was wearing his dark green silk shirt and his very elaborate green and black patterned waistcoat.

"Can we find a vase?" she asked.

"Of course". He should have thought about picking some of these daisies as he could see how wonderful they would look among the books and wooden book shelves.

"Where's Lou P?" asked Sara as they headed towards the kitchen.

24

"She said she was coming" David called back. He produced a large earthenware jug.

Kelly murmured "perfect" and dumped the flowers into it, filled it with water, jiggled them about a bit, nodded to herself and walked back into Abra Chat.

"This is Peter" said Kelly, waving in the direction of the camera. David nodded and caught the movement of Ross coming down the spiral staircase.

"This is Ross – Alexander Rossington – old friend" he said in return.

Sara looked up from the book she was reading and took in the height, the width, the golden curls, blue eyes, square jaw all encased in designer clothes.

"My God ! A Greek God!" she shouted snapping the book closed and looking interested for the first time since their arrival.

"I thought you said there were no Greek Gods, just Goddam Greeks" said Kelly, quick as the flash of her silver earrings.

"So I did" laughed Sara.

Ross, who was used to the effect he had on people of all persuasions, continued down the stairs and said with a smile that oozed charm.

"Then I think I have just discovered my Achilles heel."

To which they all exploded into laughter.

"Can't be a Greek God" said Sara, "they had no brains."

"Too busy with other bits of their anatomy" laughed Kelly.

"Which is why the Goddess's ended up with all the work" finished David.

Ross smiled and looked at the two prototypes that had so fired his friend's imagination.

The door was suddenly flung open and Louise staggered in under the great weight of a rather large basket.

"Looby-Lou" shouted Sara rushing over and flinging herself at the teenager. Kelly extracted the basket so that their hugging could be more even. They were obviously delighted to see one another. Kelly put the basket down and continued the adulation. Between bouts of "got the wine?" "remembered the cheese?" "how's everyone?" "you look great!"

25

Peter, who seemed to have the camera permanently attached to his face, continued placidly to film all activity, which made David a little wary as he moved towards the coffee pot.

The women were now disentangling and asking the health of various persons known only to themselves.

Ross had perched himself on the table and was watching all this animation with great interest.

David ventured a glance at him hoping he would remember not to say anything that may alert the women to their elevated role.

"Coffee?" he shouted above the noise and shrieks of delight.

"Please, please – yes" came a few replies.

He made five coffees and one tea. Kelly came over and saw that he had remembered she didn't drink coffee. She smiled at him, letting him know that she knew he had remembered.

When everyone had drunk their coffee, Sara exclaimed that it must surely be lunch time and if David could find some extra glasses, everyone could go outside and have a picnic. She then proceeded to dismiss Peter and his camera which left Ross and David to find glasses, cushions and rugs. Then everyone set off through the French windows and on into the field.

In the centre of the circle Sara paused, consulted Kelly with a look, got a nod and instructed Ross to place the blankets. Everyone settled down and the basket was unpacked, corkscrew found, wine distributed and plates loaded with cheeses, pickles, ham, crackers, crisps and pork pies.

After a few moments of silent munching Kelly said "The book?"

Sara looked at Louise and Louise rummaged further into the basket. Finding first a hardback exercise book, then a pen, which she handed to Sara.

Sara licked her fingers clean. Kelly passed her a serviette. The book was opened and Sara began writing whilst she said:

"Board meeting held on 3rd May, Brampton village, Hants at" she consulted her watch "1.10 p.m. Those present Director Abrams, Director Delmonte, Lou P, a Greek God and The Gypsy."

David and Ross looked at each other.

"Oh don't worry" said Kelly "we always have our board meetings outside whilst having a picnic – in fact our favourite places are graveyards."

"Graveyards!" said Ross looking even more puzzled. David just smiled quietly to himself thinking 'you just wait Ross old boy!'

"Graveyards are excellent places for both picnics and board meetings" said Sara having another gulp of her wine.

"No people, lots of peace and space and always places to sit."

"Besides" said Kelly "the dead like some more activity than the usual quick scamper through of the sad bereaved with flowers. Anyway ...... get on with it" she said to Sara.

"Alright – minutes of the last meeting?"

"Ah – there were no minutes for the last meeting – last month – because Director A and Director D were not speaking to each other."

"Oh God!" said Louise "I just wonder how many of those there are!" and she tutted in her best disapproval manner.

Ross was utterly fascinated and asked "Is it quite legal all this?"

"Legal!" all three women turned upon him as if he had said a dirty word.

"We can, and do, have our board meetings where ever we choose" said Kelly indignantly "besides as we are the only two directors, it is absolutely legal if we say it is!"

Ross held up his hands under this verbal attack, which caused a bit of spillage as one hand was holding his glass.

Everyone laughed and the building tension was eased.

"How come" said David puzzled and pausing to eat some cheese "that he gets to be a Greek God and I am a gypsy?"

"Gypsies are full of magic and wonder" said Kelly smiling at his frown "and do stop frowning DM or you will get permanent wrinkles."

"I thought they were rogues and thieves and rather unwashed creatures" said Ross leaning back on his elbow and surveying David.

"Oh they are – all of those things as well" said Sara busily spreading pate on crackers, the book for the moment forgotten.

"Well I have known times when you were more than pleased to find refuge with them" said Kelly.

"Have you spent time with Gypsies?" Ross inquired innocently.

27

"Not in this lifetime" said Sara picking up the book again.

"The gypsies – as we think of them, were the original Celtic peoples" said Kelly as if that explained everything. "They were travelling people, first in Egypt a place we remember well. When they stopped travelling and settled down, there were small pockets of them that kept travelling. They became known as gypsies.

"Just like you Pip" said Ross suddenly seeing where their minds wandered.

"No minutes" wrote Sara "due to unusual circumstances."

"I would put 'normal circumstances' if I were you" said Louise grabbing the mushroom pate.

"Are arguments quite normal then?" said Ross addressing Louise for the first time.

"As normal as breathing to these two" she smiled, the alteration in her face being transforming. "When they met they had decided not to speak to each other."

Ross frowned "but if they were strangers how could they decide not to speak to each other?"

"They had never met" said Louise "but they weren't strangers – they were carrying on some old feud or other – it was only because of me that they spoke at all!"

"Yes" said Kelly "and she was all of four years old. So if it hadn't have been for Lou P – Sara and Kelly would not have become friends – there would be no Abra Chat and none of us would be here now! So there you are!"

"Am I to put that in the minutes" said Sara getting exasperated because she couldn't hold the pen and the cheese crackers in one hand.

"No" sighed Kelly "let's get on with it. Number one, meeting held to discuss the dissolution of the Abra Chat franchise."

"What!" said David startled.

"Oh don't worry" said Sara "you will be fine. We will give you all the suppliers and things and you can get your stock yourself. It's just that we have got another project on the go."

"Right, Number two" said Kelly "the new proposal for our England/Africa project – Kalahari Kolours – spelled with a K."

"Isn't that how you always spell colours?" murmured Sara writing quickly. "Also, to begin foundation – the ASH foundation."

"ASH?" said Louise.

"African Self Help" said Sara triumphantly.

"I thought you always planned a foundation that incorporated the arts and the sciences" said Louise interested in the conversation now.

"Well" said Kelly, "we did. But … but."

"But we got sod all response from the people we invited to join our foundation" said Sara. She glanced quickly at David and then back to Kelly who scowled at her hard.

She shrugged "so we have gone into artefacts, they are easier commodities than moral issues."

David frowned at them both.

"Am I missing something here? Am I to blame for something?"

Ross, who had detected no inflections in the conversation, was surprised by this paranoia so he refrained from his intention to have another drink and watched the interplay that seemed to be taking place below the surface.

"Oh alright" said Kelly, replying not to David, but to some unspoken question from Sara.

"You were one of the people we once sent our ideas about dynamic propositions to. In the first place we wanted to look for science answers in the arts and vice versa" said Sara.

No one looked at David except Ross. They all seemed to be looking at some distant horizon.

"Care of my Publishers, I suppose" said David into the silence.

"Yes" said Kelly briefly "I don't expect you ever received it."

Ross continued to look at David "I'm sure he would have remembered if he had received it" he said gently.

"Too right!" said Sara altering the serious mood. The damn plan is 39 pages long!"

Everyone laughed quickly glad to ease the tension. Only David continued to think furiously. There was something here that was an anomaly – something he should remember …… something that cast a different light on what he knew – or what he thought he knew ……

"David! You're not eating" said Kelly watching the serious frown that had developed on his brow. Damn Sara! She wouldn't let sleeping dogs lie ever, not ever! She smiled and passed him a piece of fruit cake made no doubt by the marvellous ladies of the WI.

David stopped frowning and ate his cake, joining in the frivolous conversation that ranged from topics as diverse as the disasters of long range air travel to David's attempts at being green fingered.

During a lull in the conversation when everyone was dozing in the sunshine, a group of people appeared in the far corner of the field where a footpath cut diagonally across the ground following the stream path.

"Who's that?" asked Ross looking up.

Louise looked over disinterestedly. "Probably people from up the hill" she said "something going on in the manor house this weekend."

Ross continued to stare at them. Then he sat up and looked more interested.

"I think I know one of those people" he said standing up. "Pip – come with me, I think this could be our lucky day."

David got up and tucked the plates back into the basket and followed Ross who was now waving and calling something incoherent to the group of people. When he reached the footpath one of the group had separated from the others and was now in a loud session of back slapping and "well I never's" with Ross. The accent sounded decidedly American and David found himself cringing mentally from the onslaught he was expecting. The stranger was still engrossed amazement at meeting Ross in this quiet, out of the way place, so David held back a little and took the time to look back at the circle and the three females they had left.

They seemed to have abandoned the picnic and were now standing together in a close group laughing hilariously at some shared amusement. As their laughter gathered momentum, they lifted their arms and supported one another in a sort of slow dance of merriment. It had all the delights of a portrait of Spring and David was reminded immediately of the Three Graces. Then his eyes narrowed slightly as the laughter caught a higher, sharper, edge and unbidden the thought of the three witches in Macbeth came to his mind. The cackling, the words, the hags plotting the downfall of the misguided man with too much ambition. Then Ross spoke his name and he moved once more into the sunshine of a Hampshire Sunday in the age of rationale and technology. It seemed, somehow, less familiar than that blasted heath in the long ago world of old knowledge.

The Three Graces had, meanwhile, been paying more attention to the accidental meeting than they appeared to be.

"I would say "end of Scene One, Act III" wouldn't you?"

"Is that the one with the witches in?"

"Who cares, you almost blew it telling him we had sent BSSM to him."

"Never mind that, what is our next move?"

"Why don't we exit stage left?" said Louise picking up the picnic basket.

"What you mean completely?" said Kelly folding the blankets.

"Why not?"

"Why not!?" said Sara, "why don't we go home!"

"Home?" said Louise.

"As in really home?" said Kelly.

"Why not?" shrugged Sara.

"You mean Greece? As in Mediterranean?" said Louise.

"Why not" said Kelly and Sara together.

"Let's just go and leave dear David to find some more A-causal events" said Kelly, carrying the basket and two cushions under her arm and walking towards the wall that ran around the garden.

"What, just leave him a note saying "'gone to Greece" said Sara.

"Let's do it!" said Louise "just go and tell Dad that we are going and just go".

They had reached the door in the wall now and Sara opened it.

"It's rather like leaving the vast expanse of the unconscious out here" she said, waving her arms around the field and holding the door open, " then entering once more into the tight circle of the rational mind. The inside of this walled enclosure".

"With all its winding pathways along carefully tailored routes and byways you mean" said Louise.

"Yes, it's beautiful and contradictory, but ......"

"But it has a wall round it" said Kelly closing the door behind them " and it has rigid dimensions."

31

"Unlike us" smiled Sara "who like to be able to go through the door into the unconscious."

"But only when we are fully conscious" finished Kelly.

They laughed.

"Come you two" said Louise "It will spoil it if we can't leave the note."

They went back through the French window, returned the glasses and cushions, found a pen and paper then wrote the note in large letters. They left it on the table, closing the door behind them as they exited stage left.

It simply read "GONE TO GREECE"

Chapter Six

Of course it couldn't be as easy as that, there were things to arrange and people to meet.

The business needed a little more organising, and Louise had exams to finish – carefully forgotten by her.

Sara and Kelly had run their business alone when they had begun Abra Chat in 1988, but when Sara had had to go back to South Africa to her sick Mother, Kelly had been lost. By a stroke of great good fortune, a certain young lady happened by who was a wonder and a treasure with all the office work. In fact the smooth running of the Franchise was entirely due to Melanie. After the initial ideas and set up, Sara and Kelly had continued their other projects leaving the day-to-day running to Melanie, who now lived in the flat above the Old Malthouse in Oxford in which Sara had once lived – in the days when they ran their own publishing company. It was an enterprise that had folded due to lack of funds, sending Sara back home to South Africa once more.

They left a disgruntled Louise to finish her A level course and went straight to Oxford to talk to Mel and find out how the plans for selling the franchise were doing.

"Hell-oo" said Mel when they arrived. "I've been trying to contact you two."

"Sounds bad – what's up doc?" said Kelly. Sara, meanwhile, was trying to persuade the guys in the downstairs office, who were moving their own office furniture whilst it was quiet and Sunday, to carry her large box of papers upstairs. It seemed to be causing difficulty because a lot of laughter and shouting drifted upstairs. Mel was quiet and eventually Kelly realised that she hadn't answered.

She sat down on the armchair that faced out of the room near the floor length window that overlooked the river.

"They backed out," said Mel sitting down opposite to her, "the bastards".

"They backed out? the buyers?"

Mel nodded.

"Oh great!" said Kelly well aware that selling the franchise was the only way to keep the business afloat.

"Hell" she said to no one in particular.

Sara came in with the two guys from downstairs and the box, still teasing them about their lack of muscle power. She sensed the two still figures had only bad news and quickly got rid of the men.

"Is there a problem?" she asked sitting on the arm of Kelly's chair.

"The bastards have dropped out" said Mel in her straightforward way "no sale, no dough, no dough, no business."

"Damn" said Sara "I was looking forward to going to Greece."

"Greece?" said Mel surprised.

"Never mind Greece" said Kelly "what do we do now?"

"Panic?" suggested Sara.

"Too predictable" said Kelly, "what else can we sell?"

"The lease on this place and all the stock?"

"Haven't got any stock to sell" said Melanie going over to her files, "but the guys downstairs are interested in the lease."

"Were interested" said Kelly "until she made fun of them".

Sara smiled. "It's a good property in a great and central place – what happened to the Abra Chat idea though?"

"God knows" said Kelly getting up "I think everyone in recession stops buying books, or at least stops wanting to buy them and drink tea and talk."

"Anyway what about you Mel, we can't just take your home again" said Sara.

"Mel's getting married soon anyway" said Kelly, "forgot to tell you. How's your Dad's business in South Africa ? you didn't tell me."

Sara had been back home to South Africa to go into business with her Dad. This had seemed a good idea a year ago when her affair with the handsome and passionate Patrick had come to an end. Sara had been living with him in Pangbourne. He was an airline pilot and flew back and forth at strange hours which gave him too much scope to meet other ladies in other places – not to mention going home to his wife occasionally.

"Dad's fine, his business is fine, he doesn't need me now I have set everything up."

"So it looks like pastures new for all of us" Kelly smiled "come on let's have some tea and decide to salvage what we can. Abra Chat was a great idea it just didn't work like we thought it should."

"The blokes downstairs asked me to talk to you about the lease" said Mel getting the cups out of the cupboard "so if we say you have decided to take your business venture to Greece and don't mention Abra Chat etc., we might be able to get a good price out of them."

"Sounds good to me" said Sara taking off her shoes "as always we will leave that with you Mel."

"Whatever we decide to do next, can we still rely on you?" asked Kelly.

"Well I don't plan to retire" said Mel running her finger through her hair ,"just get married, so I hope I will still have a job when all the dust settles."

"So do we" said Sara "I haven't even got a roof over my head!"

"So what's new?" said Kelly pouring the tea and handing round the cups. "How many times have we been in this situation before?"

"Too many" said Sara moving to the settee area. "What about dear David, now we have undermined his income."

"Dear David fortunately doesn't rely on Abra Chat for income, he makes that out of writing. Abra Chat helps him to meet people and make coffee."

"He may want to give it up."

"I don't expect that would be any great problem if he does – what happens legally Mel?"

"Well if we don't sell the franchise, we don't have one, so either he becomes his own business or he closes down. It's up to him really. He owns the house anyway doesn't he, we just rent the front bit?"

"Yes. He looked to me as if taking care of Abra Chat was a bit of a liability. Besides, Lou P won't be able to help him now with exams and everything."

"Too right" Kelly smiled wickedly, "anyway I think that dear size 10 took on Abra Chat with a very ulterior motive in mind!"

"Is this sexual" said Sara looking sharp.

"Of course not!" said Kelly as if the word sexual was not part of her vocabulary "he needed to be able to observe us without us knowing!"

"Is he a weirdo?" asked Mel conversationally.

"No – well not in that way" smiled Sara "he is writing about us, but we are not supposed to know."

"Good Lord, I wonder why!" said Mel "no – just kidding" she smiled.

"He isn't just kidding though, is he fruit?" Sara replied. She called Kelly 'fruit' because her rather flamboyant surname De Monte was also that of a well known fruit buyer.

"Oh no" said Kelly, "Mr Appleby is very, very serious, more serious than even he suspects."

Indeed, whilst Kelly and Sara were preparing to accept Melanie's offer and spend the night in the Malthouse, David was morosely sitting in front of the unlit fire feeling very disappointed with his day. Not that it had been unsuccessful. The stranger who Ross had recognised was a producer and had been more than politely interested in Ross's assurance that he had something he would be very interested in. As his current project would be finished in October, he was very willing to hear more. David's depression stemmed from the moment he had read the curious note on the table announcing 'gone to Greece'. He hadn't expected them to disappear so soon somehow.

"What's up Pip?" asked Ross coming into the sitting area with a tray of tea and biscuits "you look very down for someone who has a very good chance of being extremely successful."

"Have I?" He smiled at Ross who was such a good house guest and never needed to be looked after, much preferring to do the looking after himself.

"I suppose you expected them to stay longer" said Ross putting down the tray and pouring out the tea. "I must admit it is a long time since I had such an entertaining afternoon. I see now why you were compelled to eavesdrop on them, they need a great deal of watching, otherwise you may miss something."

36

David looked at him. "That's how I feel actually" he said, "as if I have missed something and I won't be able to apply myself completely until I have understood what it is that I am missing."

"Well the point at which you went into your scowl mode was then Kelly told you they had sent a copy of their manuscript to you", said Ross who had always had the ability to analyse a situation without ever seeming to have really observed anything.

David looked at him and thought irrelevantly about the time they had been sailing a catamaran. Ross had looked at him, as he looked now, calm and analysing, except that his head and face had been wet with spray and the words he had said were "we are about to be hit by a 60 foot wave, make sure you hold onto the boat." That was a nightmare he didn't want to remember because they had lost the boat and nearly their lives, but Ross had seen it coming and given them the few moments grace they needed.

"Pip?"

"I was just thinking about our sailing adventure."

"And me 'seeing' it coming?" said Ross, not at all put out by his friend's change in tack.

"What do you see coming this time?" he smiled.

Ross handed David his tea and took his own, thinking for a moment.

"Well you started to tell me about the 'A-causal' events which lead up to you coming to live here – you were actually going to tell me about the stone circle, but you got rather side tracked by the two people who were instrumental in changing your lifestyle though not necessarily in getting you to live here. Or were they? It seems strange that you met an old friend who just happened to be selling his house, which just happens to be next door to the God daughter of one of the women who you 'accidentally' met and who suggested a suitable living to you which changed your lifestyle." Ross paused, but David had the thought now and pursued it.

"That's what I keep trying to remember – when we met they allowed me to understand that they knew very little about me and it was up to me to tell them who I was and what I did. But they must have known me already because they told us today that they had sent their manuscript to me."

37

"So who is kidding who in this relationship?"

"And more interestingly – why?" said David.

He realised it was getting cold so he put down the tea cup and sorted round the mantle piece until he found the matches. Lighting the set fire was a task that always gave him great satisfaction. It was like choosing the exact moment of maximum effect to chase away the shadows and warm the room.

"You know the only way you are going to find out what they know or have known is to ask them" said Ross watching his friend settling now with the soothing ritual of routine.

"And then they may not tell me" said David sitting down again and biting into a biscuit.

"So you might just as well take the time to tell me about the 'A-causal' events. What exactly does A-causal mean?

"It means not due to cause and effect."

David smiled at the frown that appeared on Ross's perfect brow. Ross was a 'golden boy' in every sense of the word. His honest, easy going self was quite unashamedly genuine, as was his logical straightforward extremely able mind. Every weird and wayward idea that David threw down had to be taken up and examined from all angles until it could be considered and measured with his frighteningly capable brain. Behind the screen of physical prowess and his rosettes for rowing, running and hockey, was a first in Art History and European Literature that was never mentioned.

"What's up – you assessing me again?" said Ross noticing David's intent gaze.

"Trying to decide how to assemble my thoughts, in order to run them by that elephantine brain of yours."

Ross shrugged "Whatever way it comes I'll try and field it" he threw his legs over the arm of the chair and watched the fire crackle in the grate.

"It started with a knee injury. I was walking round the field in the twilight and I fell down the ditch and injured my knee. It just wouldn't heal and one day I was talking to a friend I have known for ages and he told me I needed to use a homeopathic herb. He explained impacting – don't ask – " he held up his hand, " and he said he would send me some information in the post. He did and in the midst of this information was a piece of paper advertising the local dowsing society. The man giving the talk was a healer/dowser – someone who heals with the use of a pendulum. I decided to go. I was fascinated so I went on his course – one weekend. Whilst there, we talked about Healing circles – Neolithic ones and how you could build them. The next day I met a man who lived in West Wales and had built one of these circles. He told me where I could get the blue stone from and worked out a price for the stone and the transportation. I really couldn't afford it, it was £380, so I said thanks, but let me think about it. Next day I received a cheque in the post from my old college saying I was owed money from some lectures I had done years ago. The cheque was for £380. I ordered the circle and my new dowser friend came freely and built it for me. Those are 'A-causal events'."

Ross was quiet. He knew his friend he didn't have to ask if he was joking he knew he had just been given a list of events as they happened.

"So we are to assume that Fate or something presented a series of opportunities that were unrelated, but which led in a very direct manner to you building a stone circle?"

David nodded.

"OK – but we must ask – why? What is it for?"

David shook his head "I don't know. But I am led by these events to be relatively certain that sooner or later I will know. The answer will be part of this chain of unrelated events which when viewed together lead in one obvious path."

"You got me Pip!" said Ross untangling his legs "I don't doubt you, but I don't understand it. Let's go into the kitchen and find something to cook. That is much easier. Cause and effect. Find, cook, eat. They are directly connected."

David sighed. It was too much to keep going round in your head. Something simple like dinner would be better.

Next morning, bright and early, David and Ross decided it was time to seriously start work if they were to have some kind of script ready to send off to Elmer Greenslade the American producer who could be interested. David didn't open Abra Chat on a Monday. He usually managed to get a whole uninterrupted day of writing. Providing the phone didn't ring and he didn't get side tracked.

"How much more of 'Cleopatra's times' have you written?" said Ross getting the coffee percolated and the toast organised while David dived in cupboards looking for God-knew-what.

"It's called 'Cast no Shadow'" said David emerging with a folder from under the colander and dishes in a cupboard on the island bench.

Ross peered at the file and sure enough scrawled across the cover was the legend 'Cast no Shadow'. Ross raised his eyebrows in a question.

"I put it there so no one would find it" David explained, getting the mugs down from a hook.

"No I'm sure I would never have considered looking for a manuscript in the pan cupboard" Ross smiled. "Why 'Cast no Shadow?"

"Well originally I was going to call it 'Time', and then the sequel to Time (which is another lifetime in my two women's eternal time span,) would be called 'Time Again'. I wanted to get across the continuum that one lifetime isn't all there is and that events proceed 'Time and Time Again'."

"Perhaps you should have had three books then you could have had 'Time' 'And' and 'Time Again'."

"But who the hell would buy a book called 'And'?"

"It would be intriguing."

"Besides 'Cast no Shadow' will be more appropriate if it is going to be a film."

"Or TV drama."

"Whatever. I called it 'Cast no Shadow' in the end because I was fascinated by the idea of the 'shadow side' of people. You know the masculine side of a woman and the feminine side of a man and how 'casting your shadow' is a way of expressing how much substance or material you have as compared to Light and Spirituality, Angels being Light Beings and therefore having no shadows at all."

David looked up to see if Ross was with him so far.

"And?" promoted Ross smiling.

"And also it is about the long shadow of Rome. The masculine soldier mentality, that is opposite to everything feminine."

"Is this part of your theory, that it was the advent of the Rome Empire that destroyed the matriarchal Goddess culture of the ancients?"

"Yes" said David surprised that Ross remembered so much from their passionate conversations in the early hours in their rooms in Oxford.

"Does the manuscript get this across?" asked Ross frowning.

"I don't know. As you said before, the film won't anyway. It will be a straight forward visual experience."

"The conversation could hold interesting features" suggested Ross taking the toast out of the toaster for buttering. It was already getting cold. David put coffee in the cups and they both moved to sit at the table.

"Why do you think they went to Greece?" asked Ross putting marmalade on his toast.

David looked thoughtful as he took a sip from his coffee cup. He put it down, it tasted bitter. Every since Kelly had told him that coffee compromises the immune system, he had felt slightly guilty drinking it.

"I don't know. Perhaps it is the home of the 'Goddesses' and they feel drawn to go there" he smiled "but then I always was a romantic."

"What are you going to do about the Abra Chat business if it isn't an 'Abra Chat' anymore?"

"Don't know. I quite like having the shop there, although it is a bit of a bind, especially if I am going to have to be writing full time."

"And going away" reminded Ross through mouthfuls of toast "If the script thing comes off you will have to spend time on rewrites with me on the set."

"God, I hadn't thought of that. I suppose I really need someone to look after Abra Chat."

"What about Louise?"

"She can't do it full time – although she is wonderfully competent – better than me by a long way – but she will have 'A' levels next year not to mention 'teenage' things."

41

Ross smiled and got up to pour more coffee. He was wearing a Burgundy shirt this morning, not a usual colour for a man, but it looked superb. David scowled at him. How did he do that? Look so smart even when casual? He was sure he had only just got up as David himself had, yet David looked crumpled in yesterday's green shirt and was unshaven. Ross turned and motioned with the coffee pot. David shook his head reminding himself that he must switch to tea drinking.

"Have you got anyone else in mind" said Ross.

David thought immediately of the long legged Sally Weatherfield and having her in the shop each day climbing ladders he would need to hold.

"Not anyone who would be interested" he smiled.

"Had any more thoughts on the 'mysterious Twosome'?" Ross said leaning back on his chair whilst David put marmalade on his toast.

"Thinking about those two gives me a headache" said David "what they do and what they say don't match up somehow."

"Is it a headache you would like to get rid of?"

"God no!" said David between mouthfuls "whatever else they may be they certainly keep me occupied and guessing."

"Have you spoken to them individually?" Ross asked.

"What, you mean divide and conquer? That would be the way to go you mean?"

"Why not? You could start with the long legged one."

"Me? Why me! Anyway who says I like long legs."

Ross laughed at the consternation on his friend's face "Well actually you did".

"I did not! Sara scares me to death – besides she doesn't like me – she looks down on me."

Ross laughed again "I thought so. You have a bit of passion for Kelly, don't you?"

David scowled, then smiled at his friend's attempt at psychology. "No I don't! she is very – natural – I like her."

"And you chase after Sally long legs because you know she is too young, too gauche and too impossible to be a serious idea. It stops you thinking where your real thoughts wander."

42

David got up and removed the plates to the sink. The mo
was rather grey and drizzly now, no longer a beautiful May morn

"Ross you talk a load of rubbish – as usual" said David smili
himself "besides Kelly might be married."

"Ahh! So thoughts have crossed your mind!" Ross was
triumphant watching his friend with the far-away smile.

"No. They haven't" he said "but I always enjoy being with her.
Anyway!" he moved back to the table clearing it with purpose "who
the hell says I am too old for the beautiful long legged Sally! Who
says age makes a difference?"

"You again – actually Pip old friend. You once told me that we
can only vibrate completely and therefore intuitively with our own
age group. It is something to do with 'resonance of time' you said.
Each time has its own key signature and that becomes our sort of
background base melody line. Without it you can't really have true –
Jazz – I suppose."

"Christ! I talk a lot of crap sometimes as well! It must be a sign
of age. I'd forgotten that thing about Jazz. Anyway I am ready to
amend what I thought slightly. Whilst that is true about Jazz only
belonging to each person's age group, it changes when you bring in
the concept of past lives. You see we actually have a deep base line
melody that belongs to our past lives, or more particularly our soul
group. But as we are not usually in the presence of any of our soul
group it doesn't apply. Of course because it is such a core deep base
note it is very hard to hear. I suppose we would have to be
disconnected from all our usual vibrations by going far , far away or
something. Anyway, just remind me about it later. I must write it
down. But now I suggest you read this next section whilst I go and
ferret about for some more chapters."

Ross took the offered manuscript shaking his head at his friend.

"Where will you go for this one we ask ourselves – the bathroom
towel cupboard, under the floor boards, in with the rice pudding?
The mystery deepens!"

David ignored him and went towards the spiral staircase thinking
that Ross could be a real pain sometimes 'speak to them
individually' 'holding secret passions' well he could be right he
supposed. But if he was, it was unrequited passion, and likely to

43

remain so. Besides those two were weird, who knew where their minds travelled and where exactly they went.

Even as he thought these irrelevant wandering thoughts, the vision of Kelly pressing a bunch of daisies between them whilst she gave him a kiss drifted across his mind, bringing with it warmth and fragrance and …….. and nothing! What was wrong with him? It must be a mid-life crisis or something. He turned on the computer trying to remember what was going through his head when he had written the password. Then he remembered – God! it was Daisy!

Downstairs Ross has poured himself a third cup of coffee and settled down to visit Alexandria in the cold dawn of 50 something BC.

Chapter Seven

Ross had been gone about four days when the next strange event took place. It was about midnight and David was just dropping off to sleep with his book still in his hand when the phone rang.

He picked it up sleepily and mumbled "Hello" down a line he was convinced was a wrong number.

A female voice said querulously "David?"

"Yes" he replied more alert now.

"It's Kelly." Silence. Kelly - at this time?

"Kelly – where are you?"

"In bed."

"In bed?" pause "not in Greece?"

"Er –no. Look, David, I phoned to say I'm sorry – about the note and … and other things."

Other things? What other things? Why was she phoning at this time?

"Kelly, are you alright? Is something wrong?"

"Oh no "she laughed "I know it is a bit odd to phone at this time, but communication is easier when you are half asleep. Were you half asleep?"

"I suppose so". His mind seemed to be stuck somehow, not working at all.

There was a long pause.

"Are you still there?"

"Yes – yes" he said trying to marshal some thought that didn't centre around the vision of Kelly in bed. "What did you want to communicate that was best at this hour?"

"It's about the manuscript" so she knew that that had thrown him. He thought quickly about passing this thought off and pretending innocence, but decided that he really wanted to know something about Kelly. He did want to communicate – not just talk.

"David?" The pause had been long again.

45

"You knew all about me long before our so-called meeting didn't you" he said quietly. It was a statement not a question.

"Yes. We had been observing you for a long time."

Observing him? What did that mean? But wasn't that what he was doing to them?

"Why?" he asked.

"Why are you observing us?" she countered.

Why indeed? Should he deny it, or tell her, or stall for time? But she was quicker than he, she answered her own question.

"You are writing about us in an allegory form, I suppose."

"Yes. Are you writing about me?"

"Don't have to. I already did that a long time ago. I was just looking for you."

"Have you found me?"

"Don't know. Might have. Do you know who you are?"

Did he? Really? Sometimes did he have thoughts about a time that wasn't this one? Or did he have a very fertile imagination? Did it matter? The line was silent. She was waiting. A lot depended upon his answer, he knew that. He also knew that Kelly had somehow broken the rules tonight. She shouldn't really be communicating with him. Not now – not yet. Why was she? And how did he know it was too soon.

"It's too soon" he heard himself say.

"Yes. I know that really. I'm sorry. I'm always impatient." A pause again. Neither quite knowing how to end this curious conversation. Neither not really wanting to.

Then suddenly Kelly decided. She just put the phone down. The line went dead. One moment she was there, then she was gone and for the first time in a long time David felt lonely.

He did understand that they had been communicating. Not just holding a conversation, but actually communicating. Now they weren't. He put the buzzing phone down and listened to the silence. At least his mind had cleared now. He knew what to do. He put out the light and turned over smiling to himself as he did so.

The box arrived about a week after the strange midnight conversation.

Sara had come into Kelly's work room with a postcard that seemed to be making her smile.

"Well well well ! A postcard from the Greek God" she said

"Where from?" asked Kelly putting down her pencil. She was working out procedures for her coming lecture series on intuition.

"From New York. He says 'how was Greece? Will be back in England in 2 weeks. How about a picnic in a punt?"

"Why has he sent it to you?" said Kelly peering over her glasses.

"Perhaps I'm his type" said Sara putting the postcard down in front of Kelly who turned it over to look at the Manhattan skyline.

"Not much of a view" he said peevishly " well, I suppose he is a real blond, not like that other one you used to have. He wasn't very blond at all".

"And you didn't like him" said Sara. She took back her postcard "Oh there's a parcel in the hall for you" she shouted back as she left the room. "I'm going to the library to check some references"

Sara was working freelance for a Publisher so trips to the library were quite frequent.

Kelly went to look at the parcel. It was addressed to her in typewritten script with no other visible markings. She tried to think who would be sending her a parcel.

"You have to open it to know what it is " said Sara on her way out.

Kelly thought she would have a cup of tea first then open it.

The packing material was lots of pieces of polystyrene, so Kelly knew it was either fragile or an irregular shape. She moved the packing aside and found a sharp wooded edge. It meant nothing so she continued. It seemed to be some winged creature. She went and got a polythene bag from the kitchen and knelt down in order to remove all the packaging. It was in fact two winged creatures facing each other. She continued to empty the box until she could see that it was two angels facing each other. They seemed to be kneeling on a flat piece of wood. She eased her fingers down the sides and felt more wood. It was indeed a wooden box. She took it out and looked at it. It was a chest about nine inches long, six inches high, and three inches wide.

She placed on the hall floor and looked at it.

"Oh my God !, The Ark of the Covenant" she said to no one in particular.

The lid was firmly in place. There was no note and nothing to say who it was from. She looked at it a long time, remembering all the taboos about opening the Jewish Ark. But then if she didn't open it she was unlikely to know any more. She shook it gently. Something rattled inside. She put it down again, wondering if Eve felt like this when she had picked the apple but not yet bitten in to it. Like me, she thought , without tasting it how could she learn more?

For Kelly the need to know overrode all other drives. Whoever had sent her this box must have known about her need to know.

She opened the lid. Inside the box was a dried and pressed moon daisy and an unmarked white envelope. She looked at the flower and opened the envelope. Inside was a railway ticket from Pewsey her nearest station to Coventry and was dated 2nd September.

She was puzzled. She thought that the presence of the daisy could only be from David, but the ticket? Was he sending her to Coventry? Getting rid of her? But the Ark suggested knowledge – spiritual knowledge – a learning of some kind.

But if it was to get to know him better, why Coventry? and why so long in the future.? It was June now. How odd. Sara would laugh, she thought David was a joke. Not someone you could take seriously at all.

Kelly put the ticket and pressed flower carefully back inside the box and put on the lid. The angels were facing each other. Locked into......something ? Locked into what? Consultation, communication, prayer? Argument?

What ever it was that they were locked into the power came from these two figures. She knew all the stories concerning the ark of the covenant and they all intimated that the power emanated from between the two angels. Yin and Yang. Positive and negative. Diametrically opposed opposites. A man and a woman?

Communication when it really occurred between a man and a woman. There was nothing more exciting. Nothing more intriguing than being involved in this communication. Nothing more intimate either. Intimacy was not really about taking your clothes off. You could take your clothes off and have sex without ever being close. It was how close you got that was real intimacy. Or could it be the angels were both female, and therefore creative, with a lot of older world past, and therefore locked into a process that was beyond comprehension. Was David that clever? Was he in the process of working it out?

Kelly made a decision. There was a spark between her and David and she should follow it to see where it was leading. It was not to do with anything else. Besides, Kelly was intrigued, and that didn't happen very often.

She left the packing and took the box up the stairs and into her bedroom at the end of the corridor. Opening the door into the eves she took out some plastic bags full of last year's clothes plus three boxes containing unfinished knitting and other various projects. Then wrapping the box in an old raincoat she then returned everything to the loft and went downstairs.

Taking the packaging into the kitchen, she collected some jars of new vitamin supplies from her cupboard and place them on the work surface as if they had just arrived in the mysterious box. Satisfied that everything looked normal she then returned to her workroom to continue her planning..

The decision had been made. Kelly was keeping the box, its implied implications and her strange conversation with David a secret. As a secret she knew she could share it with no one, because a secret shared was no longer a secret. So, until she could work out exactly what, if anything, was going on she would keep it close to her chest.

The phone rang. It was midnight. The witching hour.
"Hello"
"I got your parcel"
"Did you?"
"Why so long in the future?"
"To give us time to explore the implications"
"Are there implications?"
"Always. In whatever we do"
"We always have choices"

49

"At every stage we can choose to do something or not do something"

"What are we doing?"

"I don't know. Having a conversation? Having a communication? Exploring our passion?"

"Our unrequited passion you mean"

"Do we have a passion then?"

"We have a passion for secrets, that is certain"

"No one else would understand"

"Why would they? We don't understand ourselves"

Silence. The rapid fire conversation which was almost an attack ceased.

Kelly laughed, a full rich sound that filled his hearing making her seem very close.

"I think we must be mad" she said , " are we mad?"

"Possibly. But not boring."

"Most people are boring. I much prefer plotting"

"Are we plotting?"

"Not plotting in a political sense , No. Interested in plots of our own making"

"Does this plotting have a place to go?"

She was quiet for a moment.

"You know it is my belief that people have illicit love affairs not because they are unhappy with their circumstances or because they crave different sex, but rather so that they can be involved in intrigue.

"Then why do affairs revolve around sex?"

"Because people can only contemplate intimacy within the context of a) being naked and b) once naked, sex should surely follow"

There was a pause

"Are you still there David?"

He laughed "Oh yes I'm very much here. Just a little stunned by your train of thought.

"Ah! Well that's the idea isn't it? You see we get complacent with our communications they follow a set pattern. Like taking your clothes off and then having sex. The interesting things in life happen when you alter the pattern, or change your perception."

"So you think it would be better if we were to meet someone, take off our clothes and then have tea?"

Kelly laughed " well not really I don't think it would be very practical but the idea is interesting. I just mean to imply that intimacy is about being in another's aura or the space two people can create together. Like the Vessica - the interlacing of two circles, or the gateway to another dimension"

" Don't you think it is a bit late at night to be talking about sacred geometry" David said after a pause

Kelly laughed again. "You are right. Sweet dreams dear David. Tomorrow is another day"

Before he could reply she was gone and smiling to himself he settled back down to sleep.

Chapter Eight August

David was moving the program dial rapidly through its cycle in an attempt to make the washing machine pump out the water and allow him to extract his canvas shoes from the drum. He did not hear the door knock and was unaware of anyone else observing his problem until Louise spoke from behind him.

"You'll have to get a screwdriver and take the door off" she said.

David jumped and saw in his mind's eye the water cascading around the utility room floor. He said nothing. For one thing, he was supposed to think that Louise was in Greece – his conversations with Kelly were theirs and theirs alone and for another he dreaded Louise knowing that he had shoes stuck in his washing machine and not clothes. In fact, he couldn't think what had possessed him to put them in there in the first place.

Louise peered into the depths of the drum, but the rapid spins with water still present had ensured that a thick impenetrable foam hid the contents from anyone's view.

"I'll sort it out later" said David straightening and looking beyond Louise where a tall quiet girl stood watching him through her glasses. She had that tight curly blonde hair that stuck out at an angle all over her head. He smiled at her serious face, she looked as if she could sympathise with his problem rather than expect incompetence like Louise obviously did.

"This is Leigh", said Louise ,"she has been travelling and will be here for a year."

The information seemed to be relevant, but David couldn't, at the moment, see why.

"Come through and have some coffee or something" he said, leading the way into the kitchen away from the evident madness that his washing machine had become.

"I thought you were in Greece" said David as he filled the kettle.

"We didn't go in the end" said Louise a little sheepishly. "Exams and things you know."

"Of course" said David. "Is this a social call or is there something more sinister involved in your visit? or should I say visitation thought David. She did have a way of appearing from nowhere.

"Don't be silly, David" muttered Louise, restored to her position of superiority now that Greece was behind them.

David smiled as he turned away to collect coffee mugs. A little whispering warned him to keep his back turned a little longer.

Louise sat down on one of the stools at the island bench and motioned to Leigh to do likewise.

"David ......" began Louise tentatively.

As David had no idea what it was that she wanted of him he couldn't help her in any way. So he put on what he considered his easiest of facial expressions and looked attentive.

"Yes?" he said mildly.

"I was wondering, with all this writing business that you do and me with my exams and things, whether you really needed some more help in the shop – if you are going to keep the shop I mean."

Ahh! Now the presence of the friend with time on her hands became clear. David reached for the milk and poured it into the jug.

"I was thinking that just the other day" he mused conversationally " Abra Chat has become a sort of focal point. I think it condenses lots of energies and collects them here ......" he noticed Louise's eyes beginning to give him that look again as he was in danger of drifting off into a realm of his own.

He put the instant coffee in the cups and poured on the water.

"I would like to keep the shop" he said as if he had not guessed why they were here "but it is getting to be a bit much for me and I may be writing for a screen play soon ...... I don't really know what I am going to ......"

"Well! That is why I came" said Louise. "Leigh is looking for a job whilst she is home and I thought she would be perfect for you."

David looked at Leigh with what he hoped was surprise and found her smiling at the little drama she had witnessed. "Don't feel pressured into anything, please" she said "it was just an idea."

"It sounds like a good idea to me" said David smiling genuinely "can you type by any chance?"

"Yes" she said, surprised.

"Excellent" said David "how many hours do you want to work?"

"Well – how ever many you can manage. I do my Masters degree next year and I need to save."

"Well, I usually close all day Monday, but open on Saturday so that is still five days a week. I open at 10 but there are always books to sort and invoices to ……"

"There is always something David has forgotten" interrupted Louise "but he is very nice to work for". She finished more quietly, giving David one of her dazzling smiles and making him think that the sun had suddenly started to shine.

"I can probably pay you £5 an hour" said David thinking about the possible profit margin "and extra if you type some scripts for me."

He wondered suddenly whether Leigh knew Kelly and Sara – that could be quite awkward.

Louise with the uncanny knack that she seemed to possess suddenly seemed to catch this thought.

"Leigh has lived in the village a long time" she said, "we knew each other at school."

This reassured David and also made him think again about the strange business of synchronicity. If he was going to write this screen play he needed to be available, which meant that he could not look after the shop and he also needed a secretary. Now here was Louise offering him both. The only problem was that it was Louise and Louise somehow equated Sara and Kelly and that meant ……? What? What did it mean? Oh well, he might as well just go forward with the flow, so to speak.

"When would you like me to start?" asked Leigh breaking into David's wandering thoughts.

"As soon as you can" said David drinking his coffee then remembering to feel guilty about its bad effects.

"Next week – would that be alright?"

"Fine" David smiled to reassure her that it would be fine realising that he now had an employee and would have to fill in some forms.

"Lou, why don't you take Leigh through into Abra Chat and show her where things are" he said throwing the rest of his coffee down the sink.

"Whilst you find a screwdriver for your washing machine door?" said Louise wickedly. "I bet you have something really weird trapped in there, don't you?"

David gave her his most charming smile. "What am I going to do without your watchful presence, dear Louise?" he said.

"I expect you'll do what you always do, dear David" she threw at him from the door "Panic".

Too right, he thought, it's all I can do. He opened the drawer to search for a screwdriver, but it seemed to be full of pieces of manuscripts. He made a mental note to try to organise his life a little more in the future. It was a vain hope he knew even as he thought it.

Chapter Nine

"You have to be able to distinguish the Self from the Other" said Kelly thoughtfully " and sometimes it isn't easy – not in consciousness terms – you have to somehow be able to identify your own Self, your own thoughts and your own Being."

"Christ, Kelly, sometimes I don't even know what day it is never mind which is Me – me – myself or my alter ego – you do make the most sweeping of statements."

Kelly sighed "Well we must keep it in mind. We do pick up so much from other people, that is why our emotions are always in such a tangle."

Sara frowned and gripped the steering wheel a little tighter whilst thinking of a reply to her serious friend.

"Well, my emotions get in a tangle because a) it is PMT time, b) I can't find this bloody White Horse and c) that child had me up at 5 a.m. this morning! Now I have to struggle with some concept of self you are throwing at me and try to distinguish which "me" should answer."

"There! Turn right there – no, left I mean, that brown sign that says 'Uffington', go down there ……"

Sara turned more quickly than she meant to but the mini, being a mini, maintained its hold on the road, whilst Kelly kept her grip on the child and the picnic basket, which was in danger of spilling all over her feet.

"Bloody Hell!" she muttered to no one in particular. "Alright, Sooz darling? Aunty Sara wants to wipe us out before we have even discovered whatever it is we hope to discover."

"Sorry" said Sara flashing her perfect teeth "I am listening and I do see what you are trying to say. It probably proves the point really I probably picked up all that confusion from that poor bugger we nearly ran over half a mile back."

"That idiot wandering about aimlessly all over the place, like most males seem to do?"

56

Sara laughed. "I think we are on the right road now. Tell me more about the essential 'ME'."

"Hell the essential 'YOU' is far too rich for me – but the 'ME' inside is easier. I think it's rather like spiders webs."

Sara sighed. "Are we deviating or still on the same theme?"

"Still there. You see consciousness is like spiders webs. Have you ever been in a field in the early morning when the dew is still there, and then the sun comes out?"

Sara said nothing – what could you say? You just had to wait until Kelly got to where she was going. It was usually worth it in the end, but getting there could be painful.

Kelly had stopped again in order to fight with baby Sooz who was getting a bit bored.

"Give her that bottle of juice" said Sara, "it's in the other bag."

"God alone knows why we decided to visit the White Horse whilst we have the baby to look after. We are always making life difficult for ourselves."

"No, life throws us difficulties and we have to carry on regardless."

Kelly found the bottle and handed it to the baby. Little Sooz was Sara's niece. Her brother had just come over from South Africa with his daughter. Two months before his wife had died in a plane crash and Sara and Kelly had decided that two substitute mothers might be good for her. They hadn't really come up with any detailed plan as yet, like how to fit a child into their lives.

But as they had planned this trip some days before the arrival of the baby and knew that their work had to be fitted around their personal research, they had decided to continue as if everything was normal. Which of course it was, because no one else was going to be able to understand what exactly it was, that they did. Sometimes even they didn't know, but they understood that they had arrived on this planet with a plan, and no matter what the circumstances of their weird lives, the plan was always there and always uppermost in their thinking.

"Go on" said Sara. She had seen another brown sign and knew they were getting near their destination.

"What?"

"Spiders webs at dawn or something."

"Oh yes. Well, with the help of dew and sunlight, you can see the spiders' webs – and they are everywhere! On every branch, on rocks and almost every blade of grass. Incredible webs, or bits of webs, or long strands connecting things together. It is a total network spanning the whole area."

"A bit like the internet you mean?"

"I suppose so, except the thing that is incredible is that you can see the threads and webs – the connections. But as soon as the dew clears you can't see them any more. You are just not aware of them. You can't see them – but they are still there! They were there before you saw them and they will be there after you saw them, then couldn't see them. They are always there, we just don't know they are."

"But you do?"

Kelly looked at her friend disgustedly. "That has nothing to do with it!" she said crossly.

Sara smiled. "And consciousness, what has that to do with it?"

"Well, that is the point" she continued back into her flow "I think that is what consciousness is like. A tangible substance, something we create and we leave bits of it around on stones and rocks and trees and in our houses. Bits of people's consciousness are everywhere, we just can't see it. But we 'feel' it and we experience it. Most of the time we brush it aside like the spiders webs we walk through. Then, when emotional events are part of that consciousness, we get things like ghosts or 'atmosphere' and that is also how we create sacred space, as in a church.

All those consciousness parts, vibrating on one frequency – like prayer or reverence. It somehow becomes recorded on the fabric of the building. Really sensitive people can pick it up and make sense of it."

"So stress is 'us' – 'our consciousness' walking through a load of other consciousness rubbish that people have left behind?"

"Sort of …… Look there's a car park up ahead."

Sara pulled up the hill and parked the car. There was only one other car parked there so it looked as if they were in for a quiet time. Baby Sooz was still drinking her juice so they sat quietly for a moment looking out over the hills in the vale of the White Horse. They couldn't actually see the horse from here, but there was a footpath with a kissing gate.

"Well what do you think?" asked Sara, "have we been here before?"

Kelly shrugged. "The problem with time moving on, is that everything looks so different. With us, we have to try and remember what it looked like before, like hundreds of years before."

"Shall we go and see what all that writing says. See if 'they' know anything about the place, the so called experts."

"That's a vain hope" said Kelly getting out of the car.

Sara got out. Baby Sooz didn't seem to think she was being abandoned or if she did, she didn't care. They walked over to the sign and read about 'possible' ancient peoples.

Sara tutted as she read it, whilst Kelly gave up and walked towards the gate and looked further down the valley.

"I really feel there was water down there" she said. "I'm sure that hill there was once an island."

"It doesn't say anything about that here" Sara replied "however – look down there, there is a lake or something." Sara, being taller than Kelly, could see the glint of water in the distance.

"Well – there you are then" said Kelly "let's get the pushchair out and begin our hike."

They got the pushchair out of the back with some difficulty, opened it up and placed the baby in. Then they extracted the bag with all the baby things, the bag with their picnic, and their handbags.

"Goddess - we look like bag ladies!" said Sara.

Kelly was strapping as many bags onto the handles of the pushchair as she could without it toppling over backwards.

"Christ it's not easy being mothers is it?" she muttered struggling.

Sara went to open the gate and Kelly pushed the loaded buggy through. The rough, stony pathway was difficult to maneuver and left little time for further thought or philosophy. They reached the white chalk of the back leg of the White House and peered at it.

"It doesn't even look like a horse from here does it?"

"No. Let's go back over to that hillock, and have a drink or something" said Kelly. She was out of breath pushing the loaded buggy up the hill. The sun was trying to shine and the hillsides were empty except for a few walkers in anoraks.

Sara took over the pushing for a while and Kelly removed a few of the bags to lighten the load.

"Thank Christ you didn't wear those high heel shoes" said Kelly "we would never have been able to walk up here then."

Sara was wearing a vast amount of perfume, trainers, leggings and earrings with a large baggy jumper. Kelly was wearing sandals, a flowery skirt and a jacket and she was pondering upon how incongruous they looked.

"I was reading one of those Douglas Adams books the other day. He is very funny and he said that when your memory goes, if you are really old, hundreds of years, then all you remember are earrings and smells. He reckoned that was why everyone remembered Cleopatra."

Sara stopped pushing the buggy and turned round to stare at her friend.

"Earrings and exotic perfume!" said Kelly overtaking her and swinging the dangling earrings as she went. "Come on, I've got our favourite wine in here."

Sara laughed and continued the steep push up the hillside. When Kelly decided to leave the path she did have the decency to come back and lift the bottom of the buggy so that they could carry it between them.

"Didn't we used to have chair carriers to carry us around? In our other lifetimes" said Sara breathlessly.

"That's probably why we are having to do it now! Karma or something."

"Hellfire, I wish you had told me that then – I might have done more walking."

"I doubt it – you would have been mobbed by your loving subjects and probably beheaded."

"I don't see why! In those distant days in Egypt I spent much time on grain duties. Making sure we got a good price from those bloody Roman thieves."

"Do stop moaning dear. Put the buggy down here and let's get the wine out."

Kelly dropped her end of the baby and started to empty some of the bags from the back. They had a rug and after spreading it they flopped down glad of the rest.

Sara ferreted in the bag and found first the corkscrew, then the wine and finally two glasses wrapped in the baby's extra coat.

"Open the damn bottle first then we'll get the picnic out" said Kelly.

Baby Sooz was dozing a bit so they wrapped her spare coat round her. Sara got the wine uncorked and poured a drink into the glasses Kelly held out to her. Placing the bottle in the grass, she took a gulp of the deep red liquid.

"That's better" she said "what do you think happened here on this flat top?"

Kelly squinted at the adjoining hillside. The sun was out now and was bright, but not really warm. The top of the hill was slightly indented as if something had landed on it.

"I think a meteorite landed here. That would mean that a long time later, but a long, long time in the past – it would have been mined. By dwarfs I think. Weren't they always the ones who had 'the secret of metal ores' and made swords and things."

"That would support that other weird place down there called 'Weylands Smithy' said Sara pointing down the way they had come. "The God Weyland – wasn't he lame?"

"He also was the God of Sword making, so that would explain why ancient people would be here wouldn't it?"

"Yes. There must have been horses too. Real ones. I know the White Horse was sacred – like the White Roebuck or the White Swan."

"A sign of the Goddess" said Kelly getting the picnic bag out and finding the bread rolls and cheese.

"Does it help with our period of time though?" she said pushing the cheese in between the bread.

"Not really" said Sara. "If we are trying to sort out how and when we got to England we must be trying for 100-300 AD, mustn't we?"

61

"Mm" said Kelly biting into her roll "we are going to have to leave that one just now I think."

"Oh dear. Won't Dear David be upset. We won't be able to slip him another bit of the puzzle".

"Speaking of which have you in fact slipped him any of the pieces of the puzzle?" said Sara passing a chunk of bread to the baby.

"Not as such. In fact, he is struggling a bit I think. He has put together the idea of us remembering our life times and he knows about the Goddess but he can't get the bit about matriarchy and the Goddess allowing her sons to take over."

"Not really surprising as he is indeed a man! It is going to be an even bigger shock when he realises that the Goddess is on her way back" Sara smiled her most wicked smile. "You really need to start writing some stuff for him you know. The mystery has to deepen"

"What, in case we suddenly start to become boring?"

"Some chance", laughed Sara passing her friend a sandwich, "some chance".

"Some chance" smiled Kelly eating her sandwich. "Some chance! well, pass me the book and I will record this little outing. It might give him some kind of insight into how we work. Let him see that even with our knowledge we still have to work to retrieve our past!"

"Not to mention our purpose!"

"It will unravel for him, I'm sure"

"Such faith ! I hope you are right"

Chapter Ten   September

"No compromise David, absolutely no compromise" said Kelly putting down the glass of fizzy water she had been drinking.

David frowned. "But that must mean total confrontation doesn't it?"

"We do argue a bit". She smiled wickedly, "actually all the time, but that keeps us sharp."

"You must compromise sometime" said David, leaning back in his chair and watching her. She looked very alive and fascinating. She had had her hair cut a little since May so that it didn't quite touch her shoulders, but it made it thicker and full of bounce. It suited her. She was wearing a deep blue dress with little white flowers all over it. It had a scooped out neckline and she wore some small crystals round her neck.

"No, we never compromise. We decide to differ. We once argued for two weeks about the difference between the Mother of Sons and the Mother of Daughters."

"How did you resolve it?"

"By deciding that there was a difference, noting the difference, then moving on.."

David moved slightly to allow the waitress to put his lunch down on the table. It looked very pretty. It was chicken breast cooked with Ouzo and cream and it had been decorated with star fruits, strawberries and small purple flowers.

"How lovely" said Kelly to the Greek waitress. She smiled and placed the salad and pitta bread between them.

"I'm glad we didn't stay in Coventry" she said to David, whilst finding the salt to add to her chicken.

"So am I" replied David cutting into the white flesh. "It seems a pity to eat it, doesn't it?"

"We compromised David, unlike Sara and myself. You decided we should meet in Coventry and I decided it was awful. So we drove to a place we both liked – Stratford, and felt much better."

"Especially when we discovered a Greek restaurant and that we both liked Greek food."

"I suppose it will have to do instead of me visiting Greece this year."

It was the 2nd of September and that morning Kelly had used the train ticket from her box. David had met her at the station. He was wearing his green shirt and a jacket today, as it was a little cold. She had to go up a flight of steps, along another bridge and down again before she could get to him. As she walked along the bridge she looked down to where he was standing ,not sure whether he had seen her. But he looked up and winked conspiratorially, making her smile. It was silly, but it was a secret liaison and therefore quite exciting.

"Do you only have these thoughts of 'having been here before' when you and Sara are together and working on something?" said David passing her the salad.

"Oh no" said Kelly laughing "my head is full of 'other times' or 'other memories' all the time. Well no ... that's not quite true – they sort of flash in and out of the mind at the most obscure times – probably when something has triggered them – like a place – or a person – or a conversation or just my own wandering thoughts. The trouble is it can be quite disconcerting because I 'hear' the creak of leather as I lift myself out of the saddle to look at the landscape – and then I find myself in a car with a steering wheel and for a moment it seems alien and I can't recall what year it is. The present one I mean, not the past one. Do you ever feel that? Can't remember which time you are in?"

"I seem to be 'elsewhere' most of the time. I don't think I ever know what year it is."

"That's true, Dear David, we all do wonder at times, where you really are"

Kelly smiled and David smiled back.

"I don't think I consciously catch it, like you seem to be able to do" he said.

He took some more salad. Whilst Kelly looked out of the window down the ancient paved street.

"You mean you have these 'odd' thoughts, but they remain subconscious rather than in your conscious mind where you can communicate them?"

"Yes. I suppose so."

"Is that why you are so fascinated with the relationship between Sara and me?"

David immediately felt himself to be on moving ground. This was a dangerous area. What exactly did Kelly know about his writing and his interpretation.

"It's one of the reasons" he said cagily.

Kelly laughed "Compromise David, you are compromising again – trying to find the most acceptable pathway. The one you think I will like the best. Then we can both walk down it without being attacked by Dragons."

"Isn't that good mannered? Being caring and considerate?"

"It's being dishonest" she said her blue/green eyes looking directly at him "I thought we had decided we wanted this 'communication' between us to be honest."

He sighed and went back to the salad bowl and the delightful chicken.

"You're a hard task master" he muttered between mouthfuls.

She smiled and picked up a piece of lettuce with her fingers and popped it in her mouth.

"You don't ever get something for nothing in this life – you know that. If you want to communicate with your shadow-self, you have to be honest and expect surprises."

"Can you expect surprises?" he said frowning. "What shadow-self are we talking about?"

Kelly always seemed to talk as if the conversation had already begun. Starting in the middle without the explanatory leaflet.

She took some more lettuce with her fingers and as she dipped it in the cream sauce on her plate she seemed to be thinking. He took a sip of water whilst she thoughtfully chewed the calorie soaked lettuce.

"Well your shadow-self would be the opposite to your normal-self. So it would be your feminine aspect, your Anima. Mine would be my masculine side – my Animus. So we presume that if you find a person who is very, very similar to you, but is the opposite sex, this would be very instructive in allowing you to see your own shadow-self". She paused and looked straight at him

"Isn't that why you are so fascinated with me and my relationship with Sara? Why you are writing about us? Isn't it a way of you discovering more about yourself? After all, that is what life is really all about isn't it?"

He was, at once, slightly taken aback, but also unsurprised at this turn of the conversation. Kelly continued to dine upon salad soaked pieces eaten with her fingers, whilst David seemed to be in a state of frozen anxiety, half way between being both pleased and terrified.

She looked at him closely and cocked her head to one side.

"There you are, David, now you have it, expected surprise. It really does exist."

David laughed. She really was a very interesting and amusing person so ...... so similar to me he thought.

"Are we not having a romance then?" he said suddenly.

"I don't think so – do you? It seems silly with yourself, so to speak. However, it is a very, very interesting exercise."

He smiled "Yes it is. And yes, you are right. Intellectual counterparts."

"Of course you realise that this kind of relationship is denied by 'all those who know' she said. "Well known fact that there is no such thing as a platonic male/female relationship."

"It is just a sexual one waiting to happen?"

"So they say" she laughed "that just makes it more exciting doesn't it?"

He passed her the pitta bread as she had run out of salad, but she shook her head.

"Thanks, I'm fine and you haven't answered my questions."

"They were statements, not questions."

"No they weren't, they were questions."

"I've forgotten them."

"No you haven't. Your mind works like mine – it stores information and detail – whole – ready to be used again in some other context. Some other conversation between characters you have created and are going to write about."

"Do you want some pudding?" he asked after a while of silent eating whilst he deliberately avoided her questions.

"No thank you, I'm fine. Are you buying me lunch out of all the profit you are going to make from my past lives?"

"Don't be silly" he said smiling "I am buying you lunch because you are bankrupt – or so you said."

"I am bankrupt" she murmured finishing her water and wiping her fingers.

David made a discrete sign that attracted the waitress who brought the bill and collected the plastic in return.

"And I haven't forgotten my questions. I am just allowing the lunch to go down. We will go for a walk by the river and see if your memory returns."

See if I can come up with some suitable excuse he thought picking up his jacket and helping Kelly into hers. Conversation with this woman was rather like grabbing a tiger by the tail. He didn't know how he was going to make the next move without getting in the way of those formidable jaws.

Outside it was sunny although a little cold. The air had that wonderful exciting tinge of frost that made you aware that Autumn was coming.

They walked down the street in comfortable silence. Kelly had linked her arm into David's after two steps from the restaurant. They crossed the road together enjoying the physical contact, but without the need to cover their feelings with inane conversation.

They passed the theatre and carried on along the gardens that ran by the river. People were milling about everywhere enjoying the sunshine before the colder weather arrived.

"I think we should go to Warwick" said David. "We need to be somewhere old, Stratford has too much 90's in it."

Kelly looked at him sideways and smiled "What about the wonderful Mr Shakespeare whose name appears everywhere in this 'quaint little town", she said with a rather bad simulated American accent.

"I have my doubts about him" he said, looking round quickly to see who might have overheard this terrible heresy "and I

67

certainly worry about this growing trend for everyone to become a tourist – even people who live here."

"History is so good at getting it wrong isn't it?" she said laughing at his fear of becoming a tourist.

"Which particular part are we talking about?"

"The grocer from Stratford, of course."

He looked at her, stopping suddenly.

"You mean ……?"

"William, the grocer from Stratford , who turned theatre manager due to some very interesting plays that he managed to stage."

"You knew him?" David said quietly.

"Must have, don't remember him too well – not memorable – do remember he was a grocer though and that he couldn't write. 'They' seem to have forgotten that. It was important that we found a way to hide a lot of our information though. We were in deep trouble. Witch hunts and all that."

Kelly turned to continue walking, but David realised that this was a moment he could not allow to escape. He steered her to a nearby bench and sat her down.

"So how did you hide your information?"

She smiled   "In the only safe place possible. In full view of everyone. We wrote wonderful plays that were staged. Our lines so well crafted. Our jokes, so amusing. That as time passed not a line was changed. That way we preserved our litany."

David looked at her closely, but her eyes were focussed on the middle distance and she was seeing with her mind's eye.

"Have you never wondered why the words – the language, the old English, has never been modernized, never been altered. Everything else written at that time, or any other time, has been altered. Even the bible" she was looking at him now seriously with intent.

"If it is questioned, no one pursues it" he said thoughtfully.

She shrugged "well, there you are then. I rest my case. You can read our ancient knowledge anytime you want to. It has been printed and reprinted many times and the grocer from Stratford came to be immortal, even though scholars can make no sense of his actual life or education."

68

"And the reason for that is that he was actually a grocer" said David quietly lest any should hear.

"Well – he did 'put on plays' – it was his part- time, pastime, you might say" said Kelly "but they were rather mediocre and not very memorable until we slipped him a few of our scripts. Then his life brightened up considerably. We also got a little help from old Frances too. He lived with my family you know."

David decided that he really didn't want to hear about this just now. So he got up, offered Kelly his hand, and led her towards the car park. She smiled and seemed to be unconcerned with his 'head burying tactics'. David really didn't know what to make of her. You couldn't just accept anything she said. You had to evaluate all of it, or just ignore pieces that were too big to digest. He needed time to think. Events seemed to be moving rapidly of their own volition which was not a situation that David was used to. He liked to be in a controlled environment with measured stages to negotiate.

They were almost at the car park now, but Kelly had slowed her steps until they were dragging and David had to stop to look at her closely.

"What's the matter?" he said concerned.

"Where are we going David?" she said, serious now for the first time that day.

"Warwick – you know where ……" he stopped.

"I mean you – and – me – 'us' where are we going with this relationship – this meeting?"

"Where do you want to go?" he asked, sober now, matching her mood.

"Answering with a question isn't answering – in fact you have done very little answering all day", she said scowling thoughtfully.

"Where do you want this relationship to go?" he asked, more precise now.

"I don't know" she said sighing "I really don't know. But it isn't to Warwick. I think you should take me back to the station where you found me. It's time I went home and considered – 'things'."

David searched her face for the easy laughter that had been there before. But her face was serious and a frown had appeared on her forehead. He bent forward quickly and kissed it. She smiled and the frown disappeared. He put his arm round her shoulders and began walking again.

"Come on then" he said "let's take you back. Having you to myself all day was lovely and I don't want to spoil any of it."

She gave him a grateful squeeze and they walked back to David's car in comparable silence,

On the way back to the station they talked about Ross and David's hectic days trying to keep up with the Olympian, but the conversation was light and had none of the serious overtones of their lunchtime conversation.

When they got to the station they had a twenty minute wait, so David went and bought them some tea and a flapjack. When he came to the table and sat opposite her, Kelly looked closely at him and smiled.

"Just one question more" she said.

He frowned in anticipation.

"Why the Ark of the Covenant?"

"Ah, my marvellous box."

"Was it to do with 'communication with God' or the written word being the source of all wisdom, as it had originally contained the broken Ten Commandments?"

He laughed at the speed with which her mind had interpreted the symbolism.

"I just liked the design" he said wickedly.

"Did you make it?"

"Had to, it isn't the sort of thing you can buy anymore."

She smiled, but she was waiting for his real answer.

"Source of all spiritual wisdom or something?" he shrugged and smiled, but his eyes were serious.

"Drink your tea, David, I have a train to catch" she said shaking her head.

But later, when he had waved goodbye and she was sitting on the train, bound for home, watching the countryside flash by the serious expression she had worn earlier was still there and it remained there for the whole of the journey.

70

Chapter Eleven   October

I've got no choice – I'll have to go home."

Sara was standing looking out of the window while Kelly was trying to share the crisps between the two plates. She looked up.

"Home, as in South Africa?" she said.

Sara turned round and looked at her friend.

"The business is non-existent – Kalahari Kolours is waiting for an influx of capital and baby Sooz needs looking after – that adds up to "no choice" don't you think?"

Kelly sighed "I suppose it does."

Sara came over and took her snack from the table.

"I don't understand it either – the universe seems to have reasons for us to be apart – Goddess knows why!"

"The Malthouse is gone, along with the business and I suppose your car will go next?"

"Tomorrow. I'll have to book my ticket on the Barclaycard and leave you to dodge the creditors and write the letters."

"Oh well – we've been here before."

"At least this way your house is intact and you can get a job."

"God it's all so depressing! What happened? One minute we were rushing ahead with our plans, the next the bottom has fallen out again and no one comes up with the money."

Kelly sat down opposite her friend who had opened the wine and poured them both some.

"I suppose I might as well go back and finish the degree I never finished. At least I can do that in South Africa" .Sara smiled. "Come on Fruit, let's drink a toast to the next time – we are bound to have a next time – we just don't know when or how or what."

"The trouble is we both feel that we have tried so hard with this time and got nowhere."

"All that writing. All that knowledge, that we have collated and remembered and written down."

"Not to mention our letters. That incredible record of how we started as two people who knew nothing of ourselves, or our own history, or our spiritual path and how together we developed and grew and wrote it all down so that others would know."

"Except,, no one seems to want to know. We thought we would be published by now. We thought we would be sitting somewhere each day in an office, writing more of what we know and what we remember. But no publisher understood what we were saying."

"They only seem to want to publish self-help books. Perhaps ours is too much of an "I did it my way – with my friend".

Sara laughed and took a sip of wine. The nights were drawing in now, it was almost October. The fire was lit and cast long shadows round the room. They hadn't bothered to turn the lights on yet.

"Do you remember that dream I had"? Kelly suddenly said, staring into the fire, "the one where I visited you when you had gone back to South Africa. You were in your flat and I brought you a pair of old worn sandals that were yours."

"I was in my new dressing gown wasn't I?"

"Asleep as normal whilst I am astral flying to find you!"

"And you helped me to put the sandals on, didn't you?"

"Yes. Do you think it was about journeying? walking around everywhere.? You know, the worn sandals, signifying many journeys?"

"I don't think I have stopped going off on journeys have I?"

"Perhaps we are going the wrong way. If it isn't working then perhaps we have to go a different way."

Sara looked at her friend in the half light and put her glass down.

"If we are going the wrong way and need to take a different route. Then perhaps we need to really start afresh. Get rid of all we have done."

"We won't destroy it. You know we can't do that."

"No, but we could put it all in a Time Capsule. Seal it and lock it and don't open it for ……..however many years. Then we are free to start from scratch."

"Put the letters in as well?"

"I guess so. How many times have they been back to England now?"

72

"I don't know, three or four? We do have them all don't we. All three sets?"

"Yes. At least they will be safe and we will stop carrying our own baggage around with us and be free to go in a different direction."

"Perhaps teaching. Perhaps we should be teaching rather than writing."

"Goddess knows. Nothing else has worked let's go for a complete change."

"As well as a separation?"

"It looks like we have no choice doesn't it?"

"Where are we going to keep the Time Capsule?"

"Well as it is for us we don't need to bury it or anything. We could just put it away somewhere."

"In my loft?"

"Along with all the other junk! Sounds perfect. We'll have to put everything in all the books – finished or not, all the stories, all the books we have used."

"Including Graves?"

"I think so. Nothing should escape the Time Capsule."

"We should have a witness really in case something happens to us."

"What, like we lose our memory or drop dead!" laughed Sara.

"Or our lives. Who knows, accidents have happened before."

"I know. OK let's get Louise Peabody down this weekend. I'll go back to the flat where I have lots of my stuff and some of the last batch of letters. You have the last two batches somewhere. I did bring them back from South Africa. Of course we were hoping that it might be time for our biographer to make an appearance!"

"Some hope. You need to be famous and if no one is listening to us they don't know what we have to say."

"I wonder who else but us would worry about our biographer and even leave the unknown person notes!"

"Only people who remember their previous lifetimes and know how damned difficult it is to retrieve information unless you make appropriate plans."

73

"Speaking of appropriate plans, I had better book my ticket and inform my Mother tomorrow."

They were silent for a moment. The thought of the impending separation was a vast space, with the feeling of inevitability. But beneath it they felt that somehow this separation was something they had chosen at some stage. Even though they no longer remembered why they would do such a silly thing.

"We need a box" said Sara, determined to be practical and final.

"I have the very thing!" smiled Kelly " I'll get it out."

"Will you phone Looby Lou tomorrow?"

"Yes. We will meet back here on Sunday and empty the contents of our cupboards into the Time Capsule."

"How long are we going to leave it there?"

"I suppose we need a period of time because we will need to recover it in our lifetime hopefully so not too long."

"Not twenty years."

"No. Too precise a number. Eighteen?"

"Yes. Eighteen years. Then we'll be old and all our obligations will be fulfilled and hopefully we will be able to retire on our ranch and laugh at all these strange ideas we had."

"If we need to we can always open it earlier, as long as we agree and do it together."

"What if we write something else that just has to be published and they say to us 'do you have any other writings?'"

"Do you have any other writings!!"

Kelly laughed "I'm just waiting for someone to ask us that – Christ wouldn't they be surprised!"

"I'm going to bed" said Sara suddenly feeling very weary of all the rushing and planning they had been doing for the past twelve years.

"I'll go off and pack tomorrow and collect all my work stuff. Then , I suppose I must book my ticket."

"Then plan our exit stage left on Sunday in dramatic form."

"As always dear. Dramatic entrances and Dramatic exits."

"It's all these years of being travelling players – it still reflects in our lives."

"A pity some of the respect and opulence doesn't", Sara threw over her shoulder as she made for the door.

"Good night dear."

"Good night."

Chapter Twelve

Sunday was dull and rainy. It was October, always a time of great change for both of them thought Kelly. All goings, endings and closing of circles seemed to take place in October. It was their time of change. The weather was just reflecting the mood that this parting held for all three of them. Well, four really, they had to include baby Sooz as well. She was now an important part of any future that they planned.

Sara brought the baby with her. She could walk now. The small amount of time she had been in England had seen her crawl, then walk and begin to talk. It was significant that she had done all of these important stages whilst the four of them had been together. The fabulous four as Sara called them. They didn't feel fabulous as they ate their lunch knowing that afterwards they had the task of consigning their lifetimes work together to a Time Capsule not to be opened for eighteen years.

"Remember when we met and you had just written 'A Piece of Thyme'."

"And you were clutching 'Counting an Echo' in case I didn't get the message?"

Sara laughed and put the hand written manuscript into the box.

"You wouldn't have 'got the message' either of you, if it wasn't for me" ,Louise said. "You were both behaving as stupidly as you always are."

"What, you mean the only people who can 'fall out' by letter and 'not speak' by phone call?" Kelly laughed. "I still think 'Counting an Echo ' is a fabulous title and worthy of being a best seller."

"Pity only you thought so!"

"Well you did change the title several times."

"Oh yes! What was it? 'Zimbabwe/Rhodesia' or 'Zim/Roe ' and then some number or something".

"'Echo Tango Delta' or some such thing, then it became 'Superleg'."

"Don't even ask" said Sara to Louise who was looking a little perplexed.

"Anyway, 'Superleg' wasn't the same story at all" said Kelly "you just got cold feet about writing your biography at the age of 23."

"Well, I realised there would be some changes."

"I thought these first books were intended to be a trilogy?" said Louise handing more of Kelly's manuscripts to put in the box.

"Oh yes they were. I was going to write 'An Iris for Agnes' which was about my Great Grandmother's eldest daughter, Agnes – who was my Grandmother."

"Coming down the generations" said Sara pausing to remember the excitement and awe they had felt at these first joint ideas. 'Piece of Thyme' was your Great Grandmother's story, then your Grandmother's, then your Mother's - what was that called?"

"'A Breath of Time'" smiled Kelly.

"And mine" said Sara " 'Courting an Echo' – the Irish story of my Mary. Mary O'Connor."

"Which was the reason you came to England in the first place" said Kelly thinking of the time they met " wasn't she calling you in a song or something? An Irish song that you couldn't know being in South Africa"

"I didn't know you could sing" smiled Louise.

"She can't. Fortunately it was in her head."

"So you up and left your husband, your home, your country, South Africa at that time and bought a ticket to England to find your roots and follow a song."

"And a dream. Don't forget I had the place and the people in my dream."

"So you really were 'Courting an Echo'" said Louise.

"Yes she was, and we still are. The echoes in our heads are stronger than the vibrations in our real lives" said Kelly thoughtfully. She paused as she remembered the awe and excitement they had felt, when they finally met on a train going to Manchester.

"You know we swapped manuscripts straight away, even though we were supposed to be strangers" said Sara.

"No one ever does that" smiled Kelly "not their first precious manuscript."

They laughed.

"Are we going to put Graves in too?" said Kelly holding onto the well thumbed volume of ' The White Goddess'.

"Our very own bible" said Sara "I think we have to really if we are going to come at ourselves from another angle, then yes, we must."

Kelly sighed and placed their friend and mentor, Robert Graves, carefully amongst the hand written notes. That was followed by the poetry and Sara's diary that she had kept of the events leading up to and just after their meeting.

"It's all in here you know. All the innocence and naivety. All the discoveries we made one by one. All the coming to awareness."

"All the amazement" added Kelly "do you remember – it was our most common phrase?"

"It's amazing! " they both said together and laughed.

"We used to have to have 'Amazing days' didn't we. Just spent time picnicking and being amazed."

"Are we not amazed anymore "said Sara quietly.

"We are amazed, but we are also tired. Tired of pushing our amazing energy into projects that no one understands. Tired of seeing something so perfect and complete and way beyond its time and place – then turning round and finding no one can see us, let alone the wondrous things we have created."

They were all quiet for a moment. Even the baby held the moment and the sadness, just staring at the spiritual sisters around her.

"We need to mourn a little for the people we once were. For all that enthusiasm and joyfulness that we poured into projects – that didn't quite make it."

"But they will"   said Kelly. It wasn't a question, it was a statement.   "That is why they are going into the Time Capsule. They are before their time, but we will put them all into operation one day. It just won't be this day!"

"And we needed to do it with the high octane energy of youth and innocence. We won't have that when we are ready to use them."

Kelly smiled slowly. Sara sighed. Louise began to put the rest of the books papers , poems, diaries, journals and manuscripts into the box. Followed the business plans and proposals, and finally the letters sent to various heads of state. These were never small plans, they were always huge and the leaps were high. The replies when they got replies were mainly of the type ' this does not fit our list' . Too true. Anything unique could not fit their list.

"Sometimes I think our whole purpose has been to create the idea and then launch it, so that it can be taken up and used by others."

"I know" sighed Sara "but when we do open this capsule we will have the evidence that we predicted so many things. We will have the written proof, that we knew so much, without reference to any evidence . It will make our memoirs so much more exciting."

"At least we will be able to laugh and laugh as we sit in our farmhouse in Tuscany."

"So long as we laugh all the way to the bank via the secretary, biographer and publisher, I don't mind" smiled Sara.

"You two are incorrigible" said Louise.

"You will still be saying that whilst drinking your sundowner or our stoop, in a hot place, when you are aged about forty" said Kelly.

"Is that when she retires?" laughed Sara, the sadness lifting.

"Goddess give me a chance. I haven't even started on my life yet, and you two are thinking of retiring me."

"Is that everything?" said Sara. They all looked into the box at the pile of paper that represented nine years of their lives. The time they had spent together.

"Nine. The ninth wave is the biggest wave" said Kelly.

"Are we ready to close it?" said Sara. Kelly nodded and found the roll of extra strong tape.

Together they sealed and secured their life work. Wrote on the box various legends like 'Time Capsule' 'Not to be opened until 2012 only in the presence of ......' then they all signed it, removed some of the boxes of books and pushed it slowly into the loft space.

They put back the other boxes so that it was just one box amongst many and closed the door.

"Here endeth the beginning" said Kelly.

"A bit like 'Cleopatra's Salad Days'" said Sara.

"That's in the box too."

"But the idea?......"

"The idea is very possibly alive and well and being recreated by Mr David Appleby.

"Say 'amen'" said Kelly.

"Amen" said Louise and Sara together.

Then they laughed and left the loft space and the Time Capsule ready for the closing chapters, when all the pieces of all the plots would come together and hopefully make sense. They had recreated their Archive which had been with them for lifetime after lifetime, until they had been separated and oppressed, and the memory of the matriarchal civilization had been lost.

All except, for the small group of women who had found a way of retrieving the information from their DNA. Now they needed to wake up the women of the world to their inheritance and their rightful place, before the Goddess Herself woke up in 2012.

Chapter Thirteen
The Following Year

"Leato"

Kelly blinked at the man standing in front of her. He held out his hand.

"I'm Leato"

"Oh ...Kelly"

She took his hand which was cool and long fingered and had a plaited coloured bracelet on the wrist. He smiled and went to sit on the chair next to the one she had thrown all her things over.

Her eyes followed him. He was so strange. It was the hair. It was totally amazing. Blond, curly and so much of it. He wore a fine lawn white shirt that was tucked into a pair of jeans, but billowed everywhere around him. She pulled her eyes away as he looked up and returned to collecting the notes she had gone to find before the he had appeared before her.

It was June and hot in the upstairs room. She had never been to Glastonbury before but had been drawn to this one day seminar by an author she had long admired. Joining the assortment of hippy type people making their way up the old staircase, she hadn't remembered seeing this striking man when she had first come into the building. But then she had been engrossed talking to some people who seemed to know her from somewhere.

Collecting the handouts she went back to her chair, pushing her bag and jacket under the seat. A sidelong glance told her that his jeans were old and well worn, a contradiction with the magnificent shirt.

The wonderful author, who had lead Kelly to this place, at this time, turned out to have feet of clay, not much to say, and didn't fit the image she had from his books. In fact, the more he talked the more she became convinced that the books had been ghost written and the questions on the mathematics that she had wanted answering seemed to be a mystery to him.

The slight movements from her companion were a welcome distraction from her disappointment in the course. The beautiful golden curls bounced up and down in the shaft of sunlight streaming in through the window, making them sparkle like a bright fire. Leato turned his head towards her and smiled. His eyes which she had overlooked until now were a deep violet colour and they lit up as he smiled. He wore some small beads around his neck, which seemed to be made of crystals because they too caught the light. Someone was asking a question and he turned back to listen. Kelly wondered what he did for a living. He probably worked for the water board or something equally mundane she thought.

The author droned on making it obvious that the complex geometry in his books had been worked out by someone else. Break time came just before Kelly nodded off to sleep and as everyone began to file outside to drink herbal tea and talk absolute nonsense, Kelly thought about absconding. She looked at whether the staircase exit was free, bent to pick up her things and as she arose rather too quickly, she almost bumped into the beautiful Leato who was standing in front of her without apparently having been there a moment before.

"The water board need some help" he said "but I don't work for them".

Kelly looked at him more closely, frowning. She knew she hadn't voiced this idea. He did look rather odd. He had a sort of glow around him almost like bright sunlight, although the window was on the opposite wall and not shining behind him.

"I'm an angel" he said without emotion or qualification. "I am here to help you."

Kelly gave him one of her most penetrating looks, scowled, then headed for the stairs. There was nothing you could say to that statement except "pardon?" and she had heard him perfectly well. She looked back and was unimpressed to find the room entirely empty.

That had been her first encounter with Leato. There had been others with more information and more walking away. Lack of

82

acceptance being her usual style. Except that now she realised that she had got to stop walking away and start accepting and perhaps listening. All these thoughts and previous meetings had been going through her head as she had stopped still on this sunlit day in early September, because he was standing by her favorite tree and looking at her. She had kept her eyes steadily on him while her mind had replayed that first encounter and he hadn't disappeared and she hadn't walked away so perhaps this was progress. She took a tentative step towards him and flashed through the other encounters. The second one had been whilst waiting to pick up Louise from her holiday job. He had appeared in the car next to her and she had asked him about his jeans

"If you are an angel, why are you wearing jeans?" she said sharply.

He smiled.

"I thought you would like the modern touch. Just to let you know that I am in the present and with the moment."

She had laughed at the idea of an angel in blue jeans. But she didn't ask him who he was, she already knew. She knew that she knew him, because when he was close to her she became overwhelmed. The emotion was so strong that she cried and told him to go away. He always did. She could talk to him for very short periods of time until the overwhelming sadness came and she was devastated. He led her to believe that this was to do with the parting she experienced from other lifetimes and from the higher realms, where they had been connected to each other, and to others of their soul group. She was not ready to hear this or to inquire what he wanted of her. So she always walked away or told him to go.

She had asked an elderly medium if he 'saw' angels and guides and when he assured her he did, she asked about light filled young men with large heads and huge golden hair. He recognised the description right away.

"That's what Lamurians look like" he said. "Lamuria was here before Atlantis. It was when we were in a stage between spirit and matter. They were much involved in the plant kingdom. Have you seen one?"

She admitted she had and he became very excited saying that they rarely, if ever visited now and that she was very honoured. She didn't tell him she had been very rude to him and told him to go away on more than one occasion.

She had reached the tree where he was standing now. He turned towards her and smiled. It was a devastating blast of golden light. She closed her eyes and tried not to take the full force of his energy.

"It's time you told me why you are here" she said.

He shrugged "To help you with the plant remedies."

Now within Kelly's mind an idea had been forming. A plan. A new direction. Since Sara had returned to South Africa, Kelly had been doing courses in vibrational medicine. She had always been drawn to Healing, especially making potions from herbs and plants. She hadn't studied it, she just knew what someone needed and would gather the plants and make a sort of tea to drink or sometimes place it on the outside of the body. She had also been on a course by the same man who had instructed David in building his stone circle. This course had involved removing blockages from the energy system, then allowing the body to heal itself.

Leato was watching her.

"You have done this before you know."

She knew without clarification that he was talking about previous lifetimes and not about a few months ago. She also knew that he was right.

"It would take more than your lifetime to have learned what you know now and there is more that you need to remember. That is why I am here." It was a statement.

"You need the keys to open the doors into the information you already have. You couldn't have access to that information until the time was right."

"Until I was ready?" she said quietly

"That, and until it was the right time for the Planet herself. Until Gaia the planet had moved in her vibration, and was ready. She has been undergoing some very drastic changes in the past few years."

"Is that why Sara and I needed to separate?" Kelly said

"You needed to access your own unique information. You couldn't do that together. Together you have different energy.

84

Energy that is very powerful and effects the consciousness of the Planet. "

"Just like the stone circle works" said Kelly. "It allows human consciousness to access the planet consciousness"

Leato laughed, it was a wonderful tinkling, joyful sound, high and resonant.

"So you understand that energy do you?"

"Yes, it is reliant upon the consciousness as well as the earth energies."

"David doesn't know that."

"No." Kelly frowned. Why had she never told him that?

"You have been working on your own theory with this healing you are doing, haven't you?"

"Yes, I realise that all 'illness' or dis-ease is derived initially from Trauma. And Trauma can be in different forms. It can be physical, mental, emotional or spiritual."

"That is where it can lodge" said the blue- jeaned angel "but it is always a spiritual problem. Remember that. All that ails the world is related to people not being on, or not following, their own spiritual path."

"But how would anyone know what their spiritual path is?"

He laughed again "that is the problem, only each individual person knows their own spiritual path."

Kelly frowned. She was beginning to get emotional and knew that this meeting had to come to an end soon.

"You know when you are on your own spiritual path because you become harmonious. You start to sing in tune."

"Can you hear people then, like we hear music?"

"I perceive your vibrations. Which is what people do all the time naturally. Anyway. much of the information you get from each other is not in verbal form but is about energy. How else do you think you recognise someone in a crowd? People all look very similar. Yet you always know the person you have come to meet, don't you?"

The emotional volcano that had been building inside Kelly's chest started to move to just behind her throat and her eyes. She turned her head away from the angel, but even as she did, she felt him leaving and the feeling diminishing.

She carried on waiting and as she did she wondered briefly if there would ever be a time when you could actually get used to the presence of angels.

For no reason as if quite unbidden, she thought about David and how she had not been in touch with him for some while. It was probably time she did.

Later that Year.

The phone was ringing. She had forgotten the last time it had rung.

Sara picked it up and murmured "hello".

"How is everything?"

"Diabolical! How is it with you?"

"Same"

"Goddess what on earth is going on? Has dear David done anything yet?"

"No. The only good thing is this line. You sound as if you are next door, not 6,000 miles away."

"I wish I was next door. We could go and have a picnic like we used to do."

"How is baby Sooz?"

"Not a baby anymore, going to nursery school now. I am writing the art thesis. I have decided to do Caravaggio and prove that they had lens and used them."

"You are not going to go into Galileo and his famous tower bit are you?"

"Don't think so. We fell foul of the church mafia then, I still don't trust them. They are now operating in politics so we have to be so careful."

"They always were operating in politics! How's your mum and have you got a job yet?"

"Oh God, not 'a real job' everyone thinks we should have a 'real job' and stop messing about with weird and wonderful imaginings."

"Who says we have weird and wonderful imaginings?"

86

Sara started laughing and the sound rattled down the telephone 6,000 miles away. Kelly sat down on the chair and sipped her tea.

"Anyway" she said looking out of the window at the grey sky and bare trees, "it is too cold for a picnic. We would need hot soup or better still, crumpets by the fire."

"It's 34 degrees here" said Sara "and a fire is out of the question." "Are you sure this separation is all part of the plan. It seems as if nothing is happening."

"It is happening. I have started healing like last life time and am being assisted to make remedies."

"Assisted?"

"I met an angel."

"On this plane?"

"I wasn't in an aero plane! No, I saw him with my mind.

Well he disappeared without trace. The field is narrowing. Becoming more defined. The dimensions are getting closer.;

"Does that mean you know what to do?"

"I have activated a lot of earth points, ready for the arrival of the Goddess energy. It's just that real life gets in the way."

"Tell me about it."

"It seems to be that you need to do your thing, - - like approaching everything from the art/history towards science stand point and reinstating women into the history line where they have been taken out. Whilst I need to re-establish my healing/teaching using earth energy principles. Then I could continue to write all this information from our past life times."

"Do we ever get a break where we just do nothing for a lifetime?"

"I think you have said that before, and then we got bored and caused havoc."

"Sounds about right " Sara laughed, "I suppose we just keep thinking, seeding and patterning the conscious pool"

"That sounds about it ,and let others take all the credit."

"Bugger! Don't you just hate that!"

"Yes! I really do. Do you think we could at least be rich?"

"Then we wouldn't do anything would we – just swan about having fun"

"Oh to just swan about ……"

87

"Amen to that."
"Or should it be A women?"
"Talk soon dear."
"Keep smiling. I think I will start painting again."
"Knock 'em dead!"

Chapter Fourteen

David could make no sense of the message he had just received from Ross. This was the same Ross who had always been calm, logical, well planned, not prone to sudden shifts in mood, or lifestyle. Not this …… it made no sense.

The message itself was unambiguous. It simply said "Got married this morning. Everything fine. Will be in touch. PS. Her name is Barbara, she is Canadian!

Now, David knew two things. One, that up until this moment ,Ross had been a committed bachelor and two, his last romantic obsession had been with Sara. As far as David was concerned, Ross was in Canada for a month playing ice hockey. How this had turned into marriage with someone he had never heard of and Ross had probably only just met, he could not imagine. He had hurried off to Canada in the first place to meet with some media mogul but as with most of these flash ideas, it had come to nothing and no screen play was forthcoming on the television screen or anywhere else for the young Cleopatra.

This was somewhat of an embarrassment as David was relying on the income to keep his rapidly sinking ship afloat. It had meant that without wanting to, he had to return to teaching. The Abra Chat shop had become a store room, the books being returned. The wonderful idea of community reading and relaxing put in abeyance, while David taught other people's ideas to students who were never taught how to have ideas of their own.

The phone rang. David was so engrossed in wondering what on earth Ross was up to that he failed to realise who was speaking.

"It's me, David – Kelly."

"Kelly!' God, she hadn't spoken to him for almost two years.

"Hello" he said hesitantly "how are you?"

She laughed "Still alive at least" she said.

He relaxed it was still the same Kelly. Time and distance made no difference.

"How are you?" he smiled, imagining her as he had last seen her.

"I'm well. You knew that Sara went back to South Africa didn't you?"

"Yes. But I must say I seem to have missed something because I just had a post card from Ross saying he had got married!"

"No!" Kelly was shocked too. The last time she spoke to Sara she said that she had had no communication with Ross for a while. He hadn't liked the idea of Sara becoming a full time mother. It no longer allowed her to be a full time girl about town.

"Do you think Sara knows?"

"I don't know, perhaps he sent her a post card too."

"Bastard!" said Kelly with feeling "I just hate that – that lack of communication."

David laughed. He and Kelly had not actually spoken since just after the trip to Stratford. But it didn't seem to matter, their communication could be picked up instantaneously any time.

"Well you know what I mean" smiled Kelly "Anyway how are you really. It's nice to talk to you."

"I'm OK. Had to go back to teaching and Abra Chat is a store room I'm afraid."

"Oh. I'm sorry. Look that's really what I wanted to talk to you about. Since we last met I have taken up an old passion of mine."

David laughed.

"No! not that" she laughed too, "healing and making remedies out of plants and crystals."

David was always surprised at the range of creativity that Kelly seemed to possess. She didn't just have one outlet, she had many.

"That sounds interesting" he said wondering where exactly this was going.

"Yes it is and I can earn money healing the many sick. I just wondered if I could use the Abra Chat room."

"Of course! Be my guest. You mean to do healing and making your remedies?"

"Well, no not really. I need somewhere to paint."

Another turn in the creativity it would seem.

"Paint? David said.

"Pictures, I paint pictures."

90

"Great! Of course that would be absolutely fine. When do you want to come?"

"Perhaps next week? I could come over and start to move things a bit to give me room. It has those two huge windows so the light would be fantastic and I would have the influence of the circle."

Influence? What exactly did that mean he wondered.

"Wonderful. What about Tuesday. I have a day off on Tuesday."

"That would be fine. I will be there in the morning, give us a whole day to get sorted out. Thanks, David. I do appreciate it. "

"Actually, I will be really glad that it is being used again. I hate it being empty of people when it had such potential and high hopes."

"It will be again, I'm sure" said Kelly. She paused, "see you Tuesday then?"

"Great. Bye" said David smiling to himself

Kelly back in his life? Perhaps, but you couldn't hold your breath with Kelly, she was like quick silver, forever moving at an unbelievable speed, dashing from one situation to the next. Well, everything seemed to be happening today, and for weeks it seemed that nothing was happening at all.

David checked his watch.

"Shit!" he said hurrying to pick up his jacket and car keys. No time for the toast he had had in the toaster before the post arrived with the disturbing postcard. He was late again and would now have trouble with the parking space.

Damn! Never mind, on Tuesday he would see Kelly and she was going to paint in Abra Chat. How long had she been painting? She never mentioned painting before? Had she? Oh well, he could find out soon enough he thought. He rushed out the door gulping down the coffee and thinking about getting some tea before Tuesday and the arrival of Kelly. Bit like the Queen of Sheba he thought, humming the opening stanza.

The car was iced up and freezing, he knew it sometimes happened in April but this was ludicrous. He had to scrape all the windows and try the starter at least three times before he was finally on the move, rolling down the drive and on into the day that was now running seriously late.

Chapter Fifteen

When Tuesday finally arrived, David still felt that he hadn't been able to catch up on himself. He had intended to clear away some of the boxes from the Abra Chat room, but he hadn't managed it somehow. Then he spent longer in the shower than he planned and had to rush downstairs in a state of dishevelment in case Kelly was early. She wasn't. In fact, when she did arrive, David was wondering if he had got the day wrong.

He watched her from the lounge window getting out of the car. Her hair was a little shorter and seemed curlier. She was wearing a light woollen skirt in bright purple with a plain purple jumper and a bright yellow jacket. On anyone else it would have looked ridiculous, on Kelly it looked stunning and natural.

He opened the door and she handed him a parcel wrapped in silver paper.

"Hi" she said kissing him on the cheek, then looking intently at him before smiling and crossing the threshold.

"What is this" he asked looking at the box and closing the door. She had come to the Abra Chat door and they were now standing surrounded by boxes and empty shelves.

"You won't know until you open it" she said looking round at the once vibrant place that now looked sad and deserted.

"I've made some tea" David said, ushering her through into the sun filled interior of his barn, with its high ceiling and feeling of space and openness. Kelly sighed.

"It is so lovely in here" she breathed, "so timeless".

David smiled and walked through to the kitchen to pour the water on the tea leaves. Kelly followed him, still looking round and noting the changes since she was last here.

David added the milk to the tray which he had already set and picked it up, along with his gift.

"Wow" said Kelly appreciatively, " real cups and saucers". She smiled.

"Especially in your honour" he said, carrying the tray back into the lounge and setting it down on the coffee table.

Whilst David poured the tea, Kelly took off her jacket, placed it on the arm of the sofa and sat down. David handed her the cup and saucer and as she raised the cup to her lips, she looked at David thoughtfully.

"Open your present, David" she said "it is time to tell you all the things you don't know."

"That will take a long time" he laughed "I don't know much about much."

"You knew enough to send me a box that was a message" she said, "a message that told me you know more than you claim to know."

He smiled. Conversations with Kelly were so good he could always feel his mind expanding with awaited information.

He looked at the slim parcel – it was obviously book shaped and the wrapping was silver. He turned it over and placed his finger inside the sellotape, which gave way easily and allowed the paper to fall back. Inside was a slim volume of a purple hardback with symbols under the title. All it said was 'The Journal of Isis'. He looked quizzically at Kelly as he felt his heart rate increasing and excitement working its way up to his head. He opened it and was immediately disappointed. He flicked quickly through it, but each page was the same. Blank, apart from the date on the first page which said BC 53.

"I know. It wasn't BC 53 when it was written – well it was BC 53 only we didn't call it BC 53 – obviously because Christ wasn't born yet so we didn't know we were 53 years before he was born."

"I understand that Kelly" David said. "Is it supposed to be invisible or am I supposed to write it? The pages are blank."

"Well, I know the pages are blank, David, this is just a representation – like your box was a representation of the arc of the Covenant – but unlike you – I do have the original – after all I did write it."

"When? When did you write it ,Kelly?"

93

"Originally I wrote it in what we in this time would call BC 53 and onward, but the one I will give to you I wrote about eight years ago."

"Where is it?"

"Well that's the tricky bit. You see you can have it, and it will make things much clearer to you, about Her story rather than His story (history), but it is at present in a Time Capsule."

"A Time Capsule?" David's voice sounded at least three octaves higher than normal even to him. Was this woman entirely mad?

"Well, yes, a Time Capsule."

She took a drink of her tea and leaned forward to refill her cup, looking carefully at him for signs of over stress.

"More tea?" she said quietly.

He shook his head. She was impossible! But if he wanted to gain information, and he did, then he needed to keep calm or she would be gone for another three years.

"Could you perhaps just tell me what you are trying to tell me."

She put down her cup and leaned back in the chair.

"I think perhaps I should tell you that not only do I believe in reincarnation, but I know it is true, because I remember a lot of my previous lifetimes. Not only that, I have always been a chronicler. So in my past lives I have written the information as it happened. Because of that I can remember exactly what I wrote , and when in time I wrote it. Since it was my past I can therefore reproduce it in this lifetime.

She paused. David didn't say anything. Either he was completely shocked or he just couldn't think of anything to say. After a moment she continued.

"Because, I have this long memory. This memory spans other life times. I know what my purpose is what I am here to do on this earth. Sometimes you ......" then she stopped.

"Sometimes I what?" David said looking at her for clues.

"Nothing. I didn't mean you".

"Yes you did. What were you going to say?"

Just then the phone rang, startling them both. David thought of ignoring it, but he couldn't. As he got up to go to the phone, Kelly sighed and poured more tea. This was going to be more difficult

94

than she thought . Not that she hadn't given it a lot of thought already.

She could hear David 'yes' and 'I can't go into that at the moment' and knew that whoever he was talking to he was trying really hard to get away from. With a very terse 'Fine' and then 'yes, goodbye" he was back.

He looked as if he was ready to kill someone; the anger was washing over him in waves.

Kelly had expected many reactions from him, but anger was not one of them. She waited for him to make the first move. He was silent and brooding obviously trying to work out what he knew, or didn't know, and where this conversation was going, if indeed it was going anywhere.

"Why have you been making such a fool of me?" he said, looking at her for the first time, his face closed and his tone frosty.

"I haven't been making a fool of you, David, whatever makes you think that?" Kelly put down her cup and saucer and sat upright, trying to look concerned and open.

David looked at her and scowled, not a good look on his normally engaging face.

"You didn't meet me by chance did you?"

Kelly was a little taken aback by this rapid shift to the beginning. She thought that would have taken him longer. She dared not hesitate or she would lose him and she didn't want to do that.

"I knew who you were a long time ago. We had to be sure you were who we thought you were. What we do is not a game, although the meeting was stage managed. We went to meet you and to get you interested in us."

"Why? why did you do that? Did you also somehow get this house to fall into my lap?" He was shouting now even though he didn't know why he was angry.

"David please sit down" said Kelly quietly, but with great authority.

David looked startled at the sudden change in Kelly from slightly scatty, easy going, loveable person to what? He didn't know. He sat down.

"I came here of my own free will to tell you all the things you don't know. I'm sorry if you being in the dark has made you feel out of control and therefore angry. But I didn't make you, or ask you to, write about us), I just inspired you. I didn't construct a copy of the ark of the convent and send it in a parcel. You did that, all on your own. No one has coerced you into doing anything. You have always had free will like all of us. You choose what it is you do. Just as I have chosen to come here and tell you all the things you might like to know. But you are free to listen or not to listen. To ask me to go, or invite me to stay. But whatever you decide to do, from this moment on our relationship will change. We are standing on a threshold."

Kelly stopped speaking and the room that had started off being filled with lightness then with anger, now settled into an uneasy peace while the implications of the information started to penetrate them both. Realisation of something that was out of their normal understanding crackled in the air.

"How did you know about me?" David said quietly.

"We had been reading about you and looking at what you had been doing for a long time."

"Why?" he was genuinely puzzled.

"Because we needed a new Shakespeare."

"What does that mean?"

"David please drink your tea and let me start a little nearer the beginning, then you might be able to understand what we were doing and why."

He shrugged and poured himself another cup of tea. He wasn't comfortable, but he did want to know.

"We have talked on lots of occasions and I told you strange things that didn't fit with what you knew about me or my life. You must have come to some kind of conclusion about what I have said and what it means. What exactly have you been writing about us?"

David smiled. He realised that for everything she had just said, Kelly was still playing this as a complicated game. A cross between chess and snakes and ladders perhaps. Kelly had certainly made him slither down a snake and if he was to climb another ladder, he was going to have to see the game and learn the rules.

"I have written about you both as if you are personifications of the Goddess."

"A very diplomatic answer, David, but it doesn't actually tell me anything."

"OK. I have written about you both in an historic context. I have used your personality and put you in Cleopatra's time."

"Why that time?

"African Queen and all that? Sara?" he shrugged.

"Who am I?"

"You are a High Priestess."

Kelly smiled "A Priestess of whom?"

"It's Egypt – Isis, of course."

"Good. Why did you see me as a Priestess and Sara as a Queen, as royalty?"

"Because that is how you work it. She is out front with the smile and brashness and superiority, but you are behind directing, working out the scenes and organising the structure. Very complicated structure, you are very tricky." He was still scowling, but Kelly smiled broadly.

"Not taken in by the dumb blonde then?"

"No. The eyes give it away. Not that you don't do a good job of putting everyone at ease and spreading light and harmony, but when you want your point to be made, your eyes flash and the authority enters your voice. Like just now when you told me to sit down."

"OK. So you could place us in various points of history?"

David thought for a moment

"Yes I could. When I saw you talking at the book launch, I knew at once you weren't play acting. You were in fact remembering."

"It's true. Although it has taken us a long time to retrieve those memories and to accept them. These things have a lot of propaganda to get through."

"Is that why you chose me.? I was more likely to accept your story because of my work on the Goddess and the matriarchy that had been suppressed."

"Wilfully altered, and obliterated I would say. But yes, you continued the work that Robert Graves had started. You can imagine

97

how incredible discovering Graves was for us. Confirmation for our wild imaginings."

"You have to mean the 'White Goddess' by Graves."

"What else. It took me, with my memories intact, four years to read that book. It is packed with lost connections and fantastic information. But I didn't tell you my memories David, you wrote them yourself, without any prompting from me."

"I was just fleshing out a historical character and putting my imagination to work on the powerful Isis religion and how it would have viewed the Roman Empire."

"Ah yes, the great solider mentality that walked over everything, but also built so much, so well."

"It wasn't all bad then?"

"No. They built an empire and a structure that was a joy to see. Then they got lazy. They forgot the farming principles by which they had begun their civilisation. Then they spoilt their own children. So they in turn, felt no need to work and instead got slaves to do everything. After a while, they lost control and forgot how to maintain what they had. Greed took over, as it so often does. The culture of profit. Instead of being content with enough. If everyone goes for enough, then everyone will have enough. Anyway that was then, and this is now."

"Except it's happening again, and this time, you are going to try and prevent it."

Kelly sat back and looked at David, then laughed.

"Very good David. Now you are using your brain instead of your ego. Although, it is a bit more of a task than we could do on our own."

"But the structure is what you do. You are here to rebuild – reconnect ......?

"Reform, renew, reconstruct?"

"Yes, all of those things but also to reawaken the Goddess Gene. Anyway you are part of the team. Whether you remember or not. How much of the Cleopatra story have you written?"

"I've got all the historical bit, and some of the interactions of the two women – Goddesses." David smiled for the first time, because suddenly, after so long in the wilderness of no inspiration, he was beginning to feel the prickle of excitement that meant that he was sensing the big, bigger and BIGGER picture that was possibly going on here.

Kelly watched him and saw the flicker of excitement that was quickly tempered by caution.

"It's alright, David, I'm not mad or obsessive, although I used to think perhaps I was. However, when you meet other people who have the same thoughts as you, you start to realise that perhaps you should listen to yourself even though everyone else is saying something different. So I have learned to live with my 'long memory' as I call it. It doesn't send me crazy anymore, I just expand my mind to take in extraordinary thoughts and allow myself to understand that I will not know some things until I have observed others. I also have to include living this lifetime."

"Well" David said leaning back in his chair, "that was quite a speech."

"For a blonde you mean."

"For anyone. Are you telling me that you think we have met before in other lifetimes?"

"Do you think you have had other lifetimes?"

"I don't know. I don't know that I have ever really thought about it."

"Then why was it so easy for you to write about me and Sara in past lifetimes?"

"Because I could always see you like that, you are sort of 'other worldly'. Not that you don't belong here, but you ...... sort of ......"

Kelly laughed, "you see how hard it is to get your mind and your words round concepts that are not in the conscious domain. I think perhaps you need some time to think about what we have said here today. You might even find that your memory starts to take you to places you know you have never been before."

Kelly stood up and reached for her bag.

"It's easier for women to remember we have a direct line to our ancestors. If you think about it, when my mother was in the womb of her mother, she already had the egg that would one day be me. So from woman to woman, mother to daughter, to daughter through grandmother is a direct line. When you have a son, the road stops, and is picked up again by the wife. But she will have different ancestors. Think about it."

She laughed at the frown appearing on David's face as he tried to follow the reasoning.

Kelly scrabbled in her large handbag for a moment and brought out a file.

"Here, to help a little with the writing and the understanding, perhaps. Not all the writing was put in the Time Capsule, some escaped."

She handed him the file. Written in black pen across the file was the legend 'Diary of Isis' in Kelly's unmistakable hand.

He looked up to see she already had her jacket on. She laughed, blew a kiss and headed for the door before he had time to engage his brain or react in any way. He looked down at the tea things as he heard the door bang. His cup still contained the poured tea. It was stone cold.

Chapter Sixteen : Saturday

On the second Saturday after the Kelly revelations, David was surprised by a great deal of clattering and banging from the front drive where the door to the once Abrachat stood. As he moved to go downstairs and investigate, the door was assaulted by something that sounded like a battering ram, but on opening turned out to be Kelly and two young men fully loaded with boxes and canvases.

"Were you in bed, David?" said Kelly handing him some of the things she was balancing.

"As it is 11 a.m. and you are making so much noise, I don't think so." He moved to put the things down on one of the cupboards. "I take it you are moving in?"

"Didn't I say I was?" she threw over her shoulder as she headed out to the van that was parked with its doors open on the drive. He hurried out to assist her.

"I would have given you a key on Tuesday if you had stayed long enough" he said feeling as he always did around Kelly, slightly wrong footed without knowing why.

"Were you writing?" she said as she moved past him. "I must say you have that look of someone emerging from another century."

Well you would know about that, he thought. But he was glad to see her. She might have decided to clear off for another two years.

"The Venus cycle lasts eight years, David" she murmured as he followed her in with another box that looked as if it was full of tools.

"That is why the Olympics are every four years. Half the cycle of Venus. They were originally dedicated to Venus and the symbol on the flag was ...."

"A pentangle" he filled in "I know that, but how is it relevant?"

"Four years, David, not two, we have another two to go."

The two men had finished now and Kelly went over and gave them both a hug, thanking them and saying she would see them soon. They smiled and waved themselves off taking the van and revealing Kelly's car sitting on the drive.

"Are you staying then?" he said.

She smiled "I am moving my stuff in, I have come equipped to do just that."

He looked at her. She was wearing jeans, a striped tee-shirt in lilac and purple and a long lacy knitted cardigan in shades of pink and lilac.

She smiled as he looked at her.

"I brought an apron" she said "are you available to help me?"

He laughed "I think I might be" he said

The next hour was a lesson in reorganization of which Kelly seemed to be an expert. The books that were left from the Abrachat shop were taken out of their boxes and returned to the shelves on the wall behind the door. Box's were unloaded. Shelves were taken out and repositioned to make a dividing wall between the door into David's house and the Bay window which had the door to the outside car park. This made a space to be the shop and behind this a space with tables for painting and lessons.

"If need be, I can use the tables you had for coffee for the students" Kelly said, breathing heavily and pushing the hair out of her eyes.

David was putting away his drill which he had used to attach the partition shelves to the end of the bay window and the floor.

"Students?" he asked querulously.

"Well, I don't intend just to paint you know. I will teach people how to make these wonderful energy paintings and of course we can still use the front half as a studio/shop."

David still looked a little bemused.

What will we be selling?" he asked.

"Well, you still have lots of books and you will of course be writing some more. I have books of my own and some left over from Abrachat. Plus the paintings which can hang on that wall we have removed the shelves from, and in these boxes I have brought my pottery. Did I say I did pottery? ...... no ...... well I do, and then of course there will be the special remedies which I shall be making in your stone circle" she stopped and laughed at him.

"You ain't seen nothing yet David, as they say, but to answer your question, we will be selling magic. Pure awe inspiring magic,

102

it will dance around the room and fill every article that I place on these shelves."

David looked around the transformed room and thought about how it had looked yesterday and for the two years before yesterday and he knew that what Kelly had said was absolutely and unmistakably true. It was beginning to be filled with magic.

"We need some white paint for that wall which now has holes in it" Kelly said, looking at it. "Do you have some?"

"Probably in the shed. I'm sure I do, but could we perhaps stop for lunch now?"

"That's a good idea. Do you have anything for lunch?"

"I make a very amazing omelette" he smiled. "You might even say it is magic".

Kelly laughed, "Great. Lead on, then we can paint after lunch."

David did indeed make a good omelette with mushrooms, tomatoes, peppers and cheese. Kelly made the tea and a quick fruit salad with 2 kiwi fruits, one apple, one pear and a few raspberries that were lurking in the fridge. Served with half a carton of yoghurt each they had quite a feast.

Neither were really surprised with the ease at which they worked together. They didn't get in each other's way in the kitchen and didn't try to do the same thing. Each seemed to know what the other was doing or needed next.

"It's a good partnership" said Kelly as she pushed away the pudding plates, "we didn't argue once."

"That's because you order and I follow" said David. "Once I stop being so surprised I won't be so malleable."

Kelly laughed, "we'll see. We must get the wall painted then we will be able to get the pictures on there tomorrow."

"Is there some kind of rush to finish?" he asked clearing the plates and heading for the sink.

"Of course there is. Now that we have started and it is looking so good, we have to open and get people in. We've only got two years left."

David went to get the paint and Kelly went back into the new studio/shop. She really wanted to get something in the window. It was such a beautiful bay window, with fine individual panes of glass

103

which she immediately saw needed cleaning. One of her boxes contained cleaning materials so she set about making the glass sparkle. When she had finished, she used some of her wooden packing cases to stand on the floor and put beneath the window sill. David returned with paint and some dust sheets and told her to start painting, whilst he got tools and wood and continued to make the platform which would be her window display.

The paint was white so Kelly got out some of her painting paints and stirred in a little colour until she had a vibrant, amazing, deep pink blush. Then she applied the paint to the wall after repairing the holes which the shelves had left.

They worked on, only stopping for a cup of tea whilst the wall dried a little, so that coat number two could be applied. By half past five they were finished and exhausted.

"Would you like to go and eat at the local pub, Kelly? " David asked as he swept away the wood chipping and tidied away the dust sheets.

Kelly thought for a moment "I'd love to, but I don't fancy getting comfortable and then driving home later" she said stretching her aching back.

"Then don't drive home. You can stay. I have guest rooms all ready and waiting you know."

"That would be great. I'll go and freshen up then if you show me where."

Kelly had never been upstairs in David's house and was quite curious to see what the gallery upstairs contained. He led the way up the spiral staircase and along the gallery that ran round half the barn. They passed one door and then David stopped at the second one, opening the door onto a bathroom with a sloping ceiling, a white bath under a skylight and a walk-in shower. Toilet and wash basin were along the side wall and set in deep shelf space was an upright, wooden, open cupboard supporting six shelves stacked high with butter yellow towels and expensive bath products. The walls were white with small yellow sunflowers here and there. The white floor was tiled with thick yellow bath rugs by the bath, shower and wash basin. It was full of sunshine and warmth.

"Oh – how lovely" said Kelly amazed and surprised at the beautiful, welcoming room.

"Already here" said David smiling "not mine to take credit for I'm afraid, but glad you approve. Next door here is the bedroom" He moved along the balcony a little way and opened the end door. Kelly peered into the room. It was an alcove with a sloping roof and a large sky light opposite a double wrought iron bedstead. It was covered with a patchwork quilt in a hundred shades of lavender blue and a mountain of feather pillows in shades of blue and white. The walls were lavender with a white chest of drawers on the opposite wall to the door with a mirror. A jug of blue and white flowers sat on top of a chest of drawers with a fully lined book case under the eves.

On either side of the bed, was a white bedside table with a large blue flower shaded lamp, and as she peered further round the door, she could see a white washed wardrobe fitted into the sloping ceiling wall. It was cosy, soft and airy and very, very feminine

"I know" he smiled "I do have another guest room in maroon and white, much more masculine. I don't inflict this girly stuff on Ross when he comes to stay, it's on the other side of the bathroom."

Kelly smiled "I love it" she said "it invites you to sink into that soft feathered bliss knowing you will wake up to a wonderful view over the fields."

She turned back towards the bathroom. "Where do you sleep, David" she couldn't help asking.

"There's an extension along here", he smiled as he moved along the Gallery back towards the staircase. Just before the staircase was a corridor with a skylight at the end. On the left hand side was a door, slightly ajar, which David pushed open. Inside was a much bigger room with a normal size ceiling, a double bed with covers in navy blue, with yet another wonderful view down the hill with the spire of a church just visible above the trees.

"I thought the village was in the other direction" said Kelly moving to the window.

"It is. That's the church that belongs to the estate. It is decommissioned now, but still beautiful."

105

Kelly smiled "yes it is" she noticed the room had solid wood furniture and en suite bathroom. David's clothes were scattered here and there, along with books and papers. It looked lived in and comfortable. A chair was piled high with a selection of clothes and manuscripts.

David smiled. "It spills over a bit from the work room" he said, walking back into the corridor to another door under the skylight. This room was the width of the house at the opposite side of the original barn. It was over what Kelly now realised was the garage, which was further round from the open driveway and the front of the barn which was Abrachat.

This was a high room with the far wall given over entirely to window. At least that was what it looked like. The view was up the lane towards the estate. But the lane had stout hedges disappearing into a stand of trees with the spire was just visible to the left.

Under the window was a wall and a desk flanked by open cupboards on either side. The shelves were a bit like an open filing system and contained pile upon pile of files and papers. The top of the desk contained a lap top, more books and files whilst the other walls were piled high with shelves of books. The floor was carpeted, but also had books and papers everywhere, albeit in neat piles. It also contained a photocopier, printer and an enormous cork notice board with diagrams, notes and patterns pinned all over it.

"More a memory board than a notice board" smiled Davie ruefully "I can't keep everything in my head, so when the ideas come I pin them up there until I have time to deal with them."

"It looks like a great room to work in" said Kelly twirling round to take in the expanse of space and the feel of work in progress. "I expect the return to teaching has slowed you down a bit."

"It has" said David "not to mention the impromptu DIY."

"Sorry" said Kelly quickly, not feeling sorry at all. "It will get better."

"I think perhaps it already has" he smiled, walking back to the door "ready in twenty minutes?"

"Ten" said Kelly smiling as she remembered that was his nickname from Louise was 'size 10' of the boots fame. DM – David Millhouse or Doc Martin.

106

"Kelly?" said David, looking at her far away face and wondering if she was thinking of something profound.

"I'm going" she said hurrying back to the sunflower sunshine bathroom. "Oh, can I borrow a shirt, David, this is a bit messy."

"Help yourself". He pointed to the bedroom and turned back to move some files from his desk, giving her time to look in his wardrobe on her own.

She flicked through the hangers and found a crisp white shirt she had never seen David wearing and pulled it out. As it was fitted, it wouldn't be too big and would be fine with her jeans and the cardigan which was untouched by hard work in the studio.

She hurried into the bathroom once more, jumped out of her clothes and into the shower, using some of the wonderful shower gel to quickly wash her hair. She towelled it dry as well as herself, then slipped back into her underwear, jeans and white shirt. Then she searched the bottles for some moisturiser which was there, applied some onto her face then hurried downstairs to find her handbag and hairbrush. Pulled the brush through her hair and ran her fingers through a few times. The curls were coming already, but at least her hair looked good if you didn't try to make it do something it didn't want to do. Then she turned round to find her cardigan, just as David came down the stairs.

"Wow" he said "you were quick, I thought it was a joke."

"What, my ten minutes?"

"Yes, I thought women took ages."

"Did the lady who left all her products in the bathroom take ages then?"

"Hours" said David "it was a long time ago and I never really came up to her exacting standards. She found someone better who did, and left so quickly for a better life that she left most of her stuff."

"Was it a bad time for you?"

"Only for my ego. Not for my peace of mind. Anyway Louise came and sorted me out quite quickly and Abrachat had just started, so it was all rather laid to rest. How is Louise by the way?"

"She's good. At University now, doing all the bad things that you do at Uni – drinking, smoking, sex and rock and roll – so I believe. I never got to go. Poor me."

"You don't look 'poor me'" he said. "That shirt looks better on you than it ever did on me. Shall we go and eat?"

"Yes, come on. I'm starving."

As they left through the Abrachat door, it was amazing to see it looked so entirely different than it had that morning.

"I rather think it needs a new name now" said Kelly looking at the window which was sparkling, but empty "and probably a window display but we can leave that until tomorrow"

Chapter Seventeen : Sunday

Kelly was awoken by the sound of birds squabbling over some supposed injustice. She emerged from her feathery cocoon and opened her eyes onto the wonderful view. She hadn't drawn the curtains last night, she had no need. The meal had been excellent, the tuna seared to perfection. They had chatted with the locals about nothing very much and walked round the pretty village before coming home. After a cup of tea, Kelly had borrowed a spare toothbrush and shirt and snuggled gratefully into the feathered heaven. Now she was thinking about the window display and how it was going to look.

She jumped out of bed and peered over the balcony into the lounge to see if David was downstairs. He didn't seem to be so she went into the bathroom ran a bath, sloshed a good quantity of Moulton Brown bath gel into the water, went back and retrieved her jeans and shirt, then sank into the bath and allowed herself to wake up slowly.

By the time she had wrapped herself in one of the butter yellow towels and got dressed she could hear David moving about downstairs.

She descended the spiral staircase thinking how much she enjoyed moving in a spiral and found David sitting at the breakfast bench in the kitchen with orange juice, yoghurt and cereal placed before him.

"Morning" he said "do you want me to do you some bacon and eggs?"

"No. This is fine – thank you."

They ate in comparable silence whilst Kelly thought about the window display and David thought about how nice it was to have her sitting eating breakfast with him. Then she finished quickly, gave him a smile, and started to get up.

"Will you knock in the picture hooks and hang the pictures please, whilst I do the window display."

"Of course " he smiled getting up and putting the dishes in the sink. "Have you got picture hooks?"

"Yes …. and I will put which picture needs to go where, by the wall, because they are all different sizes."

"Fine, let's get started, oh slave driver" he said hurrying off to find the hammer.

By the time he returned, Kelly had unpacked a series of framed pictures in vibrant colours, some of them with recognisable objects like trees, some looking like exploding fireworks, but all looking very alive. She placed them along the wall, explained which went with what, then made David hold them against the wall whilst she worked out some pattern that was only in her head.

"Leave space at the side here" she said "for the words."

"Words?" queried David. "To describe them?"

"No, of course not" she scoffed. "The words meld with the painting so that when you read the words and hear the rhyme in your head, your ears interpret the energy that is painted on the canvas."

David looked at her slightly puzzled.

"Remember I told you we were selling magic? Well they are magic to behold. Look it is easier for me to show you than it is to describe. But I have to find the words in one of these boxes. So before I do that I need to do this window display. So please put the pictures where I said, leaving enough space between them to be able to view one at a time and then when I find the words I will show you."

"OK" David smiled, there must be so many programs running simultaneously in her head he thought it was amazing to get just a glimpse of what was happening.

Kelly was already pulling some boxes towards the window one of which contained a pile of beautiful coloured cloth in many different textures. She chose a deep claret coloured velvet and draped it over the platform that David had created, making sure that it wasn't flat but allowing the cloth to pool in rivulets and pleats. She placed a small chest of drawers that was shaped like a triangle with a flattened top and put that at the back, on one side of the window near the partition shelves. The drawers she opened and placed more textiles from the box of packed items, which turned out to be scarves in

110

colours like jewels. Some were whips of silk, some were velvet, some were shining satin with ribbons. In the front of the window she placed three of her larger pots, one in earth colours of orange and deep red, one in calming browns and autumn golds and one in greens and blues. Behind these she stood a wooden box to give height – added a velvet green cloth and placed various sized glass bottles with old fashioned labels bearing legends like 'Banishing Gloom', 'Elixir of Life' and 'Star Potion'. Then a small easel with a painting in bright yellow and gold. Then to one side she dragged up a wooden hat stand that she had brought and from another box took an assortment of wonderfully crazy hats in yellow, green, purple and fuchsia – all sporting ribbons or feathers. Then on the branches of the stand she hung a great profusion of belts, some made of shiny metal and all linked together, some of leather in the shape of tiny leaves or flowers, all jingly and jangly.

By this time, David was just watching this modern day Aladdin extracting the most amazing things from this selection of ordinary, everyday cardboard boxes.

"Is there more?" he asked making her jump, because she had long since forgotten anyone else was there.

She smiled. "Just one very important set of items which I need you to help me with."

From yet another box she produced one large, one medium and two small exquisite quilts.

"This large shades of red one, I want to hang from the side of the window so that it can be seen, but then drape it onto the platform in folds. Could you put a couple of hooks in the window frame and the wall, so I can attach it?"

David came over to do as she had asked. "Did you make all of these?" he asked incredulously. "I made some, I designed most of them. We had other shops before our Abrachat franchise" she said sitting down on a stool.

"Our first was in Oxford. It was called 'Gats and Hats' – hence the belts and the hats. We also sold feminine safari clothes or travelling clothes that were stylish and not just practical. That was when our plan was to have a game farm in Africa – as well as writing about the Goddess and all the things we were re-

111

remembering. She smiled, David said nothing because Kelly didn't often talk about her life and it was fascinating to see the paths she had taken. He turned back to the window and stepped carefully round the display to put some cup hooks where she had suggested.

"Our next shop venture after Gats and Hats was Kalahari Kolours, all about these wonderful feminine quilts that were made all over the world, although ours were African or African inspired. Some were made there – we were desperately trying to do two things, empathise the idea the women were the same wherever they lived, because they were always operating on the principle of community. Whereas, men, with their principle of competitiveness were always in competition with each other which kept them in a state of conflict. We tried to begin something called the ASH Foundation – Africa Self Help – where we brought crafts from Africa and sent crafts back to Africa. We even got to go to ANC headquarters to put our proposal forward and get government support. It was actually the day that Mandela was elected President, but it somehow got lost in the razzmatazz that followed the making of the rainbow nation. Our timing has always been really bad."

She stopped, thoughtful for a moment.

"So you are still at the hot spots when change is taking place" David said.

"Yes. It is more about the ideas I think – although we didn't know that at the time, or we wouldn't have done it with such energy if we had thought it wasn't for real."

"Was that the only time you tried to initiate things?"

"Oh no!" she laughed. "Before that, before the shops, we wanted to create something called IFISA – International Federation for the Integration of Science and Art. We had written the plan for our real work which we called Brother Sun, Sister Moon. It spanned time and we retraced history showing where the Goddess was in time and how she had been eradicated. How the divine Feminine had lost her position and been relegated to some thing bordering on a domestic servant. Mostly she got stuck in the kitchen cooking lunch.! But that made us realise that what we were also showing was that Art and Science were once the same thing (in Leonardo's time) but had become separated. No sense was going to be found until we brought

112

them back together. This is what is happening in the millennium in 2003 Venus will come closer to the earth than she has for thousands of years and when that happens the Goddess energy which has been dormant. Will once more awaken like the Sleeping Beauty.

Anyway, the Plan for this great work was thirty-nine pages long! We did write some of it, but we only had nine months to get it together, then we would run out of money and Sara would have to go back to South Africa. Our campaign was wonderful. We had Oxford book shops ready to accommodate our debates. We wrote to illustrious people like Prince Charles, Lady Diana, Richard Branson, Robert Redford, anyone who had foundations that we could interest, as well as publishers. Our campaign was called 'The Sleeping Beauty' – who we saw as the Goddess who was about to awaken and return. We bought a jigsaw puzzle of the Sleeping Beauty asleep and sent all these people a piece of the puzzle explaining that that is what they were, and we needed their support to make this work." She smiled again "it was a great PR move".

"What happened?" said David awed and appalled at the diversity of two women on their own.

"Nothing" she said getting up "no one was willing to back us. So, all the rest of the offered help meant nothing. Sara went back to South Africa and I went back to a menial job." She shrugged and brought the beautiful Red Quilt up to him so that he could attach it, whilst she draped it to show the gold threads and the vivid pattern.

"I hope you are going to record all this David. You must write about us as you see us, because this book will be very important. In 2012 when the new energy enters, Gaia the Goddess will be fully awake and when she awakens so do all her subjects. That means that the Goddess Gene which is already awake in us, will need to be awakened in those other people. Then the world can change."

"How can I do that!" He said somewhat panicked and now clutching the red Quilt.

Kelly laughed. "You just do what you are doing. Not only writing about our past lives but recording this one as it is happening. I will give lots of "fill in" things that you don't know and then the plan will be revealed. But all in good time for now we have a shop to get ready" She started to arrange the other Quilts.

113

David knew that her information had now come to an end and he would have to start recording all these happenings as they happened. He couldn't even imagine what her next move would be. He hung the beautiful Quilt on the hook.

"All you see here are the remnants of our creative genius." Kelly sighed

"However" he said, getting down from the platform "am I right in saying that Art and Science are indeed moving together in all sorts of fields – calling itself the integrated approach and are there not many places in Africa and elsewhere, where women's crafts are brought to the west to be sold, usually to other women, and a sharing of talent and skills is taking place."

"Yes" she smiled "this is true."

"So perhaps that is what you do. Seed the ideas out into the world so that they can be picked up and acted upon when the time is right."

"That is what I have come to realise" she said stepping back from the window. "So what do you think I am seeding now, oh wise one?"

He looked around the changed and transformed room and smiled.

"Magic, of course."

"Magic , of course" she repeated. "What the world needs now, like it never did before, is magic, and that, is what you and I are going to give it, David."

The rest of the day was spent in unpacking more of the pottery which was placed on the shelves. Kelly added fairy lights to the window and got David to put more hooks in the ceiling so she could hang wind chimes and turning trails of sparkling stars. They captured the light and sent it rushing around the glittering things in the window.

They went outside to check the effect and found themselves smiling broadly, everything looked inviting and interesting.

"I do have some more things to bring" said Kelly checking the wary expression on David's face.

"More?" he asked.

114

"Well, yes. I haven't brought the knitted garments or the rainbow clothes, but there is time for them later."

"Is there anything else you do or make?" he said.

"What, besides the healing, cooking and the poetry?" she smiled.

"You know Kelly, somehow, I don't think you are joking, are you?"

She shook her head "I think it is time I went home now. You are getting fatigue from me. It happens all the time. When I first met Sara I used to give her a headache every time we met. It went when we separated. I am like Everest, you need to be acclimatised to me."

She picked up her cardigan and bag and looked round the room. "It's looking good. Thank you for letting me use it."

"Thank you" he said. "It was dying, now it is alive again. Here is your key." He picked it up from the table where he had put it earlier. "Dare I ask when you will return?"

"Oh, I will be here sometime tomorrow and everyday now. This is my place of work and I have a lot to do. Is that OK?"

"It's more than OK" David smiled. At least it wasn't two years he thought.

David left for work the next day without his usual unorganised rush and spent the day wondering whether Kelly would still be there when he got home. He declined the offer of an after school drink with the maths teacher and hurried home without any of the usual after hours chatter.

Kelly's car was parked on the driveway so he parked alongside her and collected his bag. He strolled towards the door which was now supporting a large, colourful notice announcing the "Grand Opening" of the new, exciting studio shop in two weeks time – to which everyone was invited.

Well it looked as if Kelly was preparing for a stay this time. No mention yet of the new name, he noticed, and the Abrachat sign still hung over the door. He had always been reluctant to remove it as if somehow it would be mysteriously revived - and now it looked as if it might be.

115

The door was locked he was glad to note. So he used his key and was gratified not to be avoiding boxes and a feeling of desertion that he had been for the past two years without the shop. Now it felt bright and alive.

"Hello David!" Kelly shouted from the far end where the studio was." I see you have taken in the sign." She appeared from round the shelf partition.

"I had to put something up, people kept knocking at the door – and three weeks gives us time to get organised, don't you think?"

"Plenty of time, although you look almost ready now" he said looking round.

"Well not really, I have things to organise at home and the name needs to be right."

David moved towards the inner door "Are you going to have something to eat with me?" he said.

"No, I have to go now. I just wanted to say hello really."

"Oh – ok then". He couldn't help the disappointment from entering his voice. He knew she had heard it and they both paused, looking awkward.

"I brought some more things" she said quickly, as she pointed to a rail with some clothes in rainbow colours. The skirts were in swirling patterns next to a row of plain bold tops.

"Were they from yet another idea?" he said, determined to get away from the awkward moment and return to their easy banter.

"One that didn't get off the ground I'm afraid", she smiled, adding "I love the idea of people being able to add the colour they most need to their aura."

"I thought you did that anyway" he smiled flicking through the lovely clothes.

"I do, but other people don't. Now they can have the opportunity. I didn't make them, but I did design them, and source the fabric. They were made by the team we had got together for the craft shop, the one we called Africa self help. They were made by mums who could do them in their own homes in their own time."

"Not sweat shop clothes then?"

"Definitely not. I did make these though" she said pointing to three beautiful lacy cardigans like the one she had worn on Saturday.

116

"So you knit as well!"

"I do" she looked at her watch and moved off to get her jacket and bag. "I must go David. I won't be here for a couple of days, but on Thursday I will bring some food and cook if you like. Perhaps I could stay over, then I won't have to drive back and come again the next day."

"Of course. You can bring some clothes this time. Come prepared. You can do that whenever you like" he said, "the room is there waiting"- and me he thought, but he didn't say that. He knew Kelly had made some sort of decision about him in her life, but that she was considering it at every move, so he knew not to push her.

"Yes, that would be great" she looked through the big window down towards the far end of the shop where her easel was now set up. "I really need to get back to painting soon. When I have this place sorted out" she seemed to be talking more to herself than to him. So he said nothing and waited.

She looked back at him thoughtfully for a moment.

"OK" she said, "must go". She shrugged into her jacket and found the car keys in her pocket. "Try to think of a name for the shop, David, perhaps it needs to have the word magic in its title."

"I will" he said watching her move towards the door "see you Thursday then?"

"Yep, Thursday" she waved and went out the door. It suddenly seemed very quiet and empty in the shop even with all the bright, colourful bits of Kelly's personality hanging on the walls and shelves. All these magic pieces he thought, jigsaw pieces, from her life, perhaps that was what she could call the shop. Magic Pieces, Magic Moments – no that was a bit twee – Magic Flashes – no – something - he would have some time to think about it. Perhaps he should get started on the writing. He had read the Journal of Isis which was wonderful and extraordinary and gave him all the missing insights he hadn't had when writing 'Cast No Shadow'. He could fill it in now and make it even more of an adventure than it was. He had much more of the measure of Isis the High Priestess now he had seen Kelly. He could include the Journal of Isis, or at least refer to it in some way so that it could then have a follow on book, with all its

117

wisdom and insights. Yes, that is what he would start now. He went off to make some tea with his head filled with the ideas he would use

He didn't know that this was exactly what Kelly had hoped would happen once she was there to inspire him.

"You write about your Muses, David" she said aloud as she drove off "but you understand them so little. They have to work hard to inspire."

Chapter Eighteen: Tuesday

The next morning, Kelly texted South Africa to arrange a time to phone Sara. She always marvelled at the wonderful technology that meant she could have instant communication right now, this minute. When Sara and Kelly had first met and Sara had gone back to South Africa, they had written letters to each other - long, exciting letters of self discovery. Sometimes as much as three a week, but it had taken ten days to receive a reply so answers to questions were always lagging behind. Now they didn't say nearly as much, but could talk about the moment. She made some tea and took it into the room that overlooked the garden and was always full of sunshine at this time in the morning. She opened the address book that had been efficiently compiled by Sara before she left for Africa from the several diaries and scraps of paper that Kelly had been using and losing. The number rang 6,000 miles away in Jo'Burg.

"Hello" came the drawled accent.
"Hi. How are things? Is all well?"
"Oh you know. No money, school runs, my mother. All the usual stuff."
Sara had now adopted her niece, baby Sooz, who was no longer a baby and had started pre-school. Her brother had gone back to Zimbabwe to work.
"How's the paper coming along?"
"Good. I am working hard on Gender Studies. I've enlisted the department of Feminists. Not that they understand what's going on, but at least I can get some of our ideas out into academia."
"Then you will start on Art History and put a spanner in that works?"
Sara laughed "oh yeah, but that's next. I'm doing some workshops too. It's a hard slog."
"Rewriting history always is. We just have to change the mind set."
"And you, how goes it?"

119

"Oh ok. I have taken over Abrachat and will try and sell some of our old stuff. I just need to be near the stone circle so I can work on it."

"What about the house?"

"Have got it on the market, or will have, the estate agents are coming today. Have sold some furniture and am sorting and packing."

"Well, I suppose we have to keep moving. I am going to be here for a few years, I suppose."

"Holding the points, I think it's called. Stretching the lines. We are working in the dark but we know we have to be ready for the Goddess and all the changes that are coming. Oh well - it has to be done."

"How is dear David? Is he writing?"

"Not so as you would notice. He has gone back to teaching. But if I sell the house I can offer to move in and pay him rent. That should allow him to stop teaching and write."

"He has the 'Journal of Isis'?"

"Yes. He is inspired, I think. I just need to get a group together to coalesce the energies in the circle. I know that place has to become a gateway for the new energy to enter. Just not sure how to do that yet. Still, If I am there I can do that."

"Goddess, all this work. Can't we just give it up and be normal?"

"This is normal for us! Don't forget that."

"Yeah well. Hope it goes well."

"Anything exciting happening?"

Sara laughed again "well there is a well made man who is teaching me 'Keep Fit'"

"And what are you teaching him?"

"Nothing he doesn't already know. He is most helpful to a lot of ladies."

"Ah well, it helps the days go by" Kelly laughed. " Keep in touch my friend"

"As always."

"Bye."

"Bye."

Chapter Nineteen: Wednesday

The next day, whilst Kelly was busy loading boxes with various labels and pondering what to give to whom, the door bell rang. As she wasn't expecting anyone, she decided to ignore it. But whoever was ringing the bell was not going to be ignored. She came clattering downstairs expecting someone who was lost or some such nonsense and opened the door to one of those magic moments.

Standing with his back to her a little way down the path, gazing out over the hills, was an image from a classic film. The setting was perfect with the moving sun lighting the rolling Wiltshire downs and illuminating a tall man in jeans, leather jacket and dealer boots, holding a motor bike helmet casually over one arm, with chin length black hair. He had obviously heard the door open, but he didn't turn round. He stood perfectly still, as did Kelly on the threshold of the door. Then with a slow, languorous movement, he turned his head only and as his deep green eyes met hers, he smiled. She kept absolutely still and allowed her smile to widen. He turned round, then without losing eye contact and walking in slow, perfect coordination, towards her, he seemed to blend into the beautiful morning as if he was a part of Nature herself. He stopped, and looked deep into her eyes for a long moment, then said simply, "Hi".

"Hello" she said smiling into the aquiline dazzlingly handsome face. Then he leant his head towards her and kissed her, long and silently and deeply on the lips.

A million things went through her mind like 'where have you been you bastard', 'it has been nearly three years', 'why didn't you communicate with me?' But as the kiss went on all these questions seemed to be answered and understood – this person was her twin soul and that said it all. They could not be together for long in this lifetime. He just came to give her information and strength whilst she untangled his DNA and made sense of life for him. By the time he lifted his head and his mouth from hers, all had been said without words and information had passed from his inner being to her inner being.

"You have a motorbike."

"I borrowed it. Should we go and find the crop circles?"

"I'll get a picnic. Come and help me. We'll go in my car. You only just came in time as I'm moving soon – then you wouldn't be able to find me."

"I'll always be able to find you" he said

By this time Kelly was moving down the corridor into the kitchen and opening cupboards to find bread and crackers , cheese and ham.

"I'd always be able to find you" he said once more "I found you in the first place."

He put down the crash helmet and she handed him the knife and butter.

"Actually I found you, if you remember, I knocked on your door. Well, actually, I came to see your wife."

"That's what you thought."

"As I remember it, you poked your head out of the bathroom window with those first romantic words "Oh, I thought you were the fish man".

He laughed. "Yes, but after that I came and found you."

"Mmm" said Kelly smiling as she remembered that first day she had laid eyes on him and how he had come down to let her and her painting friend in the door. He was wearing the smallest, white basket weave dressing gown she had ever seen, exposing his long, lean, brown legs and bare feet. She thought then, as she did now, that he was the most beautiful, handsome man she had ever seen, but also the least aware of it. She had written about him in her past life chronicles, but didn't really think anything about it, never believing she would ever meet him in this lifetime. But he just kept appearing when she needed something like special spring water from a holy well or a Chrystal, and giving it to her. Until she eventually took notice and recognised him. They had travelled the countryside for three months activating various sacred sites and laughing and loving. Then he had disappeared without a word, until this morning.

"I wish you wouldn't just disappear" she said putting crisps and fruit and water into a bag. He looked at her and smiled, handing her the sandwiches, but saying nothing.

"I suppose you have to don't you?"

"It's easier" he sighed "we get too close. We can't make it domestic and we would try to."

"I thought I was the one with the words" she laughed.

"Well. I've had a long time to ponder it" he said "are we ready?".

"Almost." She moved towards him and their energies collided and coalesced and they stood, transplanted in an embrace that could have lasted an eternity.

"Crop circles" she said somewhat reluctantly, he nodded and picked up the bag whilst she got her keys.

She didn't have to ask if he knew where they were, she knew he would. He always knew the place, he was somehow 'of the land' and had shown her amazing places in the past, but he could not translate the energy or understand it. That was what she did and as she did it she opened his eyes.

They unlocked the door and got into the car. He pointed the way.

"You opened my eyes you know" he said as if following her train of thought.

"I'm glad you realised that."

"Not at the time I didn't. But now I do. I'm going to Thailand".

"When?"

"In two days."

"Then this wasn't Hello but Goodbye?"

"We are never apart – space doesn't matter you know that. Besides I always leave you messages on the moon."

"I know."

Time was only a constraint of this three dimensional life. As soon as their energies came together to form a whole they were aware of this. It was as if eternity was within them. So the normal things of life became the illusion they really were. Which meant that this special Goddess man lived more in the present than anyone else she knew, and took each moment as it came. However, this

123

wonderful attitude to life made any arrangements with him almost impossible and very,very, frustrating.

They pulled up at the side of a field and got out of the car.

"Where is it?" Kelly said unable to see evidence of a crop circle.

"About two fields over" he said shouldering the picnic and the back pack. "Look, here's our first kissing gate."

Kelly laughed. They always thought it sad that no one else seemed to take advantage of the marvellous kissing gate system. James went through, pulled the gate back and leant on it smiling. Kelly took hold of the lapels on his shirt and kissed him soundly. When he was satisfied with the kiss he allowed her through.

This method meant it took a little longer, but it was much more fun and started all journeys with laughter.

The crop circle, when they arrived, was huge and consisted of a large circle with intricate spirals on the edge of each succeeding mid point. Inside the energy was high and bubbly with a distinct pattern like a dance, making the heart beat faster and the senses swim. They walked round it in silence. They had met other people on their way up the hill to the crop circle, but they were going down. So they were alone at the moment. The sun was shining and was now quite warm after the frost they had had last week. Sometimes it happened in early May as if Winter couldn't quite let go.

James handed her a print out showing the crop circle they were standing in from the air.

"They already think it is some complicated mathematical formula" he said.

"It is beautiful. It is the first one this year?"

"As far as I can tell. Just in time before I leave."

"Well that was handy" she said. "I think it is a Solomon Group energy/information point. You know like the triangle on top of another triangle making six points and often called Solomon's Seal."

"Isn't that also a plant?"

"So it is. There is my first synchronicity. I am planning to get a group together to gather information from the moon and use the stone circle as an amplifier. I also want to make some remedies in the stone circle using plants and crystals. When is Solomon's Seal out?"

"Soon. You need to find an ancient woodland. In fact, that is how you can tell if a wood is ancient, because Solomon's Seal grows there. It has white flowers almost bell shaped and large leaves."

"I'll find it. Let's do a meditation and collect this energy then."

They put the back packs down and moved to the exact centre point of the crop circle. Then facing each other they smiled and started to tone.

They never practiced or gave each other direction, they just closed their eyes and sound came from their throats. It was always an eerie and strange experience even though it seemed familiar. They always knew when to stop and stopped together, then laughed because it was such a high, energetic and wonderful feeling when they connected their spiritual energies. They couldn't explain or even express it in any way, because it was completely 'other worldly'.

"We need to ....."

"..... go to each small circle" he finished.

She laughed and gave him a kiss. Then they moved to each of the six spirals in turn starting at the one facing east. Toning each one differently and drawing an energy pattern of conscious sound that looped around the circle. Then they moved back into the centre and made the sound thread and spiral around the crop circle until it seemed to be ringing like a bell.

Then they sat quietly in the centre and allowed themselves to absorb the information that was there for them to take. It was not conscious. They took it directly into their subconscious minds and fitted it into their DNA blue print.

After a while, Kelly picked some of the corn that had been folded at the precise angle when the crop circle had been made and wove it into a crown. She put it on James's head.

"Did you know that in Roman times if a Commander had won a great battle or achieved something impossible, his men would make him a grass crown, as a mark of honour. It was more highly thought of than all the gold ones he would acquire later."

"I expect it was from a much older tradition."

Kelly laughed "Oh yes. It was actually a great tribute to a Hero who had done some marvellous deed for the Goddess. Given to the hero by the High Priestess of the day, who was the personification of the Goddess on earth."

"Then thank you" he said "I'll wear it always."

"No you won't" laughed Kelly "but you can wear it for a day. Sometimes the Hero was sacrificed to the corn Goddess. But that was before the Priestesses of Isis put a stop to all that waste. It is no wonder that the world is sadly lacking in Hero's - who would want to come back only to be sacrificed!"

"Is it time for lunch. I'm starving – also there is the beginnings of something happening a bit further on so we should go and see. In the field, energetically I mean."

"OK" said Kelly getting the sandwiches out of the back pack and handing them to him. "Anyway there will be more people here soon once they have had their lunch, ready to marvel at the wonderful crop circle."

"They might even find it more exciting now we have tuned it."

"They might. At least any who have the right reception in their energy patterns will be able to pick up what they need for the next phase of their development."

"Well. There you are, that must be why we came."

Kelly smiled but didn't say anything. It was nice just to be in this energy field with someone she didn't have to adjust to.

"I may give up the house" she said as they started on the fruit and the bottled water.

"Is it time to move on?"

"Possibly. I have to work on this DNA and regeneration", she said realising that she hadn't known that this morning.

"And the painting?"

"After today I expect there will be some new pictures. They all form part of the wake up process when they will be needed to activate the Goddess Gene"

"Good". He put his arms round her from behind and she snuggled into him.

"All will be well" he said and in that perfect moment she believed him.

126

Chapter Twenty: Thursday

When Kelly woke just after dawn, about 7 o'clock, she couldn't remember what day it was. She didn't want to wake up, the bed was warm and soft and delightful. She turned over, stretched out her hand and found James there.

"Oh bugger" she said.

"Good morning to you too, beautiful" he murmured without opening his eyes.

"You're not supposed to be here – remember? You should be gone."

"Oh bugger" he repeated in an echo of her first thought.

"Get up quick and I'll make some tea."

"OK" he said rolling over and pinning her down "in a minute."

It was more than a minute when she did go down and he got into the shower. Then she remembered that after the crop circles, they had come back home and there was a Libra full moon, so they had gone out again, to the white horse and the hill and activated some more energy. Eventually they had got back home and fallen asleep – well eventually , there had been a few togetherness hours! This was not part of either of their plans, but it seemed to be part of some celestial higher arrangement which they had had no way of avoiding. Kelly quickly scrambled some eggs and made some toast and tea. James came down just as she had put the eggs on the toast and they ate in the quiet of companionship.

It was 8.20 when Kelly let him out of the door and watched him put his crash helmet back on. It had taken half an hour to get the length of the hallway. They didn't say Goodbye. They never did, they believed in eternity, but it didn't make parting any easier.

She watched him go down the road until he disappeared in a tiny cloud of dust. Then she cleared away the breakfast things and went to get ready for her day. She tidied the bedroom and stacked the boxes she had been working on yesterday, or the day before, she couldn't remember. It was possible that the estate agent would want to bring someone. She remembered she had promised David a meal so she made a fish pie, packed her bag and set off to the once named Abrachat.

It was quiet when she let herself in and she went straight to the work room end and put a canvas on the easel. She had a lot of information to express and painting was a good way of doing it.

She had almost finished and was cutting out some shapes for the next one when she heard the key in the door. She was so surprised to find it was five o'clock and David was arriving home. She had worked through what must have been lunch and only drank her bottled water. She looked at David with such a blank look on her face that he stopped and said

"I do live here I'm afraid."

"Of course you do" she said recovering and bringing herself back from the spiralling place she had been.

"Sorry. I've been painting and lost track of time. The good news is I have made the dinner. The bad news is I haven't even got it out of the car, never mind put it in the oven."

David didn't know what had happened to Kelly, but he knew something had. She was different. In some way changed. She looked different. There was formality, not the easy banter that had been there before. But she was here and he was glad.

"Plenty of time" he said moving towards the house door. "You carry on, I'll make some tea then do some writing until you are finished."

He went off into the house for which Kelly was very grateful. She wasn't ready yet to deal with David. She hadn't got the energy.

She finished what she was doing and cleaned the brushes and the pallet. Then stood back from the canvas and looked at the picture. It was very yellow and involved trees. This was to be expected since DNA was stored in trees. She drank her tea that David had placed quietly on the shelf. She looked round this little Aladdin's Cave she had created and smiled.

Pieces of magic – treasure – eternity. Ah that's what she should call it. "Pieces of Eight." Because a piece of eight was treasure and eight was the symbol of eternity. Well laying on its side it is. So that was the new name for Abrachat, although it didn't roll off the tongue like

Abrachat had done and really would anyone understand 'pieces of eight'. What would they call it? Pieces? no, that didn't explain the magic.

She went outside to get the fish pie and wandered back into the kitchen. David was upstairs so she let the normal chores of setting the table and finding the plates and filling glasses with water bring her back to where she was. By the time the food was ready she was more grounded and ready to talk to David.

He sat down at the table smiling at how nice it was to be looked after by another person..

"How's the writing going" Kelly asked as she put the plate in front of him.

"Slowly, I'm afraid. This looks nice. Thank you."

"Slowly?"

"Mmm" he said tucking into the food. "I suppose I'm tired after dealing with kids all day and by the time I have reread where I left off, I am too tired to be creative – even when I am inspired."

"I thought that might be the case. You need to give up the teaching."

"Would like nothing more" he said between mouthfuls. "However, I need the income in order to survive."

"Yes – well – I've been thinking about that. I am in the process of selling my house – well selling lots of things really."

"Because of the bankruptcy?"

"No, no, it was a limited company, so the house wasn't involved. However, I can't really afford to live there anymore and it is time I moved on. So soon I will need to rent somewhere. What if I move somewhere like here. Then I can pay you rent for the shop and my 'room' or rooms. Then you could write full time and get the books published."

David looked at her in stunned silence and as his face was expressionless she couldn't read his expression.

"Unless you don't want me to live here – I mean you have lots of room and you could maintain your own privacy."

"You mean you want to live here? With me?"

"Is that such a wild idea" she smiled.

"No –no – I think it's a great idea - I just thought that – I mean you said you ……"

129

"David, I want to live in your house not live with you."

"Yes – yes, of course, I realise that, I'm just surprised."

"Because I went away and didn't contact you for two years? It wasn't the right time. I told you that. I had a lot of things to sort out. Anyway do you think it is a good idea or not? It is fine if you don't, I will look for somewhere else. I just thought it would solve both our problems and I want to work in the stone circle so it would be nice to live near its influence."

"I think it is a lovely idea and you are more than welcome – whatever your reasons and for however long you wish."

"Well, good. Of course I haven't sold the house yet and you have to give notice, I suppose. Anyway, before that, we have a new shop to open and we haven't got a name for it yet."

"I've been thinking. Things like Magic Moments or Mystic Connections" he carried on eating his delicious fish pie, wondering if this was why she had said she would cool.

As if sensing his thoughts, she said

"I won't be cooking every night, you know and I didn't cook in order to bribe you. It is just a practical solution."

He smiled "Perhaps you should call it that. 'Practical Solutions'."

"It sounds like some software company. I thought of 'Pieces of Eight' today because we are selling treasure, but it doesn't flow off the tongue like Abrachat."

"No. Think what you are selling. You said yourself, it was magic. So we need to convey magic."

"Oh!" said Kelly sitting upright what about Abra…"

"Cadabra!" finished David at the same time.

They both laughed.

"We must celebrate" said David "I have raspberries and cream and a bottle of wine" he jumped up and rushed to the fridge.

Kelly got up and found some bowls and washed the raspberries whilst David opened the wine and found the glasses. Once they had both sat down again he poured the wine and lifted his glass.

"To the christening of the new venture no longer Abrachat – but Abracadabra, a little magic for all."

"Abracadabra and our new partnership" said Kelly.

130

David smiled. He knew this was going to be a good day. He hadn't been late for anything all day.

For Kelly it had been a very long day. After all she had been in many dimensions. Working with mathematics that had no reference points to anything on the earth. Manipulating energies that most people had no access to and no understanding of, and which hardly touched her own conscious mind.

Chapter Twenty one: Friday

Kelly had stayed the night. She had helped David to tidy up and then drifted back into the new Abrachat to add a few finishing touches to the picture. David had given her space. He realised that something had happened and he left her to cope with it in her own way. Now waking up she could hear him downstairs, but she didn't want to go down to breakfast – she decided to wait until he had gone to work.

She heard the door shut eventually and the car start up. She got up then and went into the bathroom. Not a shower day she decided, but a bath.

She knew she couldn't and shouldn't change her plans, but she just needed a little time to adjust. Besides she hadn't sold the house and she could change her mind. Even the long term plans made in wherever we existed before we came to earth, came with built in free will and she could exert that free will anytime she wanted. All she needed to figure out was did she want that?

She sighed and sank into the bath. All these higher thoughts were fine when they were just thoughts, but actually living life was so much more difficult. She needed to just allow the events to unfold. If she sold the house she could move in here. Then she could execute her plan to activate the circle and find a meditation group and start working with the earth energies in a consistent place.

She got out of the bath and dressed deciding to let the day unfold as it would. The house was wonderfully quiet as she went downstairs and made herself a smoothie and some tea. She tidied up the kitchen then went into the shop. The sun was shining outside and bouncing round the hanging and sparkling things that were energising the room. David had typed out some flyers and four posters advertising the opening of the new Abracadabra. He must have written it this morning she thought, how kind. She felt a bit mean about not getting up earlier now, but instead she took the posters over to her work bench and drew some exciting spirally colours round the words. Then she phoned her friend who did sign

132

writing to ask if he could come and take down the Abrachat sign and redo the name. He said he would come by later that day and fit it as soon as possible.

Kelly went and unlocked the shop door so that she could look at the window display from outside and let in some fresh air. She decided to put up one of the posters on the telegraph pole at the end of the car park which was on the road and more likely to attract attention. Then she went back and continued with the unpacking and sorting of what would now be the stock. She realised after about an hour, during which time she had been completely engrossed in placing her remedy bottles on the back shelves nearest the internal door, that she had come to the decision at least that she must continue with Abracadabra.

She was just unpacking another box when someone came into the shop shouting "hello". Kelly came round into the door area to find a lady with long, straight, blond hair and a look of absolute delight on her face.

"Hello" Kelly said.

"Oh Hi. I guess you are not actually open yet are you?"

Kelly shook her head.

"Only I couldn't resist stopping when the door was open and looking inside."

"That's fine" said Kelly "come in and look round. I'm Kelly Delmonty."

"I'm Millie" she said, "it looks fabulous. Full of magic."

"That's the idea" smiled Kelly "do you live in the village?"

"No" said Millie who was probably in her late thirties, but looked much younger "I live about four villages away, but my friend, Alison, lives here and I often visit. I liked it before when it was a book shop and coffee place, but this looks amazing."

"Would you like a cup of coffee or tea now " said Kelly "I intend to still do that in here" she pointed to the area behind the dividing shelf "but I am still unpacking. However, through the door is a fully functioning kitchen."

"That would be great" said Millie "if it's not too much trouble and tea would be lovely thanks."

133

"I don't actually drink coffee" said Kelly moving towards the door "what do you do? Are you an artist."

"No - not really, although I love all these creative things. I'm a Therapist. I do massage and reflexology and various healing techniques."

"Oh that's great" said Kelly "you might be interested in my remedies. I do healing as well. Look, come through to the kitchen with me whilst I make some tea. Perhaps you could close the door before you do in case everyone thinks I am open already."

Kelly and Millie spent a nice hour drinking tea and getting to know one another better. It was another pointer for Kelly in the world of how the universe works. Because here was someone who was interested in the same things as Kelly and who knew people in the area. She was delighted to help in getting together a group for meditation in the circle. They wandered outside together to look at the stones circle. They were very secluded, not visible at all from the road or indeed any of the windows in the houses. The approach to them through the French windows and the walled garden was magical and the wonderful stones themselves glowed in the sunshine. They were always bigger than you remembered and more complex. The stone circle was 72 feet in diameter and made of blue stone like the famous Stonehenge and came from the Pressily mountains.

Millie asked Kelly if she had bought this place now and had Mr Appleby gone. Kelly laughed and explained about the Abrachat franchise and how she was just taking over the shop for a while.

"You don't live here then" asked Millie as they made their way back into the house.

"No. I live near Pusley in Wiltshire" said Kelly.

"Really!" said Millie "I used to have a barge near there with my boyfriend."

"Wow! so we have lots of connections already" laughed Kelly "although I may live here in the near future. I am trying to sell my house."

"Oh that would be great", said Millie, "but we could still start the meditation group couldn't we?"

"Oh absolutely. You find me some people and we will start" she said "I would like nine altogether. We have two already and I know two healing friends, Lileth and Tasie, they live about an hour away, but I know they would come."

"Well I have three in mind, my German friend, Gudrin, Mellissa who reads tarot and works looking after animals and Rosilin who teaches Spanish and makes remedies herself. So we are almost there."

"I guess that circle really needs to be activated. We will arrange a meeting as soon as possible – end of this week? To sort out what we need to do and how we are going to do it then."

"OK" said Millie "I'll leave you my phone number then you can get in touch and I'll ask if they are interested, but I'm sure they will be."

"Great. Here's my number. I guess I had better get back to unpacking and planning the opening. You will come I take it."

"Wouldn't miss it. I'll bring the girls then you can meet them. Bye for now!"

"Bye" said Kelly smiling as she realised that the decisions had been taken out of her hands completely and other plans were now in the pipeline. She shut the door and went back to the task of unpacking.

When she thought about what had happened this week, she realised that it had in fact been a transition time, and the appearance of James had been a closure. The end of an old cycle, in order for her to begin a new one.

Letting go was always difficult as was any change. But necessary, if we needed to move on and it would seem that she had moved on now. Nothing ever remains the same, it never did, it just takes us a while to accept that.

Chapter Twenty Two
The Opening - end of May

It had seemed appropriate to Kelly to open Abracadabra on a Saturday because Saturday was shopping day and most people would be able to attend, even if it meant travelling a distance.

The week between the 'transition week' as she now thought of it, and the opening, had been hectic and full. Kelly had been driving between Pusley and Brompton on the March packing in one place and unpacking in another. It looked as if she had a buyer for her house and she would indeed be moving into David's if all went as it seemed to be going.

The morning was bright and sunny and full new beginnings. Kelly was up and showered and down into the kitchen long before David realised it was time to get up. She had breakfast and put the crackers, olives and other goodies out on the bench ready for later when they would be needed. Then she went into Abracadabra to check that all was ready which, of course, it was. The tables that would be used when the shop was open for 'coffee and cake' were now dotted around the shop and would contain wine and nibbles later. But as the day was so lovely, Kelly decided that she could put some more tables and the chairs outside. As she was returning into the house to get the furniture, she heard the car drawing up outside.

She rushed back and unbolted the door as her favourite teenager emerged.

"Louise! How wonderful! How are you, darling. I'm so glad you could get here."

"Wouldn't miss it" smiled Louise hugging Kelly tightly "someone needs to keep Dippy David in order or who knows what will happen! It looks good. The window is lovely, and the new sign! Very you, Fruit!"

"I know, I think David is actually in deep shock. It has all happened a bit soon I think."

"Never mind the speed, it is more likely the psychedelic colours that have mind altering properties that will have sent him off."

They moved into the shop whilst Louise took in the alterations and the treasure trove of creative products that were everywhere. Although Louise had seen most of the stock over the years at Kelly's house, she hadn't ever seen it all in one small space.

"Wow!" she said "I do hope you are going to have some tables outside. People will definitely need to sit down when they have been in here."

"That was just what I was doing. Come on, shut the door again and come and have some breakfast, then you can help me."

When David came down the spiral staircase it was to shrieks of laughter from the kitchen as two of the noisiest people he knew exchanged news. It reminded him of the day they had had their picnic/board meeting in the stone circle. It suddenly occurred to him that the events that had led up to this time had all included these women who he always thought were witches. On their own they were very plausible, but together …

"Morning David" said Louise catching sight of him standing motionless on the stairs.

"Louise" he said stirring himself "how lovely to see you, how is Uni ?"

"Oh, you know – sex, drugs, rock and roll as it should be. Do you want some coffee? I have made some."

"Thanks, that would be great. What do you think of the new revamped Abrachat?"

"It looks as if it has been "Kellyed". You should have more sense David Millhouse."

David looked startled again, but Kelly just laughed and put some toast in the toaster for him.

"Come on Louby Lou, we have work to do. Leave David to get used to the changes in his life quietly."

Louise laughed, somewhat ominously David thought, as he put milk in his coffee. He still had more questions than answers with regard to everything these strange women did, but they certainly made his life more exciting.

137

By lunch time the place was heaving with people who were spilling outside into the driveway and sitting at the tables. Everyone was laughing and talking. Some were even buying. Louise was busy taking money, whilst Kelly was explaining colours and auras and paintings, whilst writing down names in a book ready for courses she seemed to be organising. People were congratulating David on the new ideas and wonderful displays. Two people actually bought copies of his books. He only knew this because Louise thrust a pen in his hand and told him to sign them. He was a little disconcerted when he overhead Kelly telling Louise that she now had the required nine moon maidens signed up, and could start the activation of the circle on the Summer Solstice. Wasn't nine the exact number needed for a coven?

He had no time to worry about that because Marian Bradley cornered him at that very minute and introduced him to two more of her very good friends, who also gushed and admired the new look shop. Then just as he was disentangling himself, he saw Kelly talking to the wonderful Sally Weatherfield who he hadn't seen for a long time. It suddenly seemed that his past was all around him. It seemed so long since that day Sara had arrived with a camera and Ross was here and he had been writing about the Young Cleopatra.

"Sit down David and have a sandwich" said Louise at his elbow directing him to a chair behind the cash till. "You look a little peaky" she gave him a sandwich and went over for a glass of wine. "Here you are. It is just synchronicity you know. Don't worry about it."

He looked at her closely and in so doing he didn't see a teenager with attitude. The eyes were wise and old beyond their years. He realised he had always known that but she was a teenager as well.

"Kelly gets excited and her energy spills all over the place. She will calm down" she smiled at him.

"Thank you" he said biting into his sandwich "it feels as if I am part of some huge plan that I know nothing about."

"Oh, you do know David, you are just not consciously aware. You should know by now that is what Kelly does – she wakes people up. She herself has been awake for a long time and now needs other people to be awake with her. It is your life path – as she constantly tells everyone – well everyone who she feels she isn't wasting her time talking to" she laughed.

"Did she wake you up?"

"Only by giving birth to me. Sorry. I know we didn't explain that. But I am Kelly's daughter."

David sat opened mouthed at this , a thousand other questions already in his head.

"No more information today, David. She will tell you when she thinks it is time" and with that she disappeared off to sell some more stock and meet her friends who had just arrived.

Kelly came over and looked at him with concern.

"Are you alright? " she said peering at him "you look as if you have seen a ghost. Is it Sally Weatherfeild?" she smiled.

God, did everyone know about his unrealistic ambitions towards Sally? That milkman had a lot to answer for.

"No" he said "Louise just told me some things I didn't know. Of course she might have been teasing me."

"What did she say?"

"That she was your daughter."

"Oh that! Yes. She is, and always has been. Even in past lifetimes – well – when she decides to come to earth that is. I'll tell you more in time. Don't worry about it."

She patted him on the shoulder and wandered off to see Louise's friends and pass round glasses of wine.

David finished his sandwich whilst scowling suspiciously at both of them, but then had to smile as the wonderful Sally came over to talk to him about the change in the shop and not seeing him for so long. She said Kelly had asked her to come and work in the shop for a couple of mornings a week which was great, as she was only temping at the moment.

God!! David thought now he would have two women around who managed to make him tongue-tied and stupid. He wondered idly whether Sally had some revelations to impart. Perhaps she was married with six children and had never mentioned it. Christ !, he must pull himself together. Events were overtaking him at such a rate. He needed to keep his wits about him, before his wits disintegrated, or were stolen by witch craft. He couldn't decide which would be worse.

The noise levels gradually got smaller as the opening party came to an end and all the curious began to drift home or move on to the next interesting venue.

David stopped worrying about being taken over by witchcraft and began to realise how nice it was to have so much life and light in the house again, It felt as if this was how this big Barn was meant to be, a magnet for interesting people, not a quiet hide-away for an introverted writer.

Chapter Twenty Three
June 21st Summer Solstice

By 7p.m. all the girls had arrived and were sitting in the closed shop drinking an infusion of herbal tea that Kelly had made in a coffee maker. It was strangely refreshing and set the mood of underlying excitement and anticipation. They sat in a circle of chairs and Kelly knew it was her task to connect these women into a group. Some knew each other, but most were strangers to one another.

"I'm going to begin by asking each one of you to state your name and say a little bit about yourself. You can choose what you think is relevant information to be your part in this wonderful collection. Please laugh or talk wherever you wish and thank you all for coming." Everyone relaxed a bit and Kelly looked round at the faces.

"I'll begin" she said. "I'm Kelly. As you can see around you, I am pretty creative and I have done a lot of different things, but it would be a sort of overall picture to say that I am always working in the energy field. My paintings are reflecting the energy of the millennium and I started painting in 2000 three years ago now. Well I actually painted before but these paintings are a new dimension for me. My remedies are about storing the energy of the plants and using that energy to enhance people's lives. The dimension-stone circle is directly connected to the earth energies, so I am most interested in being able to tap into that energy and use it to send blessings and healing to people and places that need it. It also will act as a gateway to bring in the Goddess Energy when Venus comes very close to the Earth in August."

"In other words she is a witch" said Millie which caused a lot of laughter round the room.

"Don't let David hear you saying that. He is already worried about what he has let loose in his garden."

Millie continued smiling round at the group, her long golden hair caught in a plait today. "I do massage and reflexology and read fairy cards and I, for one, am very happy to be in a group of like-minded people."

Next to her was a lovely, smiley lady, large in stature against the diminutive Millie. Also with shoulder length blond hair and lots of dangling necklaces. "I'm Melissa. I read Tarot and look after animals so I think I qualify already as a witch" she said laughing.

"I'm Rosilin" said the lady next to her with lots of dark curls and flashing eyes. "I teach Spanish (my native tongue) and make remedies for animals and sometimes people. So I think I qualify."

"I'm Dale" said the next lady "Kelly and I used to work together. Actually she employed me, but only I think because I read Tarot cards too and I had the best book ever on the cards ......"

"Which I borrowed for an extended period" cut in Kelly.

"I do do normal things as well" continued Dale who had short blond hair, a short skirt and amazing shoes.

"I'm Gudrin" said a much quieter lady also blond and very serene. "I'm a spiritual healer and a child psychologist. I'm very glad to be here" she smiled.

"And I'm Tasie" said a larger than life, louder than anyone – except Kelly – lady who laughed "I'm a loud-mouth American who loves crystals and alternative healing and creative endeavours and in fact anything and everything that Kelly does. I'm really glad to meet you all and I'm real happy to be here."

Everyone in the room was now smiling and relaxed. Tasie's presence was infectious and all encompassing.

"I'm Sofie" said a much younger girl with short, straight brown hair. "I know nothing about anything. But I love it all and I want to learn. I'm doing a massage course at the moment. I used to be a dental nurse, but the lack of conversation got at me."

You could see that this was the group comic who would keep everyone laughing no matter what occurred. Next to her was the other young member. She had dark shoulder length hair and was much quieter, but full of hidden depths.

"I'm Ashley, I used to be a nurse, but I gave it up and embraced the alternative and am a full time mum at the moment, although I do some part time telephone triage work. But this is much more exciting."

142

"And last we have me" said another attractive, but older lady, with shoulder length blond hair.

"I'm Lena, I'm a healer. I do hypnotherapy and Bowen technique. I am also an astrologer and have been part of many spiritual practices for a long time. I also paint and make jewellery."

"Oh you must bring some into the shop" said Kelly. "Now, about tonight, we are going to do a ceremony in the circle, and although it is the Summer Solstice and we will follow the Celtic calendar, we are not really going to be part of any cult. The idea of organised religion and dogma is not what we are about. This is the millennium and so we will be conducting millennium ceremonies (of the time). All the other energies and priestesses were of their time. We are going to activate the stone circle to bring the earth energy into coherence and combine it with the feminine creative moon energy. That is why our ceremonies will be at night. We will be the conscious connections between the moon energy and the earth. This will allow the stone circle to bring alive all the underground energies from the earth, and from the water. When we have got these energies right, we will then connect them with the big energy sources like Stonehenge and Avebury and Glastonbury thus connecting these energies together in preparation for when Mars comes closer to earth than it has been for – how long Lena?"

"I think it is 60,000 years."

"Ah! A long time then."

Everyone laughed. "It will be then that the Goddess energy will re-enter the earth. We will be helping to make the network to receive that energy."

"Will there be other groups doing similar things?" asked Rosilin.

"All over the world, I think. We just have to do our section" Kelly laughed.

"Don't worry" said Millie "I don't expect it will be difficult."

"No, it won't be" said Kelly "it will be fun. All I need is your commitment and your energy to want to heal and bless."

"Our good intentions then" said Melissa.

"I think we can do that" said Gudrin.

"Great. Then we will now get ourselves outside and begin. You will find lanterns over on the shelf. Someone needs to light the candles inside. Then we need these crystals." Kelly got up and put her chair away and all the girls followed suit. Putting on their costs and outdoors shoes and chatting happily to each other.

Ashley found the matches and lit the lamps. Kelly put on her robe and collected her staff which was decorated with swan's feathers and tonight an orange silk scarf. She passed a beautiful Turquoise glass goblet to Sofie to carry and some special water in a bottle that came from the white spring at the Challis well in Glastonbury. Dale took charge of the silver dish decorated with the symbols of the zodiac and containing walnuts. Tasie and Lena carried the stool to make the altar and the white cloth to go on the top of it.

Kelly led the way through David's lounge (who was out for the evening, either by accident or design) and out through the French doors. Just as they were all winding their way through the walled garden to the gate that leads into the field, a loud honking drew their attention to a string of geese flying above them. They were making a perfect V formation with one out front and nine flying behind.

Kelly laughed

"I am an air sign so all flying creatures are very important symbols for me, but none more so than geese. I think we have just been given the seal of approval from the spiritual realms."

"Wow! How amazing is that" said Ashley "does it mean we are meant to be doing what we are doing then?"

"I would say most definitely" said Kelly opening the latch on the gate and leading the moon maidens into the field.

The ceremony consisted of the maidens walking round the stones first on the outside going wider (anticlockwise) and then on the inside going clockwise. After this they gathered all the energy into the centre, where the altar was formed. The table cloth was laid over the stool, the lanterns placed around the altar forming a circle. Crystals and the silver dish of nuts were next, then the sacred water in its blue glass goblet.

Kelly sent out love and blessings and asked for help to bringing the circle to harmony. Then each stone, one by one, was surrounded and toned, the sound of the Ohm carrying on the night air, like

144

moving water. They stood in silence for a few moments feeling the harmony of the vibration they had created.

Then, holding hands in a sort of snake, Kelly led them in and out of the stones weaving a complex pattern with their feet on the inside of the circle, eventually arriving back at the middle, where they joined the head to the tail and sounded the Ohm again.

By this time they were breathless, energised and laughing. Kelly then gave thanks for the gift of food and the blessing of wisdom, ate a nut and passed the dish round.

Next came the water, "without which there would be no life" said Kelly. She gave blessings to the earth for the gift of water, spilled a little on the ground first, then took a sip herself, saying "Blessed be" in the way of the Goddess. Then she passed the cup to the person on her right who took a sip, said "blessed be" and passed it on.

Kelly smiled to herself thinking that these girls learned very quickly, and the energy between them was open and loving. She closed the ceremony and led the way out of the circle taking their things with them.

As they made their way back to the gate, Kelly looked back at the stone circle and was aware of a brightness around the stones. A glow, that was the aura of the circle. She smiled. They had achieved more tonight than she ever thought they would, and she was pleased with her new little group. All she had to do now was to keep David calm and keep him from panicking, until the energy aura from the stone circle got big enough to work its magic through to the house. Then he would be calm and accepting. Well, that would be the theory anyway. Time would tell whether it was the truth.

Kelly thanked the girls and saw them out of the shop, making sure they all knew the date of the next ceremony. Then she locked up and went home herself. Best to let David consider the changes when he returned.

After all he may not notice anything and the house may look as it had done when he left that morning. Little did he know that enormous changes had already been wrought , and were most definitely, irreversible.

As Kelly drove off the owls were hooting, a little uncertainly she thought.

No-one had fooled them into thinking that nothing had changed, they were well aware of the energy patterns in their territory, and they were different.

So different that Kelly herself was a little surprised. For the most part she worked intuitively and as a thought occurred to her she acted upon it. This meant that she herself was often surprised with the results.

Chapter Twenty Four

The next day was Sally's first day in the shop. She had already been in and taken instruction from Kelly on where everything was, how the till worked and how to find anything.

Kelly decided to leave her to it and spend the day with her clip board deciding what furniture could go where and to whom, what she would keep and take with her. The sale of her house seemed to be progressing, so she needed to make these decisions whilst she had the chance.

The day passed without her seeing anyone, but she felt on top of things by the time she had a bath, something to eat and had fallen into bed.

When she drove to the shop the next morning, David had already left, but after opening the shop she made her way to the till and found a note from him.

It invited her to dinner that night at the local pub "so we may discuss the future". Kelly sighed, she had been rather avoiding this issue although she did realise it had to be addressed. It was quite possible she would be homeless in a matter of weeks and she had to decide if it was the right thing to move in with David. She couldn't hold him at arm's length any more, she needed to make a decision. What she didn't need in her life was commitment. She was, in fact , tying up loose ends, not creating new ones. This was a temporary stop, in a year or possibly two she would have to move on. She would have to take her energy elsewhere. But first …… but first she needed David to get the information out into the world. A lot of women needed waking up. Some men too, were waiting for the key words that would unlock the subconscious barriers and allow them to remember who they were and what exactly they needed to do. Kelly was so deep in thought that she failed to notice the car driving up and her first two customers of the day, until one lady asked her if they could try on the green lacy cardigan in the window.

Kelly looked at her in total amazement for a moment until she brought herself back to the present and pulled herself together.

"I'm so sorry" she said moving over to the window "I'll get it for you. Would you both like some tea or coffee? I've got fresh homemade cake too."

Having been made welcome, the two ladies happily browsed the many treasures while Kelly took the cake out of the box and made them coffee. By the time they had settled to their morning snack, Kelly had another two customers whom she recognised from the opening. So her day began before she was ready. But people were coming to look, and even sometimes to buy. At lunch time she shut the shop, made a sandwich and strolled out to the stone circle to sit and think about the best thing to do. She felt very comfortable here with the stones and the trees. The shop was a lovely idea and David had spoken to his publishers about the new book. So that was a plan that was working itself around. David was a good friend and she didn't want to spoil a warm comfortable relationship, but she also knew that she and David had an underlying 'thing' for each other and although it hadn't been really spoken of, it was there.

"Living so close together could ruin our friendship" she said out loud to no-one in particular. She got up from the sweet smelling grass which was a little damp and went back inside to get ready for some jewellery that Lena was bringing round to put in the shop.

Before she knew it, it was time to cash up.

Whilst she was writing down the days business she looked up to see David standing in front of her

"Hi, how was your day?" he said

She looked into his green eyes and smiled.

"Busy. How was yours?"

"Rough. But it's good to be home and to see you. How did your ceremony go in the stone circle?"

She gave him an appraising look. His dark, curly hair was all over the place and touching the collar of his green denim shirt. He looked a little tired, but not panicked.

"It went very well " she said slowly "are you sure you are ok with this?"

"I thought you said it needed turning or something."

148

"I did. It does, but it is your home and you can object."

"I know and I don't" he winked at her, picking up his overstuffed bag

"Are we on for dinner?" he started to move towards the inner door.

"That would be lovely" she said returning to the till. "Did you lock the door?"

"Oh yes. No more working tonight. I am going to grab a shower and do something with my hair. I saw your disapproving look"

He was gone before she could reply so she just smiled. Actually she rather liked that "little-boy-lost-just-got-up look", it went with the wink somehow.

When about three hours later Kelly decided she couldn't really manage a pudding, David put down his glass and said

"Now. Are you moving? Are you moving in with me – my house or have you decided against all of these things and are going to do something different?"

"The house sale is going through and I would like to live in your house, but I have reservations."

"And they are?"

"Well...... You and I David......" she paused and he raised an eyebrow and smiled, but said nothing.

"You and I...... we are good friends. And such easy friendships are hard to come by."

"True."

"Well, you see I don't want us to lose that friendship. We could really bugger it up."

"Because?"

"Because David – we have passion between us!" she said in an undertone.

David laughed. "Shall I get the bill?" he said, getting up and going over to the bar.

Kelly watched him whilst picking up her jacket from the chair. He seemed to be ignoring what she had just said.

He paid the bill and opened the door for her to go out. They walked across the pub car park and on into the road saying nothing.

Suddenly David grabbed hold of her arm, stopped walking and turned her towards him.

"I know", he said and kissed her on the mouth, gently at first, and then more passionately. She pulled away first a little reluctantly.

"We can't do this. Not now. I can't commit myself to you."

"I'm not asking you to do anything" he said "we have had this 'passion' as you call it. Always. It's not going to go away and it doesn't need to be addressed. I agree our friendship is important and whatever happens between us we want to keep that don't we?"

"Yes. But this passion of ours could take over and ……"

"Kelly. Just move in, be settled, let us enjoy each other's company – if we want more it will happen of its own accord and when you are ready to move on you will."

"You mean do the present and let the future take care of itself?"

"Exactly. Let's not make problems when there are none."

"Ok. In that case I would like to move in and I may well have a date. The estate agent phoned today and says completion date is by the end of the month. How much notice do you have to give the school?"

"I have already given it. Today was my last day. That is what we are celebrating. Which means I can get on with the writing."

"Oh David, that's great!" Kelly hugged him then smiled and linking her arm through his "come on let's go home and try and decide where we can put my sofa and chair because I really can't do without them yet."

They walked off up the road carefully watched by Dez, the milkman, who had been enjoying a pint by the window of the pub.

"Looks like old Appleby might have landed himself the right girl now" said Dez as the landlord came up to collect the glasses and look out of the window.

"Well it would be about time" he said wiping down the table. "Still it's early days, isn't it?"

"Oh aye" said Dez "many a slip and all that" and he chuckled to himself.

"Course he doesn't know who she is does he?"

"No and no one but her is going to tell him are they ?" said his old friend as he moved away.

Chapter Twenty Five:
Moving Day

The month whipped past faster than an offshore breeze. It had been filled with clipboards, boxes, moving furniture and general chaos. David had been invaluable with the moving and had even done some writing. Sally had been a Godsend, looking after the shop and keeping everything running, whilst Kelly had been practicing letting go of old energies and older habits.

She couldn't pretend that she had sorted all the documents and manuscripts and pieces of paper, but she had carefully placed them all in boxes with many labels. She knew she would need at least ten years to sort through them.

Now she was standing outside her empty loft looking at the Time Capsule whilst she thought desperately. She could hear David downstairs putting the last of her personal possessions that she didn't trust to the removal men, into the car.

She ran down the stairs to find David just returning through the front door.

"Do you have a loft?" she said quickly.

"Yes. There is access to a large storage area via a cupboard door in my bedroom. Why? Do you need to store some things in there?"

"Yes. Well one very important something. It's a Time Capsule actually."

"Oh. Is it metal?"

"Metal?"

"Ready for burial?"

"Burial?"

"What does it look like, Kelly?"

"It's really just a big cardboard box all sealed up, but it's very important."

"Oh that's fine. Shall we take it now?"

"It will have to go in the van and you will need some help lifting it."

Two of Kelly's friends who had helped her move things into the shop were due to arrive anytime with their van.

"We need to wrap it up or something."

"You don't want anyone to see it you mean."

"Well obviously they will see it, but I don't want them to know what it is."

"OK. Well we've got some newspaper and Sellotape. That will make it look like …."

"A Big box with newspaper round it?"

"Exactly!"

Kelly laughed "Excellent, let's go to it before they get here."

So the all important Time Capsule was moved without anyone ever really knowing that it was all important, and later on that day it arrived outside David's loft, which was where Kelly found it.

David followed her into the room and removed a chest of drawers from across the eve space, revealing a door with a bolt.

"To stop the mice getting in I take it" said Kelly preparing to push the box inside once David had released the bolt.

"Who knows what may or may not live in that no man's land" David replied stepping inside the loft crab-like in order to pull whilst Kelly pushed.

"You will find reference to similar boxes in the journal if Isis. We seem to have been hauling and hiding our information for generations."

"Nothing much has changed then" said David finally getting the box into the loft space where it joined others from David's move.

"Perhaps this lifetime we get to release it. Who knows. I think that is the plan."

"So when do you start leaking this information?"

"Not yet, David. One step at a time, I think. Anyway, have you spoken to your publisher yet?"

David emerged from the loft and bolted the door. Then they both pushed the chest of drawers back into place.

"One step at a time" he smiled "as you so rightly say. I need to write a synopsis in my style which includes the excitement of new work and new methods. But you have to admit that moving your worldly goods has taken most of my time lately."

"It has" said Kelly walking back down the corridor towards the spiral staircase "but as from today that is over. I am – as they say – here now. Shall we have some tea before we rearrange the furniture to make room for my sofa?"

"Mmm nice", David said following her down the staircase and into the kitchen, but he wasn't really listening. He was thinking about boxes. Boxes of information. Of wisdom. Feminine wisdom, that had been sought after and battled for, over the ages. Most of it had been lost, destroyed or captured and hidden. A lot in the Vatican, so rumour had it. But somehow incredibly, the groups of resourceful women had kept this ancient knowledge alive had continually recovered their knowledge in some way, and found a way to keep it safe. Now one of these mysterious women had moved into his house and brought with her some of that knowledge. She had told him that the time had almost come to release it to the world. Until now he had thought of Kelly and Sara and Louise as being involved in some sort of elaborate game, but what if it wasn't? What if it was, in fact, bigger, much bigger, than he had ever conceived? What then? What more was there for him to know, or to find out?

Kelly was busy filling the kettle and chatting about something. She turned round when he didn't answer and looked at him.

"Not now, David. Today we move my house. Tomorrow we will think of moving the world."

Then she laughed and David lightened up and went to find the Cake Tin

Chapter Twenty Six – Turning Point October (Saturday)

The next two months evolved themselves into a pattern and Kelly and David adapted to each other and got used to living in the same space. They continued to sleep in separate bedrooms and observe their separate commitments, but they ate together and were social as a couple. It was easier than either of them thought it was going to be. They were friends, companions and it was fun.

The shop continued to flourish and the group of nine moon maidens gave their time to the various festivals and ceremonies that Kelly deemed were needed to connect the earth energies and bring the stone circle into the millennium.

David continued to write and had informed his publishers that his new book would be ready for them to see, soon. He was crafting the synopsis in the novel/history/goddess/but adventure story that he knew would 'fit their lists', so all seemed to be going smoothly.

Tonight he was sitting on the sofa watching something on television when he noticed that Kelly was pacing up and down near the French windows. He watched her for a while, but could make no sense of what she seemed to be doing.

"Are you alright?" he asked interrupting her strange pacing.

She stared at him for a moment as if she had forgotten he was there.

"We have to build a labyrinth " she said.

"Ok" David replied hesitantly "do we have to do it now?"

"Don't be silly, it's dark. It has to be outside in the field. I know how to do it, but would you mind?"

"No. Why should I? Do you need me to help you?"

"Well yes, I do actually" she said, coming to sit down next to him. "That would be great. We'll do it tomorrow."

As David had no idea what building a labyrinth would require, he decided to wait until tomorrow to find out. He didn't think it was such a big deal really. Of course in that he was entirely wrong because it was in fact a very big deal and changed everything. But that is how life is, full of things that change the world, but which at the time they happen seem incongruous.

The next morning was a warm, sunny late September day and Kelly was up, dressed and outside before David was awake enough to realise it was morning. When he came down into the kitchen the bench was spread not with breakfast things, but with bits of paper with strange diagrams and Kelly's writing. He was trying to make sense of it when she came back in clutching long garden canes and string.

"Ah, David, there you are" she said as if he had arrived from some far flung location rather than upstairs. "Great, we can have breakfast and then get started."

"Can we?" he said not quite knowing what they were getting started with.

Kelly put down the canes and string and filled the kettle. "I got croissants yesterday – shall we have those for breakfast?"

"Yes. That would be nice. What are we getting started with?" he said getting the butter and jam out of the fridge.

"With the Labyrinth" she said putting tea leaves in the teapot.

"I have been outside to dowse where we should put the labyrinth and the strongest area it seems to want to be built is next to the stone circle. Well actually, connected to it."

David had seen Kelly dowsing before so that was not such a strange thing. She dowsed to find the right plants to make her remedies and often when she needed to decide something. But he hadn't actually seen her dowsing outside. "Did you dowse like dowsing for water?"

"Yes with rods rather than a pendulum. I was looking for 100% radiating spots in the earth which would point me to 'a blind spring' that has to be the centre of the labyrinth."

Kelly had put the croissants in the oven and made the tea whilst she was talking. David had got the plates, mugs and knives out of the cupboards and set them on the island bench. Kelly moved her bits of paper and found the one she was looking for.

155

"What are the other canes for?" David asked sitting down at the bench and sipping his tea still looking at the diagrams.

"Oh yes! Forgot a bit. After the cross you then make L's in the corners leaving the width of the path. Look like this. Kelly quickly drew the key to the labyrinth. "Then you use the string to do this", she started to draw the lines that would become the walls of the labyrinth.

Whilst David looked at what she had done she got the croissants out of the oven.

"This is a seven path classic labyrinth such as you would find all over the world."

"I see that, but why are you building one and why here?"

"Because it's time to do it David", she said eating her breakfast.

He looked at her but she was thinking about something else and he knew that was all the explanation he was going to get, at least for now.

"What did you mean about being connected to the stone circle?"

"Mmm, well, I thought" Kelly said ,finishing her last bit and pouring more tea "that the labyrinth would be in the field but separate from the circle. However, when I dowsed it, it needs to be very close to the circle and I think when we lay out the string, the two are going to overlap."

"Will that be alright.?" Isn't it a mixture of energies?"

"Well, yes it is, but that seems to be what it needs. I won't know why until we have built it."

"Do you think it is a bit like Yin and Yang and how the two circles are always drawn with the energy passing from one to the other?"

David finished his tea and put the plates and mugs in the sink.

"You know you could be right" said Kelly standing up to finish her tea. "Not just a pretty face then David", she smiled.

"Not even a pretty face" he said taking her plate.

"Oh I don't know ......" Kelly said looking at his dark curls and crumpled green shirt "I quite like the gypsy look. Anyway, come on we must do this – can you take the diagram and some of the canes."

156

She gathered up all the equipment and started to make her way out of the French windows. David watched her for a moment. She was wearing jeans, a bright pink tee-shirt, three necklaces and her blond hair was tied up in a makeshift ponytail. The 'gypsy look' seemed to be in fashion this morning he thought as he hurried after her.

Laying out the labyrinth wasn't difficult once they had realised that they needed the pathways to be a certain width, but it did take longer than they had thought. Once the string was all laid in place, Kelly informed David that the next task was for him to get the lawn mower and cut the paths into the grass. Whilst he went to find the lawnmower, Kelly walked the laid out pathways to make sure that it was just one winding path into the centre. It did indeed intersect with the stone circle so that three of the stones were actually in the labyrinth, but none of them interfered with the pathway once they had made a few adjustments.

David returned with the working lawnmower and followed Kelly around the labyrinth to the centre – or heart – as they made the shape of a heart in the middle then they followed the pathway back again and the labyrinth was made. They stood for a moment looking at the spiral that now intersected with the stone circle.

The sun was now hot and bright and well past lunch time.

Kelly smiled "Looks good, but no time to eat though. I will have to go into the shop and help Sally as it will be afternoon tea soon. Sorry it took so long".

David looked at their handy work. "It was very interesting. It feels different somehow."

"I know. We must leave it to settle now and do the dedication tomorrow night when it is the full moon."

"We ....?"

"Yes, David,, you and I . Yin and Yang. Male and female energy. Look, go and finish your chapter or whatever and I'll cook for us later. Just have a sandwich or something now."

"Ok boss, see you later then."

David took the lawnmower back to the shed whilst Kelly retrieved the string and garden canes, then hurried inside to change her tee-shirt and have a quick wash before going into the shop to get tea underway.

Sally was organised as usual and had remembered to collect the cakes and scones from the wonderful WI ladies. She had put the coffee percolator on and dashed back to serve someone in the shop. Two of the tables were already occupied, so Kelly filled the kettle and went over to ask them if they had ordered. Sally looked relieved when she came back and saw that the scones were on the plates with the jam and Kelly was adding the cream.

"Sorry, Sally, I meant to be here before now" Kelly said, pouring the water onto the tea. "Has it been busy?"

"Nothing I couldn't handle" smiled Sally, picking up the plates

"I really enjoy working here you know, it is so bright and energising. I think that is why everyone likes coming."

"I have got those extra tables and chairs" Kelly said following Sally to the tables with the tea and milk "so if you can carry on here , I will get them outside and attract more people who might be passing."

Sally had already opened the new awning that Kelly had installed to take the bright sun off the window. It was a deep sunshine yellow with a yellow and white striped edge. Kelly put the two new tables with four chairs each under the awning. The seats were yellow and white striped and she had two yellow table cloths to complete the continental feel.

As Kelly walked back into the shop, a car drew up and four people piled into the empty chairs. Sally laughed as she went outside to take their order.

"You were right, it now looks irresistible" she said to Kelly.

The next three hours flew by as the new tables started to pay for themselves. All the scones and cakes were gone and there were spaces on the walls and shelves where pictures and pots had been sold. Whilst Sally cleared up, Kelly replaced the pictures with more and got out some of the jewellery she had not had time to do before.

This was made by Lana, one of the moon maidens and looked amazing by the till and on one of the shelves.

"Why do you change the pictures so often?" asked Sally as she started to add up the money in the till.

"Because I want them to be seen" said Kelly "they are keys, they open energy pathways for people. That's why they are not for sale. I mean some are for sale but these are part of my awaking project. I intend to build a huge indoor labyrinth, each pathway painted in is own colour with the paintings in that colour and the poems that match them alongside. The idea would be that people walk round this labyrinth and it moves their energies. That's why I want people in here, to see them. Although some of the paintings I have are priced high enough to make sure that only those who really want them will buy them. Then I can assume that they will be seen by all the people that the buyer is associated with"

She looked up at Sally to see if she thought she was crazy or interesting.

Sally nodded "All your things are like energy doors aren't they? I always thought that they don't make you think, they make your 'feel' something – sort of remember something from deep inside."

Kelly smiled "I can see that I chose the right person in you Sally. Now please pay yourself for the work and get off home. We have been busy today – so thank you".

"I enjoyed it – really". She took her wages and slipped off out of the door which Kelly quickly locked before anymore customers tried to come in.

Then she remembered the seat covers and table cloths and went back to retrieve them and tip the chairs against the tables to show they were not in use. As she came back into the shop, David came in the door from the house.

"Hi" he said stretching "you sounded busy. Did it go well?"

"Very. The new tables outside worked wonders. How about you? How did it go?"

"Well. In fact I have finished! Written the synopsis and sent it off to the publisher – well sent the first 3 chapters."

"That's great – how did you get it done so quickly?"

"I had written quite a lot so I decided that I would leave the 'Journal of Isis' just as you had written it. I interspersed it with the historical story I had started writing and kept that as a narrative in the third person – an observer. It lets you hear Isis's voice in the first person, present.. But fill in the historical information that the reader will not necessarily know. I think it works really well."

Kelly was clearing up and putting things away whilst David was telling her this.

"It's going to be very different from your normal style."

"I know. It's much fuller, rounder, it's, it's ...... not just the masculine perspective."

"No. it's His story or History meets Her story (the female perspective) it should cause a stir if nothing else."

"Kelly, I'm sorry – I mean about the male thing – I mean I'm not sorry I'm a male – I just mean ...."

"Thank you, David, an apology on behalf of the male species. How nice." She smiled, he looked different somehow, more ...... erm more ....

"Shall we go and eat out tonight" she said quickly. "Celebration?"

"Yes that would be nice. I'll go and have a shower. Shall we just go down the road?"

"Yes, we can walk then. Half an hour?"

"Ok" David said over his shoulder on his way upstairs.

Kelly decided to just nip outside and just check on the labyrinth. It looked quite magical. The air seemed to be misty and thick as if the two energies were mingling and blending. She dowsed to ask when the dedication should take place. Tomorrow, and the full moon, and David, were confirmed. Then she went inside to have a shower and go and eat. She was aware that it had already been a long day and could feel the shift taking place. Poor David he didn't know just how much was going to change.

Chapter Twenty Seven:
Sunday

As the next day was Sunday, David felt justified in turning over and sleeping some more. In fact he wasn't really sleeping he was thinking about last night. Kelly had spent a lot of the time between eating just looking at him. She had put her hair up and wore some long earrings which sort of jingled as she moved her head bringing his attention to her exposed neck which he had kept wanting to kiss. He knew his attraction to Kelly was always there, but most of the time it was damped down. Like a fire that was awaiting the air needed to , to set it alight

He smiled at his analogy because Kelly was an air sign and he was fire sign. Something was going on, but he knew he just had to wait for it to unfold. He decided a cup of coffee would be nice so he got up and pulled on his jeans. He drank less coffee and more tea now, but sometimes he just needed the caffeine hit. He went downstairs quietly in his bare feet and started the ritual of putting the percolator on.

He was thinking about the book and all the unanswered questions that knowing some of the past had brought up, when he felt a hand on his naked back. He jumped out of his skin and whirled round to face a sleepy headed, startled Kelly.

"Sorry!"

"Sorry!"

"I didn't mean to make you jump."

"I thought you were in bed! I didn't hear you – why didn't you say something."

"Sorry – sorry I couldn't resist" Kelly smiled then turned round to go back upstairs.

"Do you want some tea?" David said to her back.

"Yes – great" she hurried off back to her room and David thought how weird she was acting. What could be wrong with her.

He made the tea, whilst his coffee sent its wonderful smell throughout the house. Then took it upstairs to where Kelly was back in bed with the duvet over her head. He put the tea down and a muffled thanks came floating up. So he left it and went back to his coffee.

Dez had arrived with the papers so he retrieved them, going back to his room to involve himself in world affairs. At least the ones according to the news paper, and not Kellys extended perception.

He must have fallen asleep because by the time he got up, showered and went downstairs, Kelly had gone, leaving a note to say she was off to see Louise and would be back to make dinner - adding that he was not to forget they had a ceremony to do tonight.

"Weird" David said to himself, but he had much grass cutting and many papers to sort out, so he had breakfast and got on with it.

Leamington Spa.

"What is going on actually" said Louise between mouthfuls of curry and poppadum.

"It's Mars – bloody Mars – it's closer than it has been for 60,000 years."

"Do you remember that or have you got this information from elsewhere?"

"How old do you think I am!" squeaked Kelly.

"Old enough" smiled Louise.

"No, astronomers and people are all putting out this information. Anyway, I had to build the labyrinth to be ready for this new information that is coming in. I think it is going to act like a transformer and transform the energy into a form that we can absorb through our chakra system."

"Is it like that time you visited a Greek island and came back telling me you had all this information. You then produced it with a flourish and it was a crocheted spider's web?"

162

"It was all the information.! I had woven it into that web. Then I put it on a tree to allow the earth to absorb it."

Louise laughed "You are pretty crazy, you know."

"Yes I know. I also know that you have got to be in the world at the moment doing 'normal' stuff. At least for a while, but it doesn't mean I can't run my thinking past you and get your wisdom. You are still No. 6 and you do remember your past lives."

"Some of them, but I am trying to forget for a while and just be a student."

"I know. I know. I'm sorry. Sometimes I just need to talk to you."

Kelly ate some of her curry and had a drink of water whilst Louise told her some of the fun things she had been doing. They were eating in her favourite restaurant in Leamington not far from the university.

"Anyway, how is David? How's the writing coming on?"

"Fine. Good. He has finished and sent it off."

"Great. I told you he could do it, he just needed a bit of pushing."

"Yes well so far so good. He is rather – lovely."

"Oh yes? I thought you weren't 'getting involved' because "this is a temporary step", to quote you."

"I know – I know all that" Kelly smiled then sighed. She looked round the restaurant at the pictures and outside the window where the sun was shining.

"Leamington is such a pretty town" she said. "Let's go and walk in the sunshine and I can buy you those jeans you need."

"You're not changing the subject are you?" said Louise finishing her beer.

"No. I know I have to go to France and sort out all the energy lines around the so-called Cathedrals, which we remember as Temples and are in the formation of the sign of Virgo. Goddess knows what other energy lines will be activated once this new energy arrives. It means that the Goddess will be waking up and then there will be some fireworks, I can tell you."

"Don't tell me! I need to be normal for a while". Louise put her napkin down "come on, old woman, pay the bill and let's shop. I'm sure you will work it all out as it happens."

163

Kelly stood up and got her jacket and handbag off the chair.

"I'm sure you're right. The shop thing is going great. I am selling my stuff which gives me money and gets the energy out there and our 'new Shakespeare' is shaping up. So we just need to relax and let it happen."

Kelly paid the bill and they emerged onto the wide Regency style high street, with its white buildings decorated with tumbling hanging baskets.

Louise linked arms with her mother as they walked up the street, happy in the moment of unexpectedly being together.

"Thank you for lunch – it's lovely to see you" Louise said.

"And you" Kelly replied squeezing her arm and removing her sunglasses from her head to her nose. "Anyway you have to get on with this literary course you are doing, because sometime in the future, we are going to have to interpret the information we left in the writings of the original Mr Shakespeare."

"Yeah, yeah. But not just yet. Now we shop. I have seen this rather nice top that would go with the new jeans. I'll show you."

Kelly laughed and prepared herself for serious shopping, putting off all thoughts of David and the newly appointed labyrinth till later.

Kelly arrived back as promised before six o'clock with salmon, broccoli and asparagus for dinner.

David had put some more tubs out at the front of Abracadabra which made a nice dividing wall between the car park and the outside seating area. He had also cleaned the house and done some tidying in the walled garden.

"It looks very nice" said Kelly as she came in with her shopping.

"I got some raspberries and strawberries from the farm shop" he said following her into the kitchen. "How was Louise?"

"Great. She is fine. We had lunch and went shopping, then I dropped her back to her uni. It was nice to see her."

"Yes. About Louise….."

"I know. I will tell you" Kelly interrupted quickly.

164

"But not just now?" David finished.

"No. Not just now. We have to go to the ceremony tonight."

"Ok woman of mystery. What time are we doing it?"

"The moon is in the right place about 10 past 10 so we will start at 10 I think. Plenty of time. Let's have a cup of tea and I can get the vegetables ready to steam. Then we have a shower and eat. We need to be cleansed and you need to wear white."

"For purity."

"Something like that. Anyway , tea first."

David poured the boiled water onto the leaves, shaking his head slightly. One thing was certain, life was anything but dull with Kelly around.

When David came back downstairs with his dark curls slightly damp and wearing his almost white chinos and white Indian cotton over shirt, he was surprised to see Kelly dressed entirely in red. He stood at the kitchen door in amazement. She wore a long red shiny skirt, with a frill round the bottom a split at the side, together with a red sequined top and red high heeled shoes. She had curled her hair so that it was bigger and bolder and she was wearing red lipstick.

"I thought you said we had to wear white" he squeaked – it was the only thing he could think to say. She turned round and smiled at his white outfit.

"I said you had to wear white, I don't remember saying anything about me."

She put the apron on so she could wash the raspberries and do the fish. As there was no answer to this, David got the knives and forks and glasses and went into the dining area near the French windows overlooking the walled garden. He opened the doors to let in the smell of the honeysuckle and roses that climbed up the walls.

Next he found the candles, condiments and the white table cloth, then set the table . He guessed they would be drinking water so he found some sparkling water and poured it into the glasses. By the time he had finished, this strange powerful lady came through from the kitchen with their plates.

165

"Nice" said Kelly setting down the food "very nice", she repeated turning to look at the open French windows.

"Thank you" David replied, as she put down the plates.

"It's the red lady and the white knight. You know, like in Chess."

"What, we are going to fight?"

Kelly sat down and smiled at him through the candle light.

"It's the emphasis of the male and female principle. White light is strong pure and bright. Red is passion, the driving force, the life underpinning everything. Red is Power. You see........ Strength and Power....... Male energy is like a lightening rod, it holds energy and keeps it steadfast. That's what you will do, hold onto me. You have the strength to hold the position...., to ground me, whilst I become a channel and allow the energy outside to combine with mine and bring it into the circle."

"How do I do this?"

"It's easy, David, you male, me female, you don't have to think it. It just is. Eat your dinner, it's delicious. I'll tell you what to do as we are doing it"

Kelly put some salmon in her mouth and waved David to do the same, so he did, taking surreptitious glances at this strong woman sitting opposite him.

She smiled at his puzzlement.

"You haven't seen my cloak yet" she said.

No. I bet there are a few other things you are not telling me he thought. But decided not to say anything just yet. They had time to eat their dinner, and it was a nice night, no rain or clouds. The moon was going to be clearly visible and probably very powerful, just like Kelly had intended.

"Why do we need all this stuff?"

"Because we do. Ceremonies involve 'doing things'. Hurry up David, it's quarter to already and we haven't even got there!"

Kelly was having trouble walking in the now dew-soaked grass. Her high heels were sinking into the ground and she was trying to hold her billowing red cloak up slightly to stop herself from tripping over.

David was walking behind loaded down with cloths, a stool (for the altar), the singing bowls, water from the challis well in Glastonbury and two large crystals. Kelly was carrying a lantern with a candle and some incense which was smoking. She had already smudged both of them whilst muttering ominously about it being David's job to smudge, as he was a fire sign. But as he didn't seem to know anything yet, she would have to do it. She also had a silver dish full of walnuts and which was inscribed with the signs of the zodiac.

She stopped suddenly. David almost piled into her. He peered at the back of the wonderful red cloak and was a little taken aback to see a dragon imprinted on it. He was rather glad it was getting dark so that the neighbour's were less likely to see these strange goings-on. Although there was no way that anyone could see into this field or get into it without climbing the fence.

"You need to wait here now" Kelly said "whilst I open the gates. You have to have a different door to me."

As David could see no gates or doors anywhere, only the stone circle, he just stood quietly and waited. Kelly put down the items she was carrying and produced from about her person somewhere a stick that looked very much like a walking stick with feathers and some orange silk tied onto the top.

Then she went to a point between the first and second stones and sort of drew a gateway or door in the air. She smudged it and muttered some words he couldn't quite catch, made some symbols with her hand and then moved on to the space on the other side of stone no. 1 and no. 16. She repeated the process then came back.

"Right, I have opened the doors. Now I will go through this one with all the sacred furniture, then come back to the other door – there" she pointed "and you will come through the male entrance. I will greet you. You must give your name as you come in."

"Right", David said forcefully, handing her all the so-called sacred furniture.

He waited where he was until she had set up the stool/altar and placed a white cloth on it. On top of that went the candle, the two crystals , the goblet with the water, and the dish with the walnuts. From her pocket (or somewhere) she produced a small packet and suddenly David knew that it was salt, Himalayan old, old, salt from the mountains. And suddenly this ceremony didn't seem strange. It seemed familiar. As he moved towards the entrance, the male entrance , he felt the air about him getting thicker and sort of misty. Kelly held out her arm in welcome and David moved forward, stopping in the gateway

"I am Wind Dancer" he said without even realising that that was what he was going to say.

Kelly smiled and cocked her head on one side. "Welcome Wind Dancer" she said "I am Ravens Wing", kissing him on the mouth.

He had kissed Kelly before, but this time it felt completely natural and very familiar. He stepped through the gateway and followed her into the centre of the circle. Taking the matches he lit the candle in the lantern and took the smudge stick and turned towards first the east, then the south and north and then the west, inviting the four directions into the ceremony. Kelly watched him for a moment then took the salt and made a circle around them in the middle.

"Welcome back to awareness" she said, as she took the water and blessed the earth, spilling a little on the ground. Then she gave thanks for the gift of water and drank some, saying 'blessed be' and passing the cup to David who drank some and repeated the words. She then repeated the process with the walnuts.

Next she took the silk scarf from the stick she had brought and removed two feathers, placing one in her hair and one in David's.

"It is time to combine our energies" she said. "Do you give me your right arm freely and with love?"

"Yes" he said without hesitation and held out his arm.

Kelly tied their right arms together with the scarf then she moved closer so that their right arms were diagonally across their hearts. Then she moved closer still until there was no space between them. She encircled his neck with her left arm and he did the same with her waist. He was now so close to her that he could see only her eyes which looked large and luminous. She smiled and he felt her energy expand and surround him like a warm cape. He was breathing her breath and it was filling his being. He kissed her mouth which

seemed to be full of light and laughter, then he didn't seem to be standing in a stone circle in his field. He was spiralling into the night sky in a shower of golden joy and Kelly was no longer this blond haired European. She now had long, dark plaits and wore a buckskin dress of the softest material and she was spiralling and showing him how to dance on the wind. They were suddenly free of the earth and in that moment he knew how they had placed all their knowledge and wisdom into the stones of earth, so they would be able to retrieve them in another time, another era when it would be needed. They had left their knowledge and ability to wind dance in the rocks, where only those with the ancient wisdom would be able to read it.
He felt the jolt as Kelly disengaged herself and stepped slightly backwards. He opened his eyes and she smiled giving him a moment to come back.

"We need to gather the energy from the stone circle by walking a winding path, then take it into the labyrinth. We have to stay connected" she said.
He nodded and she stepped back a little further releasing their arms from their chests. Then she turned round so they were both facing the same way. Kelly, with her right arm behind her, David with his in front and she started to walk in a spiral round the inside of the stone circle. She was chanting quietly and after a few repeats, it became hypnotic and David joined in the chant which he seemed to know, but had no logical explanation for knowing.
When she had enough energy stored, Kelly made her way into the labyrinth and began the winding walk that would lead to the centre.
It was only when she had reached the centre and they were both standing on the heart shaped grass mound now facing each other that they both stopped chanting.
"We allow this energy to flow from us into the labyrinth" she said "we are connected. All is one. Blessings, love and light. We allow the energies of Yin and Yang to form a harmonic whole as the moon goes into Libra, the sign of harmony and balance. Blessed Be"
"Blessed Be" repeated David.

169

Then Kelly repeated the position of closeness they had adopted before and when they were close as they could be she kissed him again. This time it was like an explosion of fireworks which seemed to start in his chest and expand outwards and upwards. It was as if his DNA coding was reading and combining with her DNA coding. As if they each had half of a puzzle, or a lock and key. He could feel the opening of so many locked doors.

She was both a minefield, and an unbelievable expanding experience. Somewhere at a deep level, he realised that if this had happened before, he would have been in danger of imploding and not being able to return. He knew suddenly, and clearly, why she had told him again and again 'that it wasn't time yet'.

He got it now. Being close to her without being too close had somehow allowed him to be sensitized. As if she had been building a structure, for him to be able to survive this explosion. He was again awed and grateful for her painstaking work on his behalf. Because he didn't really know who she was, but he did know that he had worked with her before in previous lifetimes. But had until this moment he had been completely unaware. Yet , he had always felt close to her, as if she was familiar. He knew he could trust her whether he understood or not.

All these revelations may have been instantaneous or they may well have been kissing for hours, even days. David had no way of knowing. So much was happening that it made a nonsense of time and space, which he seemed to be floating above. After a while, he became aware that the explosions were lessening and he was drifting back down to a place, in a labyrinth, in a field, kissing a very unusual woman.

They released each other at the same time and took a breath, then hugged each other.

David noticed how cold he suddenly was, but Kelly was hot like a summer sun.

"Ice and Fire" she said answering his question before he asked it.

"Equal and opposite....... Dynamic opposition.......... It's how the energy moves.

Come on, we have to walk out now."

She led the way back round and round the labyrinth still tied together until they reached the centre of the stone circle.

"We give thanks for all the help we have received in this ceremony. We allow the energy of the Goddess to flow into the labyrinth and back into the earth. The Goddess will awaken. Blessed Be."

"Blessed Be" David said automatically.

Kelly smiled and undid the binding on their arms. She waved her arm about and did some more muttering which he understood was the closing of the ceremony. Then she took both his hands in hers and said

"Three ohm's now", took a deep breath and started to tone.

He followed her and although he was still cold, he was beginning to calm down a little.

"Come on, we can leave all these things here for now."

She took his hand and walked back towards the edge of the circle, taking him to the gate he had entered. He stepped through it and waited whilst Kelly exited her own gate, then using her stick closed both gates.

The lantern in the centre of the circle was still lit and gave a wonderful eerie feeling to the already strange, distracted state that David felt himself to be in. Kelly turned round to face him and suddenly grabbed his lapels and pulled him closer towards her.

"God, you look good enough to eat" she said and kissed him again, this time with human passion.

He groaned as he became aware of her hot, red, curvy body pressed against him. The coldness he had been feeling was immediately replaced by a raising heat. His hands slipped round the silk form that was moving against him. He put his hand inside the cape and felt the naked flesh inside the top that Kelly was wearing. This was earthly passion and good old fashioned lust, different from what had happened in the circle. This was woman and man, not just Yin and Yang.

Kelly broke away slightly and started to giggle and so did David.

"Come on" Kelly said breathlessly, still giggling, "let's go inside."

171

They held onto each other and still giggling and kissing, they managed at last to get back into the house, shut and lock the door. Kelly threw off her shoes and the cloak and dragged David up the stairs. At the top of the stairs they paused while he removed her top and she removed his shirt.

"Guess what" she murmured close to his ear whilst he was busy kissing and holding her breasts which he had freed from her bra, whilst noticing it too was red. As he had his mouth full and couldn't answer, she continued, "the red lady wears stockings and suspenders".

"Oh God" he groaned, letting his hand run over her hips and thighs to confirm the truth of this extraordinary statement. She laughed and undid her skirt, stepped out of it and headed towards his bedroom.

He watched the incredible sight of her bottom covered with skimpy, red lace whilst red suspenders hung down her thighs holding black stockings.

He hurried after her, catching her as she went through the door. They tumbled together towards the bed and collapsed in a tangle of arms and legs and kisses, then all coherent thought disappeared as the passion took over. The last thought David remembered, was that he was far too tired for this, but the soft warm and comfortable excitement seemed natural, and he wasn't tired at all.

Chapter Twenty Eight:
Monday of the new week

David's first thought when he awoke was that he had been having a wonderful, if somewhat erotic, dream. He smiled to himself without opening his eyes. Then he opened them quickly and checked the other side of the bed. There was no one there. Then he checked the floor by leaning over the edge of the bed. Only his clothes. He lay back and thought about it. Did it happen?

He jumped up and went into the hallway, no clothes there either. Then he went along the corridor to Kelly's door. It was slightly ajar so he pushed it open and peered inside. He could see Kelly's blond hair in amongst the lilac duvet cover. At least she was still in the house.

"Go and make the tea, David" she suddenly said, making him jump and wake up a bit more. She hadn't moved, but she knew he was there. "And yes. It did happen. I just like my bed better. Tea. Please."

She turned over the looked at him.

"You might like to put some clothes on. I'm doing an art class this morning and Marion Bradley is coming" she smiled at him as he groaned and hurried back to slip on his jeans, then make the tea.

So it did happen, he thought, well what now I wonder?

When he got back with tea after narrowly avoiding breaking his neck on Kelly's shoes which were exactly where she had left them, she was already in the shower . Realising the time and remembering she had five new art enthusiasts due at 10 0' clock, and nothing ready for them, she knew she had no time to do anything.

Abracadabra didn't open as a shop on a Monday as retail was always slow on that day. In fact, Kelly didn't open the shop Monday or Tuesday because she did her own things on these days and had also planned to do teaching – painting being her first one.

David left her tea where she could find it and went to get a shower himself. When he emerged with damp hair and clean clothes on, Kelly was already downstairs making a smoothie and rushing around the kitchen.

"Hi" he said, not quite knowing how to do this now their relationship had changed.

"Hi yourself" ,she said smiling. She came over and kissed him "you look delicious, I just don't have time."

He laughed and realised that nothing had really changed, that Kelly and he were still comfortable with each other and still friends.

"Did you plan last night" he said getting the cups out and making more tea.

"No" said Kelly pouring the now mixed smoothie into two glasses.

"But it was inevitable it would happen sometime. I just want you to remember what I said about not wanting a relationship. I'm not staying. Well, not for ever or anything."

"I rather got that idea from the writings" he smiled.

"So, is this alright?" she said looking at him "being close and living in the same house, but not playing happy families? I do my life, you do yours and we meet in the middle."

"Sounds like a good idea" he smiled, realising she was worried he might be thinking of making an honest woman of her.

"I don't know whether it will work, but it will be fun trying."

"That's what I think" she said, sitting down at the breakfast bar and handing him his smoothie. "Here, I've put extra protein in to make up for all that energy you expended last night". She gave him a saucy look.

"I thought you said you didn't have time for any of that", he said his green eyes flashing with memories of the energy he had expended.

"No I don't. Will you help me get ready in the shop?"

"Sure" he said sitting down and drinking his smoothie. "There's always tonight."

She laughed and checked the time on the wall

174

"Let's move it or they will be here. I am really having Marion Bradley and her friend Fiona, who is, she tells me, is 'a very good friend of yours'".

David groaned,

"She's a very nice lady, but do I have to see her? I thought when Abrachat closed I was done with all that."

"It's good for you. Writing can be a very lonely and exclusive business. You need to keep your social skills honed. Anyway you will have to charm them and make coffee whilst I get the tables ready. We are now running seriously late! Like seriously" she said getting up, finishing her smoothie and moving towards the shop all at the same time.

"I should have got ready yesterday, but I just needed to see Louise."

David had followed her and started to put the coffee on.

"What do you want to do with the tables?"

"Just help me put three together down the wall and two together here. Then I'll get my easel and they will be able to see what I am doing and follow my lead." "OK" David said, moving towards her and taking hold of one end of the table. "Talking of Louise, did you say she was coming next weekend?"

"Yes, it's stay at home week or something , is that OK?" You do realise that my home is her home."

"Yes and Yes " said David, "but I would like some more information on that subject." "And you shall have it" said Kelly hurrying to put the easel in place in front of the door into the lounge. "But just now I need you to open the door to Marion and her friend, who are my very first art class students and need distracting whilst I get ready."

"You should have done all this preparation last night! Whatever were you doing that made you forget?" said David cheekily, as he moved towards the door to welcome the beaming Marion who was always delighted to see him.

David did his host duties whilst Kelly got paints and canvases organised without anyone realising that she was behind schedule. She then demonstrated how to cut shapes, glue and arrange the shapes on the canvas. Explaining as she did what the theme of the

175

day was, what they were trying to achieve and how to do it. David slipped away as they started to relax and enjoy themselves. He could see it was going well and he was no longer needed . He had notes to write and things to get in order, most important of which was his head. That seemed to be floating a mile above his body. The strange events of the weekend were beginning to tell on him and he needed some serious quiet time to try and unravel them

Chapter Twenty Nine

It was two days before they managed to have the conversation about Louise, due mainly to the fact that on Monday night after the art class Kelly had gone back to Pewsley to visit her old neighbours. it was a long standing arrangement that she had forgotten all about until she consulted her diary.

On Tuesday David was called to his publishers to discuss the new book which had now been read by his editor, who needed to know more about this new style of writing and his inspiration.   One of the conditions that Kelly had imposed upon him was that his source material had to remain secret.

By the time he had managed to convince the editor that a three book deal with more revelations of the mysterious two women was possible, it was late and Kelly had already gone to bed – her own bed.

On Wednesday morning they had met for breakfast, but Kelly was off to do some dowsing of a house, so David had only managed to ask about the existence of more source material and about the circle of women.

All she had said was something about 'Shakespeare writing more than one play' before she disappeared to talk shop with Sally. The rest of the day he had spent looking through the plays of Mr Shakespeare to see if he had any inspiration for the next two proposed books.

Obviously Cleopatra was there, in Mr Shakespeare, full of life and strange happenings.   Perhaps he should be working on places, not the stories themselves.   That didn't make much sense, so he decided to make dinner and keep Kelly in one place long enough to get some answers.

When she came home she was delighted to see the table set and cooking smells coming from the kitchen.   It was only pasta with chilli prawns, but it was one of her favourite dishes.

"This is lovely – thank you – sorry about the rushing around" she managed between mouthfuls, "but I am here now – free night, so ask your questions."

"I think we can relax and eat dinner first . Are you OK?" he smiled, passing her some bread.

"Deadly tired. That was quite a ceremony we did."

"Not to mention the afterwards. That wasn't part of the ceremony was it?"

"No, that was just you and me", she laughed. Deciding that he could only handle the truth a little at a time and if he had really thought about it he would know that they had just performed the oldest ceremony known to man. But only really remembered by woman. "So the publisher likes the book but wants more?"

"Yes. Doesn't want me to go back to my old, dry style I suppose. I went through Shakespeare and didn't get any clues."

"No, I didn't think you would. It hasn't stayed hidden all this time for just anyone to be able to access it. You would have to know what you are looking for. It Is in fact our litany, so it would only make sense to the initiated. That is why it had to stay in rhyme form. Can you pass the wine please?

Anyway, don't worry about that, because when something is really important, it is a node point in time. Which always means that we have two lifetimes in quick succession."

David looked at her with a more than usual blank expression on his face

"So" she said slowly " that means that there is a follow on lifetime. Making two books ......"

"Should I be taking notes or something?" said David trying to eat and follow this conversation.

"Don't be silly, I'm just talking. Anyway I have the next lifetime written – it might be a bit controversial because it is also the time of Jesus". She paused and but David didn't say anything. For one thing he didn't want her to clam up again.

"The last one is Celtic because we all get a bit scattered and shaken up by events – anyway the next one which would be the third one, is in England. Just write a bit of a profile for the Publisher, outlining the times and areas and I'll get you some information."

178

"It's not in the time capsule then?"

"No. It escaped the time capsule. I couldn't find it when we were putting things in."

She pushed her plate away and he handed her a bowl of raspberries and strawberries.

She smiled "Now, Louise?"

"Yes – Louise who is her father? and where is her father? and why did she live up the road and you lived somewhere else?"

Kelly laughed, "actually we both used to live up the road."

"Is the violin maker her father?"

"Not her biological father, but he was a bit of one. As were others in our group. We are all friends …….. in fact your friend Dez the milkman knows I used to live here before."

"Yes?" said David.

" Yes……… anyway, Louise's father is a pirate."

"A pirate!!"

"Well a River pirate, I suppose."

"What on earth is a river pirate?"

"Well. He lived on a river boat, and as he didn't have a real job, but always had money, I decided he must be a pirate."

David looked at her in expectation so she realised that she would have to say more.

"I used to be a sort of traveller, in my wild youth. You know, hippy style, we lived in a van my friend, Janey, and I . We were attached to a group. The group consisted of Indigo, Jake, Pete, Marie, Linda, Ruby, Rus and Spud.

Sometimes there were others who stayed with us for a while. Some of them had lived before in a squat in London – all of us just exploring and living the alternative lifestyle. We would go from festival or carnival to festival in the summer. We would make things to sell, often food or jewellery. We would play and sing folk music and perform poetry. Sometimes we would go down to Kent and pick fruit or go across the channel to the vineyards and pick grapes. We made money where we went, then spent it on more travelling.

I did a lot of my writing and remembering whilst I was doing that. Sometimes in the winter we would stay in a friend's house or just move further south to get warm. We were a community.

Then one spring we met the river travellers who did the same thing, but on the water. We joined them for a while going to the summer festivals by boat. That was my time of the River Pirate. Dashing, exciting, dark and daring. I stayed with him when the others were going off to France. Janey had already got it together with Indigo. So we sold our van and she went off with him. He is the respectable Mr Evans, your neighbour!" Kelly laughed at David's rapt face.

"But I thought he was Gerald Evans. The violin maker"

"Sure, he is, but who the hell wants to be called Gerald. He always wore Indigo waistcoats, and for years, that is the only name I knew him as. Anyway, whilst I was 'messing about in boats' as Ratty would say, my little Lulibug decided to make an appearance. We decided that she had obviously thought I was getting too far from my purpose in life. So she had to come to earth and steer me into the right river."

David was looking a little puzzled.

"Louise is like Sara and I. She remembers her times before. We have been in previous lifetimes together. She remembered when she was a child, usually as nightmares about the bad times."

Kelly was silent for a moment, thinking, so David poured her some water not daring to go and make the tea in case she stopped talking again.

"So how long did you stay with the River Pirate?"

"Long enough to make babies. Less than two years. Probably twenty one months. Twenty one is my number, so important things happen in multiples of twenty one. Anyway, I realised that commitment was not his style and commitment to him wasn't mine. Of course, the universe had been busy. Indigo's Grandmother died and left him the huge house up the road. Which is also attached to six acres of land, along with outbuildings and all sorts of farming things. The only stipulation was that he couldn't sell it. He had to live in it. She wanted him to settle down. She also left him some money, so not wanting to give up the lifestyle or the community, everyone parked or sold their vans and moved into the new commune. So when I left the river for a more settled life I had

180

somewhere to go. The guys in the commune became her fathers and the girls became her mothers and we all continued to be alternative.

When Lulibug was five years old I met Sara on a train. She had come from South Africa looking for something, following dreams and a song in her head. We recognised each other, or rather, we remembered we were in the middle of an argument even though we had never met!

But our darling, wise, child remembered all……. And somehow got us to speak to each other again on the train journey. We were both writers, we both remembered other lifetimes and we both had written them down. When we compared notes, we realised we were two halves of the same puzzle.

Then the fun really started.   But that is another long story. Anyway when I needed to move, Louise wanted to stay and go to school where she was and then college.   I had taught her myself when she was younger – with the help of the others. Janey and Indigo got married long ago, so Louise lived between us. It was too complicated to tell you at the time and I didn't want to alarm you too soon."

Kelly stopped talking and David went to make the tea. He now knew something about her life, but not much about the mystery of her life. It did explain his conviction that he had indeed met the three witches. In that he had been spot on. He smiled to himself remembering how much they all scared him at first. Was it just that he knew Kelly better now and she seemed to make it alright?

He brought the tea in. Kelly was still sitting at the table looking out on the garden and obviously thinking.

"So",   said David decisively, putting the tray down in front of Kelly who started to take the cups off and stir the tea.

"You didn't actually have to stay with me then?" he cocked his head to one side.

"You mean I could have stayed with Indigo and Janey?   She smiled and poured the tea.

"I could.   But they have their own family now and besides you can't go back."

"Oh" said David a bit deflated.

"And, of course, I needed to start the shop", she went on noting his expression. "Besides I wanted to live with you, gypsy man." He looked up and saw she was teasing him.

" But you didn't know whether you wanted to at first."

"No. I was worried about getting trapped, about getting too comfortable and not being able to move on. You know I must move on at some stage."

"So you keep saying. Can we just do the 'now' time and think about that later?"

"Great idea" , she said as she passed him a cup, "and no more questions now, I said I would explain about Louise and I have."

"What about the question of what happened to me during that ceremony?"

"Ahh – yes – well, that needs a bit more time before we approach that particular subject I think. Drink your tea, we have some catching up to do of a different kind. This time you can come to my bed."

The sudden change in tack took David unawares, exactly as she knew it would, and as he felt the new familiar heat rising up his body, he decided that she was right. Sometimes the talking has to end and the action has to begin. He was definitely up for that in all senses of the word.

"Hi, it's me. How goes it?"

"Not well, my aunt just died. Heart attack."

"Oh Goddess! I'm sorry, was it the one in South Africa?"

"Yeah – Mom's sister. If it's not one thing, it's another. Anyway, how's it there, are we on schedule?"

"Think so, the publisher wants a three book deal."

"Well, we have that and more. It does make you sick though doesn't it. All that time and energy we spent in trying to get published, but because he is already published and a man it is fine."

"Yes, well, we 'never fitted their lists' did we?"

"Story of our lives. Anyway how can we 'fit their lists' when they are deciding what people want to read."

"Hey let's not go there, we knew changing the world would take some time and a little effort."

Sara laughed, "what's going on with you anyway?"

"Oh I am selling our stock and working on the earth energies. Have got my group of priestess's back, so it is going well."

"What's going on?"

"What do you mean? I just told you.

"With you! It's David! have you been using your usual methods with him?"

"Whatever do you mean!"

"Don't come that with me. Shag him by all means, but don't get involved. You know you are on your way here. You know you have to do to the Isle de France and sort out all that unfinished stuff with the Temples"

"I do know! I know. It's fine. I'm just keeping it at arms length, it will be fine. As soon as the book is published I can move on. He has to be inspired, you know that."

"I also know you! how often you get waylaid."

"OK. I hear you, don't worry. How's motherhood?"

"A real drag. She is lovely, but the whole process – Goddess how do women do that , again and again?"

"Another of life's mysteries I would say."

"Me too. Keep in touch. Have to write a course on gender studies for the university now."

"OK. Take care. Speak soon."

"Me too. Keep in touch. Have to write a course on gender studies for the university now."

"OK. Take care. Speak soon."

"As always."

Chapter Thirty: Sunday

"Nine months. It's like having a baby."

"I know. It's also May again, a year since the launch of the shop."

Kelly was stacking some paintings that her students had produced, whilst Louise was choosing a necklace before she went back to university. The early morning sun was streaming into the shop, sending rainbows round the room from the crystals suspended in the bay window.

"So when is the actual date?" said Louise trying on a green and turquoise geometric design that a new jewellery maker had brought in.

"The end of October predicted, but I think it will be more like the end of the year"

"What takes so long?" Louise tried another necklace in shades of purple.

"I don't think it's a long time actually to publish a book. Anyway, thank Goddess it is happening at last."

Kelly went to help Louise undo the necklace.

"Come on, we have to get you to the station. Which one do you want so I can write it down?"

"The green one, I think it will go with my new top. We are having a party next weekend."

"Oh good, can I come?"

"No you can't! You are too old and no one has their mother there. Anyway, won't you be doing something romantic with 'dear David'?"

"Don't be mean, you know you like David . And yes, I might be. Anyway I have to leave soon you know, I have to go and investigate the Isle de France and the cathedrals in the shape of the constellation Virgo, it is ...."

"Don't tell me!" said Louise "you know I have to do my teenage stuff and try to be normal and in the real world."

"I know, I know, I'm sorry. Enjoy being nineteen and take good care of yourself my darling."

Kelly wrapped the necklace in a bag and handed it to Louise.

"You know I'm going travelling this summer don't you? I can't come with you to France."

"Yes, I know. Have you settled on Canada?"

"I think so. Helen and I are working it out. Besides you don't intend to come back do you?"

"Not for a while." Kelly went and gave her daughter a hug, "whereas you, my Lulibug, have to be back to start your next year in September."

"Anyway, we are going to get a house for next year, us girls, and perhaps Pabs. I will see if I can keep it longer or probably join you somewhere. We can keep our stuff here can't we?"

"Of course" said Kelly making her way into the lounge and collecting together some of Louise's things. "I will be leaving stuff here including the Time Capsule, so I will have to be back at some point and I haven't sorted out the shop. I will talk to Sally and see what she thinks."

Kelly put Louise's spare shoes in the bag just as David came in the room.

"Hi you two. You are watching the time I hope, trains and all that."

"Yeah, we are just going David. Thanks for a nice weekend" Louise went over and gave him a hug, which surprised and delighted him as he always felt disapproval from her. Perhaps she's growing up he thought, then decided against that. Louise had always been grown up.

"Come on old woman, let's go", she said grabbing her bags and putting her jacket on at the same time. Kelly grabbed her keys and moved towards the door. She always hated it when Louise went off, it was such a comfort to have her around.

David, sensing this, said "I'll start the clearing up whilst you are at the station. Shall we go to the pub for lunch?"

"That would be nice" smiled back Kelly over her shoulder, realising that it was nice to come back to David – comforting. Oh Goddess, she mustn't get comfortable, that would never do. Besides she had to get him started on the next book. The vague ideas had held off the publisher for now, but she knew he was supposed to be well into the writing. That would involve another in-depth conversation.

"What did you tell David about my origins?" said Louise as they settled in the car and buckled on their seat belts.

"The river pirate" said Kelly adjusting the mirror and starting the car.

"Oh God!" Louise started to laugh.

"Have you told him about the name changing?"

"Err – no. I thought it might be too much."

"But the river pirate isn't?"

"Never mind about that, I am more worried about Sara and what she is up to."

"Has she written that stuff about Da Vinci being a Buddhist?"

"Probably. She says she now has evidence that he had lens from China and used them to paint his pictures. Ever since we went to Vinci and saw that stone by the little river, dedicated by the Buddhists, she has been convinced."

Kelly drove out of the drive and down the road towards the station.

"Well it is part of the 'A-causal field theory' isn't it? I mean she had already come up with the non-Christian, but Buddhist theory. Then use of lens and cameras in art. So you can't blame her when you find an inscription in Vince of all places, from Buddhists. "

"I don't have any difficulty with the theories. I'm sure if I put my mind to it I will remember it is true. After all we were around at that time and did spend time with Da Vinci. It is just she is going to blow the art world apart, whilst dear David will be drip feeding the truth of the crucifixion in his second book."

"What, you mean too much at once?"

"Not just that, we don't want too many enemies at the door do we?"

"That's a bit rich coming from you! I thought the whole point was that you need to show how wrong history has got it, because the history was rewritten by the victors."

"Yes, yes, who then wiped out all evidence of the female society that had kept the harmony for so long.

"Anyway you said David definitely was a Goddess man."

"Yes, I know that. You know that. Sara is not too sure, and David himself has no idea."

"He didn't re-remember the lifetime you wanted him to then?"

"No. He remembered a much older one. Probably, because it was a dedication ceremony. I needed him to remember the lifetime he is just about to write about."

"Perhaps when you give him your written account 'Je Suis' isn't it called?"

"'I Am'. In French. Yes. A play on words, with the word 'Jesus'"

"Whoever he was?"

"Goddess! Anyway, darling, don't get your head round this. Go back to Uni and be nearly twenty – fall in love or lust – get drunk – be wild. I'll see you soon or at the launch or I may just come up."

"OK, loved one". She leaned over and kissed Kelly as she pulled on the handbrake at the station.

"I'm sure you will work out some formula to make the energies work. You usually do. Love you."

"Love you, Lulibug. Take care. Got everything?"

Louise reached over, got her rucksack , slammed the door and with a wave, rushed off to her life.

David turned the dial on the washing machine and smiled as he watched the bed clothes start their journey to being clean. He remembered the time when Louise had found him in front of this machine, panicking because he had his shoes inside and the door was stuck. Now he was washing her bed linen whilst she was returning to University and her mother, who he didn't know at that time was her mother, was now his lover. Time had changed so much.

They had all slipped into a nice routine. Louise came home here, or Kelly visited her in Warwick, usually on her own but sometimes with David. The shop prospered. The courses were ongoing. The coven met regularly, laughed a lot and never let anyone know what they were doing. David and Kelly had mutual friends and did social things together, as well as doing their own things apart. Sometimes,

Kelly came into David's bed, sometimes he went into hers and sometimes they slept apart.

David had been writing the story of their meeting. About the extraordinary circumstances that seemed to be happening to him. Ever since that first meeting with Kelly and Sara at the book launch of his last book, events seemed to have taken over. These were definitely A-causal events

He realised now that it had been no chance meeting, but was in fact part of a carefully constructed and meticulously executed plan, of which he had hints but absolutely no real idea of what was happening. He was being manipulated he knew, but for what, why, and how this 'long term' clever plan involved him, was a complete mystery.

The fact, the only fact, he did know was that Kelly wanted him to write about their 'other' lifetimes.

The door banged, announcing Kelly's return from the station. He went to put the kettle on. She wandered through to the kitchen and he watched her for a moment. He was always surprised how ordinary she looked. Wonderful and lovely, but just a person, wearing jeans and long sleeved tee-shirt. Perhaps it wasn't until she looked at you with the full force of whatever it was behind her eyes, that you became aware of the feeling of who she was. She was a twelve foot being living in a 5ft 2inch body.

"Why are you staring at me?" she said without turning round. It always unnerved David how she knew he was there without seeing him.

"I'm not staring", he said even though it wasn't true. "I was just thinking."

"Oh God, not more in depth conversations today, my brain hurts. Anyway, what have you been writing all these months?"

"As you haven't given any instructions for the next book, I have been writing about meeting you and Sara and how I came to write the book. It's bound to be of interest to the readers."

"Yes it is. I suppose you are trying to figure out about the energy field."

"Well, I was just writing what happened actually."

Kelly took the milk out of the fridge, then handed him a mug.

188

"As long as you don't give anyone my address or the ability to find us, that will be fine." She moved to the lounge area and sat down on the settee.

"Why don't you want anyone to find you?" he said sitting opposite to her and putting his tea down on the coffee table.

"Possibly because we have been hounded, killed, destroyed and ridiculed throughout many life times and we have no reason to think that this one will be any different. Did you know that the Witch Laws were only repealed in 1945 in this country? They are probably still in existence in other countries.. They want our knowledge. They don't want the women of the world to wake up to their heritage. Come on David, use your not inconsiderable brain and join up all the dots. You have written and researched the Goddess and her wilful destruction. You must have asked yourself 'why?' on some occasion."

"I might have asked it, but I didn't get any answers."

"The Secret of Life" she said sipping her tea "women have it. Men want it. The trouble is most men and women are unaware of that fact except for the people in power. But still the conflict continues."

"Isn't that a bit paranoid?" said David leaning back and putting his feet on the coffee table.

"Only if they are not really following you, or out to get you. If they are, it is being wise."

"What about this next book? Do you have another manuscript?"

"I do. Unfortunately, I don't at this moment know where it is. All this moving and packing means I have lost it."

"Lost it! It's not in the time capsule is it?"

"No. Put the damn time capsule out of your mind. I think you writing about how we met and what happened is a good idea."

"Trouble is, I don't know what is happening."

"I know, and if you are writing that as you yourself, learning things, it will let the reader into the mystery slowly and gently. Tell you what, when you have written all the stuff from your point of view, I will add a few bits – like the conversations between Sara and I or Louise and I, so that some information is gleaned."

"That's a good idea, then I can read it and perhaps understand what is going on."

"I could give you the energy diagram for the field of consciousness in which we are operating if you like." Kelly smiled and David realised it was time to quit whilst he was ahead. Too many of these high octane conversations on an empty stomach was not good for him.

"Come on let's go to lunch" he said, getting up and offering Kelly his hand.

She went over to get her jacket whilst he contemplated that once upon a time his main conversationalist had been Dez, the milkman, and his main preoccupation was the length of Sally Weatherfield's legs.

Life was definitely simpler then, but not nearly as engaging. Kelly was a full time challenge and he had begun to realise that he didn't really want to be without her. Another difficulty on the road. Although thinking about Dez the milkman, he realised he must have know about Kelly because she had lived in this village before David even knew it existed. He could have told him. Another mystery to unfold.

Chapter Thirty One : Monday

"I've just had the predicted launch date" said David

Kelly was coming back into the house from the field. She was loaded down with baskets containing various plants and herbs. He was used to her disappearing in the early mornings, only to return with her baskets filled with all kinds of earth's bounty.

She moved into the room that was divided off from the open plan lounge on the same side as the shop. This had previously been used as a dining room. David had always had his dining table and chairs by the French windows in the lounge area. Dividing the high ceiling barn into cosy areas was the only way to make it work. This small room had ended up as a sort of storage area, until Kelly took it over as her plant room.

She had drying racks hanging from the ceiling; a large table for working on, and David had put shelves all around the room. As it had windows on two walls, light streamed in all day and made it an ideal work room. The shelves were now filled with jars and jars of dried plants and flowers with wonderful coloured labels that Kelly made herself.

All of them were hand drawn and hand written. She had told him that this was part of the magic. The energy that came from her hands went into the conversion of the plant, making the magic concoction that it would become. This was where she made her remedies that she used in healing. The production room where magic was made!

By the window that overlooked one side of the walled garden she had a small table with two comfortable chairs, where she conducted her healing sessions. If David had ever needed proof of Kelly's status as a witch, this was it. She had gone into this room and was now arranging the plants and flowers and putting string on them in order to dry them. The room also contained a small fireplace so in winter she could have a real fire. All of this added to the sense of things ancient. When she had first asked if she could use this she had been wandering around muttering what sounded like ' damned

Angels', but David thought he had misheard until she opened the door to the small dining/junk room and then said

"David I have got an angel breathing down my neck insisting I make some remedies. Do you think I could use this room?"

He had been so shocked that he didn't ask any questions , just suggested that they move all the boxes and spare furniture into the garage. Like most garages theirs had never been used to park cars in it.so it seemed like a good idea. Kelly had worked on the conversion with her normal efficiency, enlisting her moon maidens at various stages. It now seemed to be a part of their living environment.

"So" she said looking at him, "when is this launch date then?"

"Oh, it's in July . But I should tell you something. I have had to use a "nom de plume" because it is so different from history and legends so......I have decided to use a woman's name."

"Oh" she looked immediately shocked, then quickly recovered herself. "That's great, really good." She started to laugh. " A sort of double bluff".

He went over to her and gave her a hug, brushing her hair out of her eyes and kissing her forehead. She leaned against him feeling the warmth love and comfort that was there.

"You really do surprise me sometimes David. In the best possible way!"

She pulled away and started to tie up her plants once more, realising that he knew what she was thinking and why she was suddenly sad.

"Is it the end of a cycle?" he said quickly.

"Something like that" she said.

"But we are so ...... "

"No, we are not 'so' anything". She paused. "I've got the girls coming tonight, I have to get some blackberries and gooseberries that I picked last year out of the freezer in the kitchen. I am going to make magic pie. You can have some if you like."

"Will it stop you from going away?"

"Oh David, don't. No. It won't. I have to go. But I will come back; I am leaving lots of things here."

David walked back out of room wondering if he should never have finished the book. But then the book was the reason she had come to live with him in the first place. Perhaps remembering your past lives wasn't always a good idea. Perhaps you must remember bad times and partings and sad times. He decided that he must stop thinking small and start thinking in bigger terms. He went back to write about these extraordinary things that had happened to him and the even more extraordinary women that he had met and how the story about the story was winding, round and round like the labyrinth itself.

"Girls, I want to put something to you tonight". Kelly had her nine ladies sitting in a circle in the art room/coffee shop area of Abracadabra.

"God, you sound a bit serious tonight" said Millie, "what's up?"

"Nothing. Look you have been doing these ceremonies with me now for two years. We have covered the ceremonies that need to be done for the year cycle. You know what they are for, both in the personal sense and in the earth cycle. You understand them – yes?"

They all agreed and added their enjoyment at doing them.

"You're not thinking of giving them up are you?" said Lana, " we really enjoy the group, its great to work together."

"Good, that's what I hoped. It's just that I am going to have to go away soon.

Shock went round the faces.

"Away? But I thought you were happy and settled here" said Melissa shaking back her blond hair.

"We also thought you and David were now a couple", said Tasie in her American drawl. "Are you leaving because things are not good?"

Kelly sighed "No nothing like that. I never planned to stay – it was always a temporary thing really."

"What about the shop?" said Roslin, always the practical earth one.

"The shop is going to stay – well I hope it is. I haven't put it to Sally yet, but I hope she will take it over. So any of you selling things through here, it will be fine. She will need some help, so do

193

think if any of you can work some days, or source some more magic things for the shop to sell."

"Oh, I'm going to Morocco in a couple of weeks" piped up Dale. "Shall I get some of those lovely burners and lamps and beautiful silk scarves?"

"That sounds great. Please all do that. Look, that's what I am trying to say to you. The magic doesn't go away if I go away. You are the circle now."

"Is that the magic circle?" said Millie laughing.

"Yes, I suppose it is " said Kelly. "By creating the circle physically, we have created it consciously and that is how you make magic. By conscious, positive, intent, and the weaving of light. Like rainbows. Which is why, the Goddess Iris, is the Guardian of the stone circle. She is the Goddess of the rainbow and therefore light. Like the iris in your eye. Anyway enough teaching, I'm not here to teach you today. I just wanted to tell you that I need you to continue to do all the ceremonies and continue with all the things I have started here. Will you do that?"

"Yes, of course we will", they all nodded or affirmed their answers.

"Will you come back?" said Gudrin.

"I will come back, but I don't know how long I will be away. I have got to go and activate some other places on the earth, and possibly make my way to Africa. I just don't know how long that will take me. I need to know that this point here will remain active. Does that make sense to you all?"

"Not really, but we have learnt to allow what you say to work its way through to us. Anyway we will keep everything going, won't we girls?" said Millie.

"Great. In that case, what I intend to do before I go is let Millie have lots of lists and information about what has to be done and when, so she can be organised and let you all know what is happening.

"OK?" said Kelly to Millie, who nodded.

"So, Millie will take your place" said Dale "but that means we are short of one person, we won't have nine."

194

"No, but I thought I would ask Sally if she will join us. Then it connects the circle and Abracadabra nicely. Don't forget that you can recruit more if you find them, but the nine will be your core cell. At the Summer and Winter Solstices you can invite male persons, but only at those two ceremonies do you need the Yang energy. The rest of the time you are moon maidens."

"Ooh, I'm glad I can get to be called a maiden again" said Melissa, "I never thought that would happen".

Everyone started laughing and Kelly got up to collect the basket and the candles to take outside, happy to hear the light-heartedness with which the group energy was operating. It told her that all would be well in her absence, although she had never thought that leaving the girls or the shop was going to be a problem. At a later stage she would ask Roslin and Sofie who made remedies to continue with that and Lana and Tasie who painted , to continue with the art classes. The only real headache was David, he was not going to take her leaving lightly in any way.

"Come on girls, time for the ceremony" shouted Kelly above the noise and excitement of the group now realising that they were in fact The Group. They all carried something outside through the French windows where they waited for Kelly to put on her robe and lead the way. They followed in single file, singing the blessings of love and light.

They didn't see David standing in the shadows by the staircase, deep in thought as the air was filled with the eerie sound of moon maidens singing.

Chapter Thirty Two: Tuesday

Next morning was unusually sunny and bright. Kelly had avoided David by sleeping in her own bed, after a late night with the girls which had turned into a celebration of life in general. The magic pie had helped and there had been excited plans about what they were going to learn before Kelly went away.

She had been vague about when exactly she was going, mainly because she didn't really know herself and also because her plan was to have everything in place and then just slip away quietly. She was used to doing things in secret. She heard David getting up and hurried downstairs to be busy in the kitchen. When he came down she had made toast and scrambled eggs.

"Morning" he said in a non-committal way.

"Hi" she said, "want some scrambled egg?"

"Just what I need today" he replied, moving to make the tea then seeing she had already done that.

"What are your plans for today?" he asked sitting down at the breakfast bar. The sun was streaming in the window and making pretty patterns on the bench and the floor.

"Well, I have to have lots of discussions with Sally when she comes in, but that's all I'm really committed to. Why, do you need me to do something?" she said, putting the eggs on the buttered toast.

"I do actually, I need you to accompany me to the river where I have arranged to borrow a boat, take a picnic and .... "

"'Simply mess about in boats'" said Kelly, quoting.

"Well, it's the sort of day when Mole just had to drop everything and run outside. Spring and all that"

"Was 'Wind in the Willows' one of your favourite books too?"

"Absolutely". David cut into the toast and buttery egg whilst trying to act casual, as if he had just thought of the picnic idea and not been planning it since last night.

"You know, that does sound quite wonderful."

"OK that's settled then" said David "whilst you talk to Sally, I'll get the picnic ready and then we can be off. Bring a book and your parasol and I will row you to a suitable spot."

Kelly laughed. "How did you know that Ratty was always my hero. He rescued Moley from the drudgery of the normal, and got him to see the world."

"I didn't think for a moment that you had ever been in the 'drudgery of the normal', but it does look like the very first picnic day don't you think?"

Kelly was eating her eggs and smiling so David guessed that he had got it right.

Stage one he thought, make myself indispensable and very useful. She liked initiative, he knew that.

"So Sally, what do you think? You take 80% of the profits, I keep a hold in the business for 20%, plus whatever is still left of my stock and the remedies and some rent to David, then the business is yours. The girls in my circle are already primed to collect or make stock for you and you, of course, can get stock from wherever else you wish."

"It sounds great. I love it here and I am planning to live with my boyfriend (when we find somewhere to live). The house share I live in isn't suitable, but I would really like that, thank you so much. My own business. Wow!"

"Well at least you know what is involved and all about it. The other thing is, would you like to join the circle of girls who do the ceremonies. Then you get all their help and support and the two things come together."

"You mean I will be involved in making the magic"

"Something like that."

"What about David? Is it going to be alright with him?"

"The shop? Yes, he will be busy writing, it will be fine."

"It's just he did run Abrachat before. I don't want him to feel 'taken over' or anything."

Kelly smiled at the beautiful, long-legged Sally, who she knew David had always had a yearning towards, long before he knew she was a really intelligent and nice person. She thought he would have enjoyed being 'taken over' by her.

Sally was putting the cups together ready for the morning coffee whilst Kelly was putting fresh flowers in the little holders they had on the tables. It was such a bright and happy shop, she knew she would miss being here each day.

"David is having his book published" she said to Sally "and he is writing another so he will be very occupied. Just make sure you keep a separate shelf for all his work", Kelly laughed.

"Goodness, it will be a shrine" laughed Sally "and I would like to join the stone circle girls. Thank you, Kelly, very much. My own business, In this lovely place - wow!"

Kelly went to hang up the new necklaces that had arrived yesterday.

"I thought you had a picnic to go to" said Sally coming over with a duster to dust the counter and the shelves.

"I do" said Kelly, smiling at the thought that she had never thought of dusting until the dust was actually visible.

"I'll see you later. Start thinking about who you would like to help you in the shop part-time. One of the young village girls, perhaps?"

"I will, don't worry. You go off and enjoy the day 'whilst you can'."

"Bye Sally."

"Bye."

Chapter Thirty Three: The River Picnic

"Well, I do have to say David, that there is nothing, simply nothing, in the world ...."

"........ quite like messing, simply messing, about ...." Quoted David.

".......... in boats". They both laughed together.

Kelly was sitting in the stern on a cushion with another cushion behind her back while David rowed slowly, but strongly, down the river. A fully packed picnic basket was between their feet and the sun was shining.

"I really think I should be wearing a long dress and have a parasol" said Kelly trailing her hand in the water which she found was actually quite cold.

"I think jeans and a jumper are better" said David who was wearing the same. "It's only May , it might be warm and sunny but you know the old saying 'never cast a clout 'til May is out'. Its not summer warm".

"Anyway why haven't you brought me on this boat before? Have you used it before?" she said looking at the confident way he was rowing the boat.

"Many times. It's my thinking place. Somehow moving through a space, especially water, seems to sooth and help you think, don't you think?"

"Yes. What have you got on your mind to think about?" she said quickly.

"Today is about having fun. Remember, that was what the Rat in 'Wind in the Willows' was trying to teach the mole, who spent all his time making tunnels underground. Sometimes you have to do things just for you."

Kelly laughed "That's right, and this is fun, thank you."

"You ain't seen anything yet kid" he smiled, "We are actually going to a little island up ahead."

"Not in a backwater like the one in the book where they found little otter?"

"Yes. But I can't guarantee that the God Pan will be waiting for us."

"Well ...... you never know."

"I do know. No work today, just you and me having a picnic."

"How lovely" said Kelly turning her face up to the sun and leaning back.

David smiled and rowed on. When he got tired he scuppered the oars and let the current take them on for a while. He knew that rowing back was not so easy as it would be against the current when he rowed back. But that was later, now he had Kelly all to himself and intended to impress her. She was very tricky and could not be grasped firmly in any way.

"Can you see the island now up ahead?" he said glancing over his shoulder.

She looked and could see that the river got wider. One half going to the right whilst the main bulk of the river flowed passed on the left side, wider than the right and faster flowing. David headed for the right and negotiated the overhanging branches and reeds until they were half way down the island and now completely hidden from the main running water.

"I'm going to row very close to the island now. Do you see where the bank gets closer to the water?"

"Yes, I think so."

"OK. Look out for two wooden stumps."

As the boat got closer she could see them. David turned round again to check.

"Now guide me to them so that we come alongside. Then take that rope attached to your end and when we are close enough, wrap it round the stump."

Kelly did this without too much difficulty and secured it. David pulled the nearside oar into the boat and did the same with a rope on his side.

"You step off and I will hand you the picnic and secure the oars. Because lovely as this place is, we don't really want to spend the night here do we?"

Kelly laughed and carefully stepped onto the bank then took the picnic basket and the cushions. Just a little way from the bank was a perfect little clearing that was already being warmed by the sun. The trees and bushes were dense on the other side of the bank, so you couldn't be seen from this place and river traffic could go by without you ever being aware of it.

"What a perfect place" said Kelly opening the basket and taking out the rug. Wrapped in the rug was a copy of the magical book 'Wind in the Willows' by Kenneth Graham and a thermos flask. She laughed.

"So we can start with a cup of tea and read our favourite bits. You do seem to have thought of everything, David."

"Well. We haven't started on the picnic yet. I might have forgotten something." He took the other end of the rug and they spread it out and put the cushions on the rug.

"You pour the tea and I'll read the bit about messing about in boats. Then we can find the bit about little otter going missing."

When they had laughed their way through Ratties description of what was in their picnic basket, Kelly wanted to get out their own. Although David had included the very English roast beef and mustard sandwiches for himself, he had made cream cheese and smoked salmon with watercress for Kelly, who didn't eat meat at the moment, but did eat fish.

When Kelly found strawberries and champagne and tiny chocolate truffles, she declared the picnic decadent. But later, when David dipped the strawberries in the champagne and fed them to her between kisses, she amended that to lunchtime seduction. No more encouragement was needed and although it was too cold to remove all their clothes, they managed very well, even falling asleep for a short while after their exertions in the warmth of the sun.

When it went colder they decided to head back, packing the boat and setting off without too much difficulty. Once Kelly was again sitting in the boat watching this very surprising gypsy man rowing her home, she announced that this had, in fact, been more than just 'a perfect moment in time' this had been a perfect day.

David smiled. Step one in his plan had been successfully orchestrated. He might not have been able to figure out Kelly's plan, and he knew she had been manipulating him ever since he set eyes on her, but today he had been able to fight back. A little planning, a lot of research, and most of all the ability to listen and remember had paid dividends. Plus, he too had had a perfect day, especially when he had wrapped a satiated, almost naked, Kelly in the blanket and she rested against him and had fallen asleep. That had been his perfect moment because in that moment she had felt safe enough to trust him.

Chapter Thirty Four

The phone was ringing and Kelly ran out of the Remedy Room to catch it. She already knew who it was.

"Hi"

"Hi. How are you?"

"I'm good. Am sorting out the shop and making plans."

"Great. I've booked my ticket for the week before the launch and a week after. It's all I can manage."

"That's fine. It gives us time for a board meeting or two, make some more plans and visit some key sites."

"How is it going with the stone circle there?"

"The energies are all connected, and I have connected them with Glastonbury, Stonehenge and Avebury, plus the other labyrinths I know about."

"What about when you leave?"

"Ah – well, I thought of that too. I have arranged for the group – the 'moon maidens' to carry on doing ceremonies."

"That will keep the energy grid active?"

"Yes. It is very powerful earth energy from the stones but it needs female consciousness, with the right intent. Which is what the group, all have in bucket loads. They understand they are holding a gateway in the earth energy, which is all they need to know."

"You do realise that once the book is launched and out there, you can be tracked down."

"Yes, I do. Which is why I will be leaving soon. After the launch and when you have gone back to Italy".

Sara had met an Italian and was now living with him in Italy.

"I would like to think that we are not being pursued anymore and they have all become interested in material things so won't worry about our revelations."

"They were always interested in money, but they are more interested in Power. They have to hold onto their constructed ideology or the women of the world might start to remember their heritage and take back what is theirs".

"Don't use any key words; you know we can't trust the technology. Just keep a low profile and I will be there soon. Anyway it is high time we did some serious swanning about and having fun. It seems an age since we laughed about things.

"I know. Soon, then. What date are you arriving?"

"28th June – I will hire a car so you don't need to come and get me."

"OK. Is baby Sooz ok?"

"Fine. No longer a baby. Going to boarding school now. How's Louise?"

"Good. Trying to be a student and nineteen. It will help when I go off I think. Anyway this is your phone bill. Take care and be good."

"Don't be ridiculous! 'good' is boring. You be careful of commitment."

Kelly laughed, which set Sara off laughing.

"Take care, dear – I look forward to seeing you."

"Me too. Bye for now."

"Bye"

David moved quietly away from the extension phone. He hadn't meant to listen – he had been about to make a phone call himself, but he needed information and sometimes he needed to remember how these two women spoke to each other. At least now he knew how much time he had and that was good. He knew about deadlines, he could work towards deadlines. "Dead-lines" , how very telling a phrase.

Chapter Thirty Five : 23th June

"David!   Looking charming as ever" ,boomed Sara as she came in the door.

David was wearing one of his waistcoats, probably to annoy Sara who believed in ultra smart, not hippy type, dressing.

"And you look as polished as ever" he said, going over to give her a hug.

Sara was slightly taken aback as she was used to completely unnerving David, not have him assess her so easily.

Kelly laughed and took Sara's dark red leather jacket off her.

"You forget" she said, looking at her friend , " David has spent the past years writing about you. I think he now has your measure."

"Huh" she said, but smiled. "Then I guess he will know that I need him to bring my bags inside."

"I'm on my way" said David, feeling confident for the first time ever in the presence of these two together.

"Tea?" said Kelly moving towards the kitchen. "I like the outfit."

"Milan" said Sara moving towards the kitchen with her friend, her new boots clicking on the tiles. "I told you about the Caravaggio thing. Well I hope the book is going to come off. I went to Milan with this rather Caesar-like Italian who likes to spoil me."

Kelly put the kettle on and took down the cups whilst Sara sat herself down at the breakfast bar.

"You mean he is older and rich" she said.

"Something like that. You know I like power."

"Of course you do. That's what No. 1 is, Power."

"Whilst you my dear fruit, are No. 5 and Magic. You look good and the shop is lovely, very different from Abrachat, but very you."

"Do you like the yellow umbrellas outside?"

"Lovely, but I can't see how anyone would want to sit outside yet."

"No. it's colder today, but we did have some days of sun. In fact David and I went on a boating picnic". She handed Sara her tea and a piece of the cake she had made in her honour.

"Very romantic", laughed Sara, "whereas my kind of romance is going to the designer shops in Milan and being bought beautiful things. Did he read poetry to you?"

"No, but he did read to me". Kelly sat down opposite Sara and they smiled at each other.

"Is our plan coming together then?" Sara asked.

"I think it is. And so far, no opposition. Although that just might be a matter of time, and the fact that David writes about these things anyway. Perhaps we are just paranoid."

"Then again, perhaps they just haven't found us yet."

"Who hasn't found you yet?" said David coming into the kitchen. "The cases are all in your room". He sat down and Kelly passed him some tea.

"The patriarchal power group who don't want any change in their status quo" Kelly answered.

"And who certainly don't want women to come to awareness and remember who they are."

"I wish I could remember who I am" said David, having a piece of cake. "Sometimes it is on the tip of my tongue."

"Best you don't try to remember yet" said Sara looking at him. "You do know that you have to deny all knowledge that we gave you any information at all."

"Like Shakespeare. Yes, I do know. He made a very good job of it. No one has ever suggested that any of his work was written by a woman."

"You had better forget that you know that too" said Kelly frowning. "I know you think we are crazy and it is some kind of a joke, but it isn't."

"I know that Kelly" said David looking seriously at her. "I have read Isis's journal and I have listened to all you have said to me."

"Yes, well sometimes, she talks too much. Don't forget that" said Sara sharply. "Only remember that we owned the franchise for Abrachat, and then Kelly made your shop into Abracadabra, and you don't even know my forwarding address."

206

"I don't" said David "and I have just got you two tickets to the book launch along with my other honoured guests. Anyway how exactly did you get invited to that first book launch where I met you both. Just by chance ?"

"We gate crashed!" said Sara laughing again, 'it's easy isn't it, fruit?"

"Very" said Kelly pouring more tea all round. "You just keep talking and look as if you should be there."

"Not to mention getting the 'Kelly glare' if someone asks you for your invitation" said Sara remembering. "Believe me, they don't ask again."

"Anyway, at this book launch we will say hello and then just wander about, o when we eventually get there, and we will stay well out of the limelight.

"That won't be easy for you will it?" said David smiling.

"We'll manage" said Sara standing up. "I'll go and unpack and freshen up now."

Kelly stood up too. "I'll show you where you are. It's funny really isn't it, I've put you in what was always Ross's room. Have you ever heard from him?"

"Not a peep. Very odd. What about you David? Have you heard from him?"

"Not since the mysterious marriage. No. He seems to have faded off the radar."

"Oh well."

Sara and Kelly moved towards the staircase.

"Are you going out this afternoon?" David called.

"Yes" said Kelly.

"OK. I'll make dinner for about 8'ish? Does that sound good?"

"Perfect" said Sara "but let's go for 7 shall we? Travelling is hell, and I need my beauty sleep."

"You're not going to go on about your skin again are you?" said Kelly following her upstairs. "We have always been tied up with problems with your skin, no matter what century we are in."

"That's because we have to rely on my face so much" answered Sara.

"Rely on your face ! what about all the damn ……….."

207

The voices faded as they disappeared into the bedroom and David smiled, marvelling at how these two women seemed to argue all the time, yet still think in the same manner. Probably, it had something to do with keeping their feet on the ground, and their heads in more than one dimension, whilst still being able to live some semblance of a normal life. Not to mention the other time frames they seemed to inhabit. He didn't envy them one little bit. It was one of those strange things about knowledge, once you knew something, you knew it for ever.

Chapter Thirty Six

For the next four days, David saw very little of Kelly and Sara except at breakfast and dinner time. They had been to see Louise at her university house for a day, the other days he didn't know about. Their talks which lasted long into the night didn't exclude him, but were never slowed down for him, and seemed to range from information and map references to various sacred sites, crop circles, stone circles, labyrinths and sacred geometry, almost in the same breath. They tended to treat him rather like an indulged child, with affection, but without letting his presence interfere with their train of thought.

He felt privileged because he realised that they were allowing him to be their silent observer and witness, knowing that one day he would work out what they were doing and what they were talking about. Then he would write about it, although of course that always assumed that he would live long enough to be able to work it all out.

"Did you hear that size 10" Sara's voice cut through his reverie.

"Size 10 ?"

It was the night before the lunchtime launch party and Sara and Kelly had been talking about what they were going to wear. David had zoned out to think about his observer / witness duties and thought they were talking about shoes.

"Size 10. DM. Doc Martins ……… your initials – it's what we used to call you. Your code name" said Kelly.

"Oh! Did you ask me a question?" he said.

"We were talking about our biographer " said Sara taking, a sip of her wine.

"Have you got one?"

"Well, that's what we were asking you. Not that we want you to write or have our biography written just yet. But we thought that we would tell you about the letters now"

"When we met – in this lifetime – on a train" continued Kelly, pulling her legs under her and getting more comfortable on the couch.

"Goddess, don't start all that time ago or we'll be here all night" interrupted Sara from the other end of the couch. "Just suffice it to say, David, I went back to South Africa to raise some money in order to come back and stay in England and in that year we 'kept in touch'. By letter."

Kelly laughed. "You could say that. Actually sometimes we wrote to each other three times a week."

"The problem was that it took ten days to get a letter, so we were always following an echo."

"That being said" continued Kelly, thinking back to the wonderful feeling of receiving those words from someone who was on the same wave length, "the letters are totally amazing and not disjointed at all. It is a fantastic record of how we woke up, and came to our awareness, of who we were, and who we had been in past lives".

"It that when you started writing?" said David pouring himself some more wine and offering some to Sara.

"Oh no" she said holding out her glass, "we had both been writing before, it just meant that the memories came faster and we could discuss them. Then the writing came faster."

"Anyway" said Kelly declining the wine, "the very interesting thing is that even in our 'just aware' state ...."

"When we thought of ourselves as 'two housewives' and nothing more" laughed Sara.

"We still wrote notes in our letters for our biographer" finished Kelly.

"Did you?" said David surprised that anyone would have the forethought to write any explanation of their own writings, especially in a letter to a friend.

"Yes. We have always known how important our letters were. We kept them very carefully – and secretly. Then put them together when we got together."

"In fact" Kelly said smiling, "the letters are very well travelled. They have been back and forth between England and Africa many times."

"How long a period did you write to each other?" asked David.

"There are three batches. The three times that Sara came to England to live. We started a new project – it failed – then she had to go back. Each time we wrote to each other."

"We worked it out once; we have more words between us than the complete Shakespeare."

"Wow" David breathed "where are they now?"

They looked at each other for a moment.

"They are in the time capsule aren't they?" he suddenly realised.

"If anything happens to us, they belong to Louise and baby Sooz,, but it would be good to know that you might like to do our biography, and the letters would make fascinating reading" said Sara.

"Especially as they are about how we came to our awareness."

"Thank you" said David "I am honoured. I hope it doesn't fall on me for a long time, but I will take care of your knowledge and wisdom for as long as I need to."

"Oh good, that's that sorted out then" said Kelly sitting up straighter. "Now to the important things – what are we going to wear tomorrow?"

"Also David" said Sara, "tomorrow we are just casual acquaintances. Don't introduce us to anyone, whatever you do."

"No, then we can be our disruptive selves. I think I'm going to wear that turquoise outfit I showed you. Try to have a calming effect around me."

Sara laughed so hard she spluttered her wine.

"That will be something to see – you having a calming effect! I'll wear that lilac suit. No feathers this time though, we need to just blend in."

David got up and took the plates into the kitchen shaking his head at the crazy notions of these two, especially together, ever being able to just blend in.

He was also aware that tomorrow was some sort of end of a cycle. He had met them at his last book launch and he felt that they were now planning to leave at this one. They hadn't announced their entrance and he knew they would not announce their exit. Sara had six more days before her return flight and he suspected that Kelly was planning to leave soon after. He would have to work fast if he was going to be ready. He knew, without being told, there would be no forwarding address

Chapter Thirty Seven: Launch Day

"Well this is very déjà vu, don't you think?" Kelly was sitting opposite Sara in the same café in Oxford, where they had once sat drinking tea, before they went to meet the Author David Appleby and get their project underway.

"It seems a long time ago. So much has happened."

"Yes. When I came back to South Africa – was it the second or third time and we thought we had cracked the making money thing, with Abrachat. We expected to be able to retire to the proposed Game Farm."

"I don't think we are ever going to be able to retire. Anyway, we decided we didn't want a Game Farm in Africa."

"No. We decided we didn't want any visitors, people, or animals. We liked the Game Farm idea though."

"Goddess, we do have some extraordinary plans. All we need now is for you to start on about Leonardo da Vinci being a Buddhist and we will be back where we started."

The waitress arrived with tea and hot, buttered teacakes with which they had decided to fortify themselves, before they went to the launch and drank champagne. They had left early in order to have some time together and to arrive separately from David who left early for some reason of his own.

"Yes. Well, don't think I have given up about Leonardo. I want to take that stuff you have written about him, and get on with proving my point about his religious persuasions."

"Not to mention his other persuasions! Anyway, I need to concentrate on all the Temple stuff we wrote in Brother Sun, Sister Moon. I keep telling you it is too soon to do anything about Da Vinci. Besides, you need to help me go through all that writing in order for us to make our next five year plan."

"Yeah, ok, we can do that tomorrow. I'll continue on the art history , and on the now time. Whilst you can do the earth energies and geometry in preparation for what is to come."

"And hopefully we will meet in the middle somewhere."

"Anyway" said Sara sighing and passing the tea to Kelly who was busy cutting her teacake whilst it was still warm, "it wasn't in the last plan that I would go back to SA again and that you would have to sell up the house was it?"

"No. But I am beginning to think that we can't spend too much time together. Our combined energies seem to alter the time/space continuum too much, all sorts of weird things start happening. Besides we are very detectable when we are together."

"Only because we actually create things. ..... AND we do it really, really fast."

"Here's a serviette, don't spill tea on that lovely suit" said Kelly, trying to avoid getting butter on her delicate dress. She had taken her linen turquoise jacket off and hung it on the chair. Sara's suit was a designer fitted jacket that had no room underneath for anything else. With her pencil thin skirt and three inch heels she looked taller and skinnier than ever. Her dark hair was cut shorter now and made her look elfin with enormous green eyes.

Kelly's dress was pea green and turquoise with little sleeves and a V-neckline. The jacket was plain and lined so it did give her some protection from the chill in the air. Her shoes were soft green leather and not so high as Sara's.

"We do look a bit as if we are going to a wedding" said Sara, wiping the tea spills up. "Perhaps we should have worn hats."

"We could have designed them in our spare time" said Kelly.

Sara laughed "as if ...... spare time! "

They both thought about the fun they had had when they did design the hats for their shop, 'Gats & Hats'."

"Let's not think about failed ventures. This is celebration time. We wanted this information out there without it being from us and it is going to be now. The process of activating to Goddess Gene can begin. Hurrah!"

"Eat your teacake and let's get ourselves to the book launch. We will be late now so we should blend in nicely."

214

"I hope we will be in time to hear dear David reading some of his wonderful new book" said Sara now eating her teacake.

"I wonder which bit he will read."

"Goddess. I hope it's not the bit where I have to flee the country and wear peasant clothes. Did you put that in?"

"Of course I did. But I don't actually know whether he has added all the things that were in the diary of Isis. Actually, I haven't read it. Come on, hurry up then I can buy a signed copy."

Sara laughed as they both hurried to make the deadline and enter the next stage of their plan.

David hadn't actually seen Kelly and Sara so he didn't know whether they had heard him read his excerpt or not. There were a lot of people milling about which was very gratifying, but he hadn't been able to look for them because so many people were asking him questions and writing down his replies.

"So what was your inspiration for this change in your style?" said someone called Ellen, who was obviously from a high brow publication and who liked to know the reason behind the writing. This was the question he had been waiting to field all day. The publishers had decided in the end that he should keep his name and they would make much of his changing style.

"Just my observation of women over the long period of time", he smiled at her. "Once you realise that women are a lot brighter than they allow men to know, you also realise that they must have been keeping some secrets from us for a long time."

"Really?" She narrowed her eyes suspecting she was being taken for a ride.

"Shirley Valentine was written by a man if you remember, and most women seem to be able to identify with her. Also you must be aware of Willie Russell saying in interviews that he spends time trying to overhear women's conversations because they are so interesting. I have been listening to a lot of conversations in a lot of places."

"Can I quote you on that?" she smiled.

215

"Please do. Who knows, I might score some brownie points with the female population."

He could feel his arm being pulled by his editor, Gillian, so he excused himself and moved to the desk that was piled high with his new books. She pushed him into the chair with a 'start signing' instruction. So he started. Lots of people who had been chatting and nibbling the food now moved towards the desk to receive the first batch of signed copies, all quoting various names that they wanted included. He did hear Sara and Kelly laughing at one point, but even though he looked up he couldn't see them.

It was after he had paused for a drink then started on the second session of signing, that he suddenly caught the unmistakable smell of flowers that always made him think of Kelly. He looked up and, sure enough, she was handing him his book, smiling.

"Hello" she said "good turn out."

"Yes." He said taking the book, "glad you could make it."

"Oh, we wouldn't have missed it for the world" she said, "We liked the bit you read. A good session of plotting in the back room of a Temple somewhere in Egypt usually catches peoples' attention."

He smiled and wrote something quickly before anyone could look over her shoulder, closed the book and handed it back to her.

"Thank you for coming" he said, as she made way for the next person.

She knew he had interviews lined up all afternoon and wouldn't be back until later. Sara was deep in discussion with someone about the difficulties of living in South Africa, so Kelly found herself a quiet spot and opened the book. On the fly leaf in David's beautiful copper plate writing, it said...

'To Isis. With love and Thanks. Joseph'

She smiled quietly to herself and went to rescue the poor man from Sara.

When David did arrive home later that night he could see by the picnic basket and the minute book that Sara and Kelly had had their board meeting in the circle and probably now had their new five year plan worked out.

He also knew, from the board meeting that he and Ross had once been allowed to attend, that even if he looked at the minutes he would be none the wiser as to what it meant. The minutes were always interspersed with the oddest of things, including the latest fashion statement.

He smiled and followed the sound of laughter into the lounge area.

"David! Hi" Kelly came and gave him a hug. "Congratulations on a great job, it has the look of being a best seller."

"Hope so" said David, noting that she had changed now into her jeans and a long sleeved tee-shirt in jade green. Sara came over to congratulate him and gave him a hug. She too, was now in jeans and a pink shirt. They both looked animated and relaxed.

"It's our celebration too, you know" said Sara.

"And we have cooked you a special dinner" said Kelly.

"Well – you have cooked, I have peeled and been drinking."

"My friend can drink like a fish" said Kelly giggling.

"Did you put some wine in the fish?" said Sara suddenly.

"In the sauce – yes."

"What are we having?" said David accepting a mug of tea which Kelly had just poured for him from the tray.

"Salmon, new potatoes, broccoli and asparagus. Rhubarb crumble with custard and cream."

"Great! He sat down beside Kelly, as Sara drifted off somewhere either by accident or by design. Kelly smiled and squeezed his hand.

"Thank you" she said.

He kissed her gently on the mouth. "I never knew whether you had bewitched me" he said smiling, "but I never cared either. I did it willingly."

"When you signed the book 'Joseph' did this Joseph have a surname or anything else to identify him with?"

"Once of Arimathea and later of Glastonbury, I believe."

"Ah, that Joseph" she smiled. "In that case you should really have addressed it to Calpa – my given name – in that time. Short, I suppose, for Calpernia – but she changed her name later ……"

217

"Don't for Goddess sake go into all that name changing business. It drove me crazy then, and it still does. I keep wondering who I am supposed to be", Sara shouted coming back into the room.

"Don't be silly. You have always been you, no matter when it was. Anyway you have changed your name enough times in this lifetime already."

"Yes", said Sara sitting down on the opposite settee with a new bottle of wine and a corkscrew, "but that was to avoid creditors."

"It always was" said Kelly, getting her a wine glass from the table.

"No it wasn't , in that lifetime we are talking about, it was for religious reasons. Anyway, do get rid of that tea Kelly and let's start on the wine. Have you given him the damn manuscript yet!"

"No. But he has remembered who he was in that lifetime."

"Well that's a start then" said Sara pulling the cork out of the bottle.

"Excuse me, I am still here you know" said David, laughing at the speed with which these two could argue about something that happened in another time.

"Oh yes, do you want some wine!" said Sara offering the bottle.

"David, I have now found the manuscript so I will give it to you. This is the one that is about the next lifetime, after Cleopatra. I'm sure you will remember some more things when you read it" said Kelly. "Come on, sit down at the table, we can eat now."

"When you do remember," said Sara moving towards the dining area and picking up the bottle, " do argue with our little chronicler here, who sometimes writes things that are not quite clear and not quite how it happened. Sometimes she can't remember it all."

"I'm sure I will be intrigued to learn more of your past triumphs", said David sitting down at the table. Kelly had disappeared into the kitchen to put the food on the plates.

"Misdemeanours you mean", laughed Sara, "every lifetime we seem to spend half our time trying to remember what the hell we are supposed to be doing or not doing. Even with the writings – if we can find them." She was now eating a piece of freshly baked bread from the basket.

"Then, of course, we have to find each other and try to undo the programming of the current lifetime."

"Which *you* do, mainly when you are asleep" said Kelly bringing two plates of food.

"Ah yes, dreams and portents, what would we do without them?. Anyway, eat your dinner David and enjoy today, time enough for our nonsense another day."

"Amen to that" said Kelly sitting down with her plate of food. " Here's to 'new beginnings'" She raised her glass and they all chorused "new beginnings".

"And Harmony" said Kelly, "our ultimate goal – the red rose and the white rose together – the Yin and the Yang energy reunited in harmony."

"To harmony" they all said together.

"And don't for Goddess sake get all poetical " said Sara, laughing.

David recorded the scene in his mind. It was, without doubt, a piece out of time, and although he wanted to ask more about the Field of 'A-causal events' and exactly how these two women saw it, and manipulated it, he knew it was not a conversation for tonight. Because tonight was the end of a cycle and the new one had not yet begun. All he knew for certain was that he wasn't going to let either the information, or the chronicler, slip out of his life. How could he! There was so much he still needed to know. But that was for tomorrow and tomorrow was another day.

Chapter Thirty Eight: The final curtain

David was standing anxiously looking out of the window just inside the shop (where Sally was getting very fed up with him coming and going). First he would stand at the front door window which was next to the shop on the house side, then he would move to the shop windows and peer down the road from there. These were the possible places from which Kelly could arrive.

This was the second day he had spent his time doing this particular ritual.

Sara had left early the following day after a brief thank you, and a goodbye hug. Kelly had driven her to the airport with a lot of hurried, last minute things they seemed to be remembering. She had waved breezily to David as she left, and had not been back since.

David had always known that there was a chance that Kelly would decide to go back to South Africa with Sara, but she had said, more than once, that she also had things to do, in and around the cathedrals in France.

Although he knew that she was going to go, sooner rather than later, he didn't think she would just go without saying anything.

Then again, he didn't rule that out, she was indeed prone to the spontaneous. He had checked in her wardrobe and the bathroom and she hadn't taken anything with her. Even though he knew he couldn't act on his plans until Sara had left, he was beginning to think he may well have left it too late.

Sally came up beside him.

"David, I've made you some coffee, do come and sit in the shop and have some coffee and cake". She took hold of his elbow.

"You can watch out of the window from there" she smiled. "Anyway, aren't you supposed to be getting some agreement organised?"

"Yes. Yes, I am. Thank you, Sally. I'll have the coffee then I'll do that."

"She will be back you know" smiled Sally over her shoulder as she went back into the shop.

"Who will?" said David innocently. But Sally just shook her head and got the cake. The shop door opened and Marian Bradley walked in with her friend, Fiona.

"David! How lovely to see you. We just popped in to get a copy of your new book" she boomed, coming towards him.

Sally had been busy giving the new book and the advertising, pride of place in the window of the shop. The cover in jewel-like colours picked up the early morning sun and fitted in well with the mysterious look of the Abracadabra trade mark.

"Nice to see you Marion – and Fiona. Do come and have some coffee with me" said David, "then I can personalize one of the signed copies if you would like me to".

He smiled wondering what she would make of the concepts he had tried to convey. Who knew, perhaps this was exactly what she had been waiting for all her life. They sat down and David went to get them both some coffee and walnut cake whilst Sally placed two copies of the book on the table.

"It looks very exciting" said Fiona tracing the gold pyramid with her fingers.

"You are right" David said, passing the coffees out, "It isn't like my normal scholarly, dry writing, this is more exciting."

"But historical?" said Marian.

"Oh yes" David smiled sitting down, "almost as if the characters had told me their own story."

Fiona giggled. "I take it it's about Cleopatra?"

"Indeed it is" he said "but so – so much more. Would you like a copy each and signed to you?"

"Oh yes!" sighed the ladies together.

"That would be super" said Marian.

Let's hope all the other women in the world feel the same way David thought to himself. Then we will, in fact, be spreading the word. He wrote the small personalized messages in the books and chatted easily about the new proposed extension to the pub and the mysterious outpouring of incomprehensible wisdom that was doled out each morning by Dez along with the milk and papers. When the shop door opened and Kelly came breezing in with a large box of something for Sally and smiles and hellos for the people in the shop, David didn't at first see her. When he did, he picked up the coffee cups and went over to the sink to rinse them.

"Hello" she said coming past him to go through to the house, " have you taken to helping in the shop now?"

She was smiling, so he smiled back, deciding now was not the moment to start questioning her as to her whereabouts. She seemed to be carrying lots of bags with various things in them.

David went back and made sure Marian and Fiona were happy with their purchases. Then he phoned his friend, Kevin, who was also his solicitor, and asked about the contracts he was having drawn up. His assurance they would be in the post today was one less worry. Now he could go and find out what Kelly was doing.

She was in the remedies room putting some of the dried herbs and bottles into boxes. It looked very like packing to him.

"Hi" he said leaning casually against the door, "how are you?"

"I'm fine thank you" she said.

"Did Sara get off ok?"

"Yes. Fine. We managed to get everything done, but like always it's a rush. Are you ok?"

"Of course, fine. I was a bit worried that was all."

"Oh" she said "Oh I see. You thought I might have gone off with Sara."

He nodded slightly.

"Well. I have to say it did cross my mind. But I can't, I have more things to do"

She carried on putting various things in boxes, then continued.

"Actually, I came back earlier this morning. I went to see Indigo and Jen. Haven't seen them in a while"

She wasn't looking at him, but he knew what that meant. She had been to see Louise and taken some of her things to Indigo's and made a plan that Louise could go back to them if she needed to at any time. He could feel her withdrawing from him and closing lots of doors. He knew it was time to act now.

"Will you be here for the rest of the day?" he said moving himself from the door frame and adopting an action position.

"Yes, of course" she said looking up "why?"

"No reason. Be back in a minute or two."

Then he went outside via the shop to the car park in order to phone the man who was awaiting his phone call.

"How long will it take you?" he asked

"Can have it there about half past two mate." Came the reply.

"Great. Good. The girl in the shop can sign your bits of paper" he said and rang off quickly.

A word of confirmation from Sally and he was speeding back into the house. Kelly had left the Remedy room now and was upstairs in her bedroom. She had the wardrobe doors open and lots of clothes on the bed. David backed away from the door to the top of the spiral staircase without her seeing him

"Kelly!" he called " Do you want some lunch?"

"Yes. That would be great" she shouted back, "just salad or something. I will come down soon."

"Ok. Fifteen minutes then?" He started back down the staircase.

"Ok."

He hurried into the kitchen, opening the fridge door to get out the salad ingredients. He had two large stuffed mushrooms. Taking them out of the package, he placed them on a tray and into the oven, making sure he turned it on. Glancing at the clock he started to chop the salad . Ten past one. Good. He had only a short time now to wait.

Chapter Thirty Nine

Kelly was indeed sorting out her clothes. Deciding on which to take and which to lay in the boxes. She was sad to be leaving here. She loved the house and the walled garden. She had enjoyed the shop and making the remedies, but it had always been temporary. She had to move on. She had to go now, whilst she still could, because David was very comfortable to be around. She liked his energy, and she was beginning to be more than just fond of him. It was time to go. She finished the box and placed it in the bottom of the wardrobe then went downstairs for lunch.

David had set the table in the dining area overlooking the walled garden. The sun was shining in through the open French windows. She didn't ask why they were eating here, rather than in the kitchen, instead she sat and enjoyed being looked after. There was a single red rose on the table.

"It is imported I'm afraid, they are not ready in the garden yet."

"It's still lovely."

"It should be white really. Have some hummus, it's that fresh, organic you like."

He passed it to her and she took some pitta bread.

"Do you remember when we met and went to Stratford?" she said quietly.

"Yes. We had pitta bread there, at the Greek restaurant."

"It seems a long time ago."

"Only because so much has happened to us. And in the process our lives have changed. Come on, no sadness, let us enjoy the now-time."

"Sounds like something I am always saying" she smiled.

"It just shows how much I have learnt." He said passing her the bowl.

"You will never guess who I heard from this morning."

"Who?"

"Ross! Got a letter."

"Really? What did he say?"

"He said he had a son, a mortgage and a job and asked if I had ever kept in touch with those strange women who had board meeting picnics in the stone circle."

Kelly laughed. "Will you reply to him?"

"What! , and tell him I am now their official biographer? I don't think so. It would take too much of a leap of faith,."

David said a silent thank you to Ross for getting in touch at this particular time, because it had made Kelly laugh and remember all the light-hearted moments they had shared. The sadness had threatened to overwhelm them. They chatted amicably and Kelly told him about seeing Louise and her new friends. By the time they had eaten some fruit and had a cup of tea sitting on the bench in the walled garden which was always sheltered and warm, Sally came through to tell him his 'package' had arrived.

"What package?" said Kelly.

"It's a surprise. You sit here and promise not to move whilst I go and check it out."

"Ok" said Kelly, closing her eyes and lifting her face up to the sun and allowing the wonderful, peaceful feeling to envelop her.

David was back before she even had time to wonder what this surprise could possibly be.

"Ok. Now you have to be blindfolded" he said producing a scarf from the shop.

She looked at him. She could see he was very excited about something, but she had no idea what it could be.

"You haven't built another ark of the covenant have you?" she said standing up to allow herself to be blindfolded.

"Not quite" he said.

"Ah! it must be Noah's Ark then."

David froze imperceptibly, but he was near enough for her to feel it.

"Don't guess anything" he said, taking her hand and leading her in through the French doors "and keep your eyes shut."

He led her through the house to the shop which was fortunately empty of people. She heard Sally open the shop door and David warning her to step down into the open space out the front.

"Ok Kelly" David breathed "I'm going to take the blindfold off now". He moved behind her and untied the knot.

There, in front of her, parked and ready to go was a motor caravan. She looked to the right and the left, but could see nothing else.

"It's a …… sort of Winnebago, only smaller" she said puzzled.

David moved to her side where he could look at her.

"Kelly. I'm coming with you. Wherever you want to go I'm coming too. I can't let you do this on your own."

She stared at him in surprise. All the reactions to her leaving she had imagined, but not this one. This was a complete surprise.

"But , what about the house, the shop, the writing?"

"Sally, her boyfriend, and two more friends are going to rent the house, the contract will be signed tomorrow. I can write anywhere – we now have modern communications. If I need to come back for something special, I can fly. All we have to do is pack what we need and go."

Kelly looked at him and felt a great weight lifting off her heart. She didn't have to do this alone. She threw her arms round his neck and hugged him. Realising that what she always looked for was a man who could surprise her and this one had really surprised her.

"And do you know what the last, most important thing of all is?" he said quietly in her ear.

She leaned her head back to look at him.

"And what would that be?" she said smiling.

"No forwarding address. No one will ever know where we are."

"No forwarding address" she repeated "that has always been my preferred exit line. Every time, every lifetime"

"Now it's mine too.

Exit stage Right.

226

The Goddess Gene
Ju Suis

Available December 2013

The Goddess Gene
Cast No Shadow

Available 2014